ROHAISE

ALSO BY SHANI STRUTHERS

EVE: A CHRISTMAS
GHOST STORY
(PSYCHIC SURVEYS
PREQUEL)

PSYCHIC SURVEYS
BOOK ONE:
THE HAUNTING OF
HIGHDOWN HALL

PSYCHIC SURVEYS
BOOK TWO:
RISE TO ME

PSYCHIC SURVEYS
BOOK THREE:
44 GILMORE STREET

PSYCHIC SURVEYS
BOOK FOUR:
OLD CROSS COTTAGE

PSYCHIC SURVEYS
BOOK FIVE:
DESCENSION

PSYCHIC SURVEYS
BOOK SIX:
LEGION

PSYCHIC SURVEYS
BOOK SEVEN:
RISE TO ME

PSYCHIC SURVEYS
BOOK EIGHT:
THE WEIGHT OF THE SOUL

BLAKEMORT
(A PSYCHIC SURVEYS
COMPANION NOVEL
BOOK ONE)

THIRTEEN
(A PSYCHIC SURVEYS
COMPANION NOVEL
BOOK TWO)

ROSAMUND
(A PSYCHIC SURVEYS
COMPANION NOVEL
BOOK THREE)

THIS HAUNTED WORLD
BOOK ONE:
THE VENETIAN

THIS HAUNTED WORLD
BOOK TWO:
THE ELEVENTH FLOOR

THIS HAUNTED WORLD
BOOK THREE:
HIGHGATE

THE JESSAMINE SERIES
BOOK ONE: JESSAMINE

THE JESSAMINE SERIES
BOOK TWO: COMRAICH

REACH FOR THE DEAD
BOOK ONE:
MANDY

REACH FOR THE DEAD
BOOK TWO:
CADES HOME FARM

CARFAX HOUSE:
A CHRISTMAS GHOST STORY

THE DAMNED SEASON:
A CHRISTMAS GHOST STORY

SUMMER OF GRACE

This Haunted World: Book Four

ROHAISE

SHANI STRUTHERS

This Haunted World Book Four: Rohaise
Copyright © Shani Struthers 2022

The right of Shani Struthers to be identified as the Author of the work has been asserted by her in accordance with the Copyright, Designs and Patents Act 1988. All rights reserved in all media. No part of this publication may be reproduced, stored in a retrieval system, or transmitted in any form or by any means, electronic, mechanical, recording, photocopying, the Internet or otherwise, without the prior written consent of the copyright holder, nor be otherwise circulated in any form of binding or cover other than that in which it is published and without a similar condition being imposed on the subsequent purchaser.

Authors Reach
www.authorsreach.co.uk

ISBN: 978-1-7399581-2-1

Most characters and events featured in this publication are purely fictitious. Any resemblance to any fictitious person, places, organisation/company, living or dead, is entirely coincidental.

Let us learn from the past to profit by the present and from the present, to live better in the future.
William Wordsworth

Acknowledgements

Rohaise was inspired by a trip in the summer of 2021 to Delgatie Castle in Turriff, Aberdeenshire. An incredible place, steeped in history, we had the privilege of staying for a week there, a magical and sometimes eerie experience! Like Kenna in the story, I immediately became intrigued with the mysterious Rohaise, a woman whom so little is known about and yet what we do know, is fascinating. This is her story, totally imagined of course, but suffice to say, when I was writing it, it took on a life of its own, the words just bursting from me. No book is created alone, so many people are involved in the process. A HUGE thank you to my beta readers, Rob Struthers, Vanessa Patterson, Kate Jane Jones, Sarah Savery, Alicen Haire, Louisa Taylor and Lesley Hughes, your feedback was, as always, invaluable. Thanks also to Gina Dickerson for creating yet another brilliant cover and for formatting. And last, but never least, to Rumer Haven for her attention to detail and editing. If you ever get a chance to visit Delgatie Castle or to stay there, take it!

Prologue

"Rohaise! Why've you stopped? Come on!"

"No…I can't… You go…without me."

The man, tall and bearded, roared with surprise. "There's no time to falter!"

She held firm, her eyes leaving his face and travelling to the wet brickwork an inch or two above her head. It stank down here in the tunnel; sludge-like water pooled at her feet, having sat stagnant for an age, moss clinging to the lower half of the walls. It was hard to breathe, let alone talk, but she must. Their lives – *his* life – depended on it.

"I can't leave. I'll stay. I have to."

"For God's sake, woman!"

Finally, Rohaise shouted too. "No, Alexander! Not for His sake, for yours."

"Rohaise—" The man reached out and tried to take hold of her, but she stepped back, avoided his touch. Holding aloft the candle that was doing its best to guide the way, she stared at him. His dark eyes blazed, just as her own surely did.

"I cannot, *will* not leave. I'll go back and conceal the entrance so they will never find it. I won't let them tear down the walls of Drumlin to get to you, Alexander, for that is what they intend to do. They'll destroy it. I'll walk out to meet them, tell them you've fled, that you've gone overland

and headed north to seek sanctuary on one of the islands there. And they'll believe me; I'll make certain of it. They'll see as truth every word that falls from my lips."

"You'll bewitch them."

She nodded.

"As you have always bewitched me."

There was sorrow in his gaze, and agony, but also something else: relief. He knew his fate if he was captured. The king's men would tear him apart, limb from limb. Hack his head from his torso, impale it upon a spear, and with it ride from Drumlin into the surrounding towns and villages. '*This* is what happens when you betray the king,' the stark message. No care if that betrayal was built on lies.

Even so, Alexander refused. "I cannot leave you here."

Aside from his voice, the tunnel was quiet, not even the scurrying of rats beneath their feet. Above them, though, all hell would break loose and soon. The troops had a cannon with them that no walls, no matter how thick, could withstand.

It was she who grabbed him, darting forward, hands grasping his arms – arms that had held her close in passion but with such gentleness too.

"They don't want me," she told him. "I'm a peasant in their eyes, a commoner. But you… Our only chance is to divert them, and I can do that."

"Rohaise…" More words failed him as he acknowledged the truth in all she'd said. Instead, he pressed his lips against hers, bruising them with the ferocity of his sorrow.

When they parted, he couldn't look at her, and so she guided his face back to hers.

"Be safe, Alexander. Live."

"Because of you…"

"Because of me. Because I *want* you to."

Now he lifted his eyes towards her. "I am nothing without you!"

His words made her gasp, the depth of them.

"I love you," she said, surprised when her voice held steady.

"I love you too." His did not.

"Then do this for me. Obey."

"They will kill you, Rohaise!"

"And they may not."

"But—"

"Remember who I am. I am no one. They may just dismiss me."

In the darkness of the tunnel, with only a single candle spluttering, time gave the illusion of disappearing too, as if it meant nothing. But it did. Time was everything, and it was running out. He had to go, and she must stay. Her mind was made up.

She released him, and he half turned, her heart – despite her efforts – cracking to see it.

They each took a step back. The pain, though, was too much.

She weakened first, but only by a moment.

Again in each other's arms, they clung harder than before.

"My love, my life," Alexander whispered, his voice as frantic as her heart now felt.

What if she changed her mind and went with him? The temptation was so great. To live life in exile, yes, but blissful if together! She had to remind herself again about the tunnel, how impossible it had been to cover fully from inside, no servants left to aid them, having taken flight too.

After breaching the castle, on finding it empty, the soldiers would, of course, turn their attentions elsewhere. They would bear down on them, surround the forest where the tunnel emerged…unless she did as she'd said and distracted them, sent at least half their army elsewhere. A terrible situation. The very worst. Yet in this moment, did it matter? All that mattered was them and the love that had not so much blossomed but exploded between them.

A moment that passed.

"Go. Leave. Now. But, Alexander, come back one day. Promise me that."

"Rohaise, if they cast you aside, if you should escape…" How he cleaved to hope. "Hide in the forest! You know every inch of it. It's your domain, not theirs."

True; the surrounding forest had birthed her, the dark heart of it. But…if there was hope in him, it was dying in her. They would never let her go, believing her to be a simple servant girl, abandoned. The rumours about Alexander Buchannan and his flame-haired lover had spread too far, too wide. They'd been reckless, perhaps, too consumed with each other.

A few more words, a promise she had to extract, one she would keep too.

"Whatever happens, I will wait for you, here at Drumlin."

"Rohaise—"

"I will be here, d'ya ken? Do you?"

"Yes. Yes, I do."

"*Whatever* happens."

"Whatever happens," he repeated, his voice ragged again.

"Come back. Let me gaze upon you once more."

"In our home."

Our home. He had called it that from the start.

"Promise me," she breathed. "Alexander, promise!"

"I promise, ma cridhe"—the Gaelic for 'my heart'—"ma cridhe fiadhaich," *my wild heart.*

"Two wild hearts together," she replied, gently pushing at him.

Alexander Buchannan not so much stepped back as staggered.

"Go," she said again, tried to smile, to make it easier for him.

With a howl, he turned and began running, the tunnel's mouth covetous, swallowing him quickly, the candle that had been cast aside dying.

No matter, tears had blinded her anyway. She lifted her hands and felt her way back.

Heaviness in each step.

Chapter One

A dream come true? It could have been. If he'd fulfilled his promise and gone with her. Up until the last minute, he'd said he would.

"Yeah, of course, Kenna, stop agitating. I'm looking forward to it. Something different. We'll make a real go of it, you and me. Honestly, I can't wait."

And then a week before…not even that, *three days*, he'd changed his mind.

"This project I'm working on, I thought it'd be finished by now, but it's not, it's…dragging on. I'm sorry. Really. But I can't just upsticks and move. But I will come, I promise. Go first, get settled, and as soon as I can I'll join you." When she'd protested, got angry, an edge had also crept into his voice. "Look, I'm under enough stress as it is! I don't need you piling on more. This isn't as easy for me as it is for you. I still have to work the day job. I've got people waiting on me for this stuff, and right now my life is here in London."

As she sat on the train from King's Cross, heading north, his last words echoed in her mind – *my life is here in London*. Whereas her life in London was over, at least for now. And yet…he'd *wanted* this, been excited for it, had encouraged the idea from the outset. And she'd trusted him, taken him at his word, hadn't thought not to.

Aged twenty-six, perhaps she was naïve still, a thought that also took her by surprise. She'd describe herself as many things – independent, fair-minded, down-to-earth – but naïve wasn't one of them until now. Kenna Jackson had met Adam Carter two years previously in a London bar, late at night. They'd been with respective friends, both well on their way to inebriation, her especially. He'd noticed her as soon as she'd entered the bar, he'd said, with her red hair, pale skin and green eyes. In a crowded room, she'd stood out.

Taking the reins, as Adam usually did, he'd weaved his way through the masses to stand by her side, eventually catching her attention and smiling at her. And she'd been lost, pretty much lost from thereon in, drunk on more than mere alcohol.

He was tall and broad, with blond hair and high cheekbones. Not her usual type, but there'd been something about him and his solid rugby build that had drawn her right in, his easy smile and the intent in his eyes, which were focused solely on her.

She remembered that her friend Sal hadn't been overly keen on him. With a sigh, Kenna leant back against the seat, a journey of no less than seven hours in front of her to dwell on all this.

Sal had spied them chatting, sidled up to her and tugged at her arm.

"You all right?" she'd said, not even looking at Kenna but glaring at Adam. Finally, she'd adjusted her gaze and said to Kenna, "Want to head outside, grab some fresh air?"

That was what her circle of friends did. They made sure the person who cornered you whilst out on the town was someone you were happy with. But that glare had been blatant if not full of dislike, then distrust, and for the life of her, Kenna couldn't think why. Adam had looked reasonable enough, *more* than reasonable. He was handsome and sexy. He was…beguiling. Had Sal been jealous? Was that the reason? Kenna had thought it but instantly dismissed the notion; Sal was sweet, not the jealous type. And yet…

Straightaway, Kenna had assured Sal she was fine, wishing she'd quit with her silent condemnation and disappear. Eventually she had, along with the entire world, it seemed, leaving only the two of them, their heads together, talking, talking, talking.

Two years had passed quickly, relatively happy years, certainly busy, each pursuing their own careers – Adam in IT and Kenna an editorial assistant for a publishing company. They couldn't spend as much time together as they'd have liked. London, that city she was leaving behind, could be brutal. So often they'd said that to each other; it was a place that demanded so much, that sucked the life from you. They could go a straight week without seeing each other, just too exhausted after long hours at the office to then trek via a packed tube to one of their flats. She hated not seeing him. He seemed to hate it too.

"One day," he'd said, "it'll be different."

"How?" she'd asked, genuinely curious.

"We'll escape."

It'd been a day in late summer, one of those hot, sticky ones you thought might never end. They were in Hyde Park, grabbing some time together during their lunch break. Not that they usually worked so close to each other, but Adam had just happened to be in her part of town, seeing a client. And so they'd walked, his arm around her, her grumbling about work as usual, him being optimistic as usual. She loved that about him. His ability to see the silver lining. She could be negative on occasion, her vision of the future a little fogged.

Not his, though. His was crystal clear.

"So come on, how will we escape the chains of drudgery?" she'd probed.

"Something will turn up. It always does."

"Like what?"

"I don't know, an opportunity of some sort. It will come from nothing, just rise up out of the ether and present itself – a chance to step off the treadmill, quit the rat race, be together all the time, you and me. The way we dream of."

"And that's it? You've nothing more concrete than that?"

"Have faith," he'd purred whilst gazing dreamily into the distance.

Silence had followed his words, and then she'd dug him in the ribs, the pair of them bursting into laughter, not because it was funny but because that's what they did. They laughed together, about everything, especially in those early days. But work had taken its toll, London did, even with someone like Adam, his eternal optimism, his shine, fading as bigger contracts came along – more money, certainly, but also more pressure.

He'd lost weight recently, wasn't quite as broad. Two years older than her, crow's feet were developing around his eyes. Any talk of escape had petered out. They'd just…endured. That's what it had seemed like. And it had been getting harder and harder to find time together to talk, to touch, to build on anything other than their careers. Sometimes she wondered whether she'd lose him, an unbearable thought. Her vision of the future might be vague, but not concerning Adam. She wanted him in it, her rock, always.

And then an opportunity *had* come, just as he'd said it would, right out of the blue.

Charlotte Skelton was an author Kenna worked with, a lovely lady who specialised in historical novels, sometimes with a dash of romance in them, sometimes grittier than that. The pair had been lunching in Covent Garden one day – talking shop but other topics too, as both genuinely enjoyed each other's company – when Charlotte had mentioned a castle that she'd visited in Scotland recently, possibly the inspiration for a future book.

Kenna now closed her own eyes as she recalled the sparkle in Charlotte's.

"Kenna, this castle's amazing! I don't mean in a fairy-tale kind of way, not like that. It's more…*raw*. Dates back to the eleventh century and was home to so many through the ages, the Buchannan family predominantly." She sighed. "Such misty times, and so much of it shrouded in mystery. History that's drenched in blood. It's all there at the castle. You can feel the weight of it even before you enter. The air's thick with it."

Kenna picked up her glass of wine and listened as Charlotte continued to enthuse.

"Honestly, I didn't want to leave the place, and that's rare for me. I love a research trip as much as the next person, but I love getting home too. This time, though, I had to tear myself away, seriously. I've never been anywhere so atmospheric, so…magical. Kenna, that's a Scottish name, isn't it? You've no accent, but is your family from Scotland?"

Kenna inclined her head. It was true, Kenna *was* a Scottish name. Her maternal grandparents hailed originally from Paisley, but she'd barely known them. They'd both died when she was a child. If her mum had an accent, it was slight, as the Jackson family had left Paisley when Kenna was young, barely two years old, to live in London. But Kenna nodded, said yes, that she was from Scottish 'stock' on her mother's side.

"Ah." Charlotte was misty-eyed again. "I often think some travesty occurred, that *I* should have been from Scottish stock too, as I truly love the land, but, nope, not a drop of Gaelic blood in me. I'm a Sassenach through and through."

"Sassenach? Oh yeah, I've seen *Outlander*. It's what Jamie calls Claire, isn't it?"

Charlotte's brown eyes were still glittering. "*Affectionately* calls her. Bloody love that series. You see? Addicted to all things Scottish. Can't wait to get cracking on this new book, be Scottish in character, at least!"

"It's bound to be a hit," Kenna replied, "as are all your books."

Charlotte only shrugged in response, something Kenna liked about her, her humility. She *was* a highly regarded and successful author, and yet, for Charlotte, it wasn't about money or fame; it was about passion – she simply loved writing, and it shone through in every word. *That's* what made her a success. She was, Kenna thought, possibly her favourite author to work with. Some…well, some believed way too much in their own hype.

Charlotte began speaking again, and so Kenna leant forward to listen.

"So, do you spend any time in Scotland?"

"Me?" Kenna was aghast. "Oh no, not really. Been to Edinburgh once for a friend's birthday, much of which was spent in an alcoholic haze."

"Not curious to explore the rest of it?"

Was she? Kenna had to think. Yes, she supposed she was. She had asked a lot of questions about the place when she was young, when it had seemed almost mythical to her, this land of kilts and haggis and clansmen. Trouble was, as an adult, the allure of exotica had always won out, she and her friends following the crowds down to Lanzarote, Ibiza, Majorca, the usual trail. Adam liked it abroad too; they'd had a couple of great holidays together, sultry nights spent under a starlit sky.

"It's just…" Charlotte continued before Kenna could answer, "you know what? There's a vacancy at this castle due to come up, something I was told in confidence by the Keeper of the Castle, if you will, the custodian. The lady that's in charge now – Jean, Jean Morgan – she wants to take more of a back seat and needs someone to manage the day-to-day running of it. The castle's open to the public, you see, from ten till four each day. You actually get to live *at* the castle in a private suite. Tempting, isn't it?"

"Tempting? Well…"

"Oh, come on, being Lady of the Manor, living in a castle, in an actual castle? It would be the most amazing experience! They want someone with Scottish heritage too; well, they would, wouldn't they, so that's me out even if I did decide to leave Dan and the kids and hightail it. What a notion, though, what an opportunity to actually live the dream."

"Isn't the castle owned by Scottish Heritage or something?" wondered Kenna.

Charlotte shook her head. "It's privately owned by the same family who've owned it on and off for centuries, the

Buchannans. Only, they live in America now, apparently, barely visit, but what the heck – they pay towards its upkeep, wanting their family history to be upheld. Something to be said for ego, isn't there? Rich as they come, according to Jean, which is strange because…the castle is amazing, but it's nothing like other castles in Scotland, the really grand ones. It's more of a home. Yes, that's it, it feels homely rather than stately, its unique allure, I suppose. So, are you tempted?"

Kenna couldn't help but burst out laughing. "Me? Why would I be?"

Charlotte's expression was more wistful. "Why?" she repeated. "I suppose…like I said, I would be if I was young, free and single."

"I'm not single," Kenna pointed out, but Charlotte, as authors do, was losing herself in a world of her own creation.

"History is important, isn't it? Without it, well…what are we? It shapes us and so has to be preserved. I mean, don't get me wrong. It's sodding hard work maintaining a building like Drumlin." She laughed before adding, "I know that because Jean told me! It's something you devote yourself to day in, day out. It becomes your life, but, by God, what a life! I'll write about it in fiction, but there's something about being there, *actually being there*, getting your hands dirty, so to speak. It'd be…exhilarating. That's exactly what it was when I was there, but so peaceful too, rising every morning, hearing the birds sing, watching from your window as trees swayed gently on the surrounding hills and nothing, absolutely nothing to break the view. And then to come back here to the hustle and bustle, the *noise*." Charlotte covered her ears with her hands. "Don't you ever want to escape the noise? It's a different life up there, and I know the weather can be harsh, but it's a better life. I honestly feel that. It's more…real. If I was as young as you, if I had no commitments, if I could invent a Scottish ancestor somewhere, I'd be like Jean and live at the castle. You wouldn't need to ask me twice."

The meal had ended, the bill paid, and Charlotte and Kenna had gone their separate ways. Although other topics had been broached – notably the discussion of more plot points for Charlotte's next novel, the reason behind the meeting – the author had never lost that faraway look in her eyes.

Back at her desk, Kenna had Googled Drumlin Castle simply out of curiosity. A castle or a glorified house, a tall building over several floors, with a pine forest surrounding it. Impressive, magnificent and, yes, most definitely alluring. She'd zoomed in on the image on-screen, tried to peer into the many narrow windows, but it was no use; they were like black eyes, empty. Lonely, that's what it felt like, *crushingly* lonely, and yet there it was, spelt out before her that it was open to the public seven days a week with tea and cakes served in a vaulted café. It couldn't possibly be lonely, must have plenty of visitors, but she couldn't shake the feeling even long after the web page had been closed and she'd immersed herself in edits for another author, sighing at the words before her with no real depth to them, another regurgitation of a popular theme, the same old, same old. She'd asked her manager if she could work on more manuscripts like Charlotte's, in the historical genre rather than 'fodder for the cannon', as sometimes that type of fiction was called – *pulp*, in other words – but her request had been denied, ignored even.

It was gone eight that day when Kenna finally reached

home, finding out from Adam via text he'd also been working late. Whilst she picked at some hummus and carrots, the TV blaring in the background of her tiny rented flat, she spoke to him on the phone, both of them initially moaning about their commute and how busy it had been even at that hour.

"This bloke, right up against me, started coughing." The disgust in Adam's voice was evident. "I mean, like right in my face, not bothering to use his hand to cover his mouth. I was like, 'Mate, can you turn your head away or something?' and he was like, 'Why can't you?' So fucking rude! He just continued to cough all over me. I was that close to punching him. How I kept my shit, I don't know. I've probably contracted TB now!"

As he talked, she thought about birdsong and imagined the sound of wind rustling through pine trees. Should she tell him what Charlotte had told her? In the end, she did, all about Drumlin and how Charlotte had loved it, found it magical, such a contrast between the two worlds.

"She also said she'd love to be keeper of the castle if she could, if she wasn't married to a London businessman, had three children, that kind of thing. If she was free."

"Free like us," Adam murmured.

"Huh? We're not, though, are we? We both have jobs."

"A job I could jack in right now."

She felt that way too after the insipid book she'd been editing all day, after her commute home, the carriage full of faces as hacked off as hers.

"And that's the thing, there *is* a job going there as keeper of the castle, or an assistant manager, I suppose you'd call it, a custodian. The lady currently in charge wants to scale down her involvement and needs someone to take over the everyday running." She bit into a carrot stick before speaking again. "Charlotte said I should go for it, grab that life by the scruff of the neck. Something noble, she called it, worthwhile. I was like, yeah right, Jean –the manager there – would be inundated with people wanting that kind of job, historical nerds, and Charlotte said that, strangely, she wasn't, that very few people had applied and all so far totally unsuitable. You actually live in the castle in a flat there. Can you imagine that? It'd be creepy at night."

"Is Jean married?"

Kenna frowned. "What? I don't know!"

"The flat. Do you think it's big enough for two?"

"Adam! What are you talking about? How'd I know any of that? Why are you asking?"

"Why?" Adam sounded incredulous, as if amazed she couldn't guess. "Because if it is, if it's a job we could both do, you and me, it'd be the answer to our prayers."

Again, Kenna was stumped by what he was saying and couldn't actually reply, giving him the room to explain himself, at least.

"We're always talking about jumping off the treadmill, aren't we? We're always moaning, you and me, about our life here, how busy it is, how stressed we are. God, we don't even have time for each other. We just work all the bloody time."

"Because we have to earn money to live," Kenna said, finally finding her voice.

"We do," Adam agreed, "and yet we're always broke, we're always tired. We're in our twenties, and we're so fucking knackered."

"So? What is it you're trying to say?"

"That we give it a go! We find out about it, at least. The

details. Anyway, I can keep my job. All I need is my laptop and my phone, and I'm sorted."

"Hey, I want to keep *my* job, thank you! I like it."

"Less and less."

True, she supposed. She felt her boss didn't take her seriously, didn't value her even though she worked so damned hard and always to the best of her ability. When she came to think of it, she was often overlooked, from the big things right down to the small. She'd been there five years, doing the same job, and no sign of a significant promotion.

Knowing this as well as she did, she allowed Adam to continue persuading her, his enthusiasm eventually setting something alight.

"Just find out about it. That's all you have to do," he said. "Probably a pipe dream, but you never know. If a flat comes with the job and it's big enough, we could live together, you and me, finally, twenty-four seven. Also, you've talked about writing your own book rather than spending your entire time editing everybody else's. Maybe in a place where you're able to think more, you could do that, pen your own masterpiece."

And so she had found out about it, emailed Jean, enquired.

Now this. She was on her way there, not with Adam but alone, a job not for two, only one, but two could live in the flat, certainly. That wasn't the issue; it was plenty big enough. As Adam had said, he could work anywhere, commuting down to London easily enough on the occasions when Zoom wouldn't do.

She'd taken the plunge and handed in her notice, relishing the stunned expression on her manager's face. She'd notified Charlotte too, who'd squealed in delight, declared herself 'so jealous' and then had to run, no time to hear all the details due to a meeting she had to attend – a certain irony in that, thought Kenna. Even so, she was excited, or had been. Until Adam had backtracked spectacularly. *My life is here in London.*

What the hell? What the actual hell?

A complication had arisen with work; he was mid-build on an online rental website that wasn't going well, had become overcomplicated and now needed his full attention…apparently. A complication with work…or with someone? Another woman?

"Go, just go," he'd said. He'd *begged* her to.

Had Sal been right to distrust him?

Tears fell as the train rattled on. So many miles to go, hours that stretched ahead of her. Going through the motions, that's what she was doing, for what other choice was there? This was her job now, the rental in London given notice on too, a new home waiting that she hadn't seen. A new life that she knew nothing of. And all his idea.

He had pushed and pushed until he'd disposed of her, sent her far, far away.

Alone.

Chapter Two

A seven-hour stretch had seemed an eternity, and yet, as it always did, time passed, and soon enough the journey was at an end, the train pulling into Aberdeen railway station, the busiest in Scotland, north of Glasgow and Edinburgh. And it *was* busy, people rushing, heads down and frowning, most of them, just as she used to frown in London. It was a little after five, commute time, and a spark in her, just a tiny spark, was glad she'd done this after all and escaped what used to be. *Including Adam.* Immediately, she berated herself. She was neither escaping nor losing him; he'd been delayed, that's all. No reason not to believe him, to think the worst. No evidence. She hadn't seen him the day before she'd left for Scotland. *He* hadn't made time to see *her*, but he would. Soon. They'd have all the time in the world together, he'd said. *Just go!*

Her chest heaved at the memory.

"Hey! Hey there!"

She was so lost in thought, she only half registered she'd walked through the ticket barrier and was in the main hall, only barely heard someone calling her name.

"Kenna, Kenna Jackson."

She lifted her head, eyes scanning the crowd. A woman was waving, slim, really quite tiny, with bobbed hair as white as snow.

"Jean!" Kenna said, walking towards her.

The woman smiled and reached out a hand. "You're here! Oh good! That's good!"

As Kenna took the other woman's hand, her own smile faltered. Jean had spoken as if she'd doubted Kenna would materialise, *seriously* doubted. No need to worry on that score, though. Between her and Adam, one of them fulfilled their promises, at least.

The relief on Jean's face as they continued to stare at each other was unrelenting. They'd already 'met' via Zoom for the interview, but in the flesh she was a little craggier with no artificial light to smooth out lines, and somewhat…harried. Noting this, alarm bells rang in Kenna's head. *Will I look harried if I stay too long?* The initial contract for castle manager – or 'custodian', as she still preferred to call it – was for a year. If she hated it, she could leave, return to London, an option she held close to her chest. She could let someone else bear the burden. And she didn't have full responsibility for the castle either, as Jean would still manage finances but from home.

A burden? Why had she thought that? It was unwarranted so far.

After releasing her hand, Jean turned and led her out of the station to where she had parked her car. The day they emerged into was a cold, crisp one, the late March sky losing its brightness. At this rate, they'd arrive at the castle in darkness.

At the car, Jean commented on how little Kenna had brought with her.

"You are intending to stay longer than a week?" Her smile didn't quite reach her eyes.

"Yes, of course! It's just…there's always Aberdeen. If I

need anything, I'll head there."

"Aye"—Jean nodded as if satisfied with her answer—"and as you know, the flat is fully furnished. It's very comfortable, actually, a four-poster bed too! You'll feel quite the part!"

Her own stuff – what little she'd had – she'd sold or left for the next tenant, the people who owned the flat pleased about that, IKEA basics, most of it. Some things had been put into storage, Adam adding his too before finally making his way up, stuff that could be sent on if they stayed. But again, who knew if they would? With no ties, that longed-for freedom – that impossible goal – had become entirely possible. After Drumlin, they could go anywhere, travel and work abroad, somewhere warm, and really start living. She just had to make it through the year first, add to her CV. *They* did. She and Adam.

In the car, Jean pulled out from the side street, Kenna unable to decide if the tall granite buildings that surrounded them were beautiful or austere. No matter, they soon gave way to countryside, an increased chill prompting Jean to turn the heater up.

"Likely be a frost tonight," she warned, "but don't fret. Contrary to reports, Scotland does have some good weather. Seriously, when the sun shines, it can't be beaten."

The countryside was certainly beautiful, hilly landscape covered in fields of gold that shimmered in the dusk, the silhouette of mountains in the distance more rugged, wilder than she'd ever seen before and punctuated with clumps of shrubs, possibly heather. It was breathtaking, and whilst Jean chattered on, Kenna leaned her forehead against the window, just…absorbing it.

London. All her life she'd lived there, surrounded by

bricks and mortar and concrete. A good life, she'd loved it, so much at her disposal. Shops, bars and restaurants in abundance. Made the most of it but had grown tired of it too. Here was something different, something…unexpected, and despite her anger, frustration and confusion at Adam's absence, that spark of excitement within her refused to fizzle out completely.

"Oh, Adam," she breathed.

"Sorry?"

Startled, unaware she'd said his name out loud, she turned to Jean. "Oh…um…I…"

"It's fine," Jean said, one hand waving in the air. "I know you emailed to say Adam was held up with work, but will he be here soon?"

"Soon enough," Kenna said, unable to provide more of an answer than that.

"Well, there's plenty to keep you busy till he arrives. Tourist season's due to kick off, and, although we're a private concern – not as grand as some of the other castles in the region, perhaps, Fyvie and the like – there's a steady stream of visitors. We've a café too, as discussed, which is popular following a visit. Two young people from nearby Tulce oversee it, Connor and Laura. Aye, summer at Drumlin can get very busy indeed."

"Sounds great," Kenna replied. "Exactly the challenge I'm looking for."

"You'll be wonderful, I know it. I could tell as soon as I set eyes on you, even if it was via Zoom. You have this…enthusiasm about you, and that's what's needed at the castle to bring life to it, to help those that find their way to us see the magic of it all."

"Magic?" Kenna raised an eyebrow.

"Aye, there's magic aplenty at Drumlin. The history it's seen, it's second to none. It's forged into stone."

Her eyes still on Jean rather than the surrounding countryside, Kenna could only nod, the prospect of the task ahead as daunting as it was exciting. She was here now, though; she'd do her job to the best of her ability, just as she had in London, and hopefully be appreciated for it this time, not just a cog in a wheel, a *tiny* cog, easy to overlook. And maybe Adam was right: the entire experience would prompt a novel of her own.

One day.

Drumlin would be busy in summer, as Jean had said, but summer wouldn't last forever. It would fall away, as would the visitors, and she, Kenna, would still be there – for a good few further months, at least. Time in which to test that quiet ambition of hers.

Dig deep.

* * *

At last, Drumlin came into view.

"There she is!" said Jean, a wealth of pride in her voice.

The journey from the railway station to Drumlin, although little more than forty miles, was via a series of increasingly twisting lanes that, in the dark, Jean had negotiated with obvious care. Consequently, it had taken around ninety minutes.

Eventually, Kenna spotted a signpost for the castle – the only one – and they'd turned up a long driveway, granite gateposts on either side and the entire estate flanked by the hills of a pine forest, countless shadowy giants that stood sentinel against the moonlit sky.

ROHAISE

Darkness might have shrouded the castle, but it was still silhouetted, something more imposing, even, than the majestic trees of nature. It stood defiant.

Towards the rear of the castle, Jean brought the car to a stop, all the while Kenna unable to drag her eyes from the building in front of her.

"Home," she breathed.

"Aye, it is that. It's been my home for many, many years, but now it's yours."

In the car's gloom, Kenna turned to Jean. "How can you bear it?" The words, once out, made her wince, as they were so personal. She was genuinely curious, though: How did you go from living in a castle to somewhere bound to be more ordinary?

Jean simply stared at her, no answer on her lips at first. Gradually, she formed one.

"It's time," she said before opening the car door. "I've done all I can. Come on, let's away now. Let's get you inside."

There was to be no tour this evening; Kenna had already been informed of that. "I'll get you settled in the flat first, and then I have to go. I've cousins visiting from Inverness, and we're meeting for dinner. Tomorrow, though, in daylight, I'll show you round properly, help you to get your bearings. We'll meet first thing."

The flat Kenna would stay in – originally where Jean had lodged – was where a porch addition jutted out. After grabbing her trolley bag, she crunched across gravel to reach it, still in awe of the castle and how it loomed over her, how solitary it looked too, as alone as she'd felt it to be when she'd seen it on Google.

As Jean opened the door, Kenna shivered, and not just

because of the cold. Tonight, she'd be the only one in this vast property, which made her feel small suddenly, more insignificant than she'd ever been; it made her long for Adam too, causing a flash of anger that he was absent, that he wasn't experiencing the wonder of this alongside her.

They stepped inside the entrance lobby, with its exposed stone walls and faded tartan curtains at two sets of windows. Jean swiftly removed her shoes and placed them neatly to one side before sighing, perhaps with nostalgia. "This way," she said.

They headed towards a door, Jean opening it to reveal a narrow staircase that curved just as castle steps curved, upwards and into the flat on the first floor.

At the top of the staircase, Jean crossed over to the wall and flicked the light switch.

"Wow," breathed Kenna, taking in yet more of her surroundings. Before her was a good-sized living room with a sofa, two armchairs and a coffee table, plus a fireplace with a log burner already lit. Kenna could feel the warmth of it from where she stood.

"As I've said," Jean said, "it's very comfortable, and there's central heating too, although nothing beats a real fire, don't you agree? Here, come through to the kitchen."

The kitchen was through a short arched tunnel and was itself a vaulted stone room but with all mod-cons, flagstones beneath her feet and a large picture window at the rear end.

"Lovely," Kenna declared, "just lovely." It was so big compared to the London flat, the kitchen there nothing but a glorified countertop that overlooked the living room. Here was something entirely separate, a place to pad towards in the morning, grab a coffee from the filter machine and sit at the long refectory table, with its tartan-clad chairs, and contemplate this new life she'd rushed headlong into.

"Right," said Jean, clearly happy with Kenna's expression, "to the bedrooms!"

"There are three of them, is that right?"

"Aye, as I've told you, it's a comfortable flat, big. It is, after all, part of the castle."

"Yes, yes, of course," replied Kenna, glancing at the thick walls to the side of her, what lay beyond them so mysterious right now.

A long passageway led from the living room, whereupon the ceiling became higher, clearly entering an older portion of the castle. Her skin prickled on entering it, imagining it to run on and on like a bridge towards another age.

"Are you all right, dear?"

"Pardon?" Kenna said, blinking.

"It's just you've gone rather pale."

"Oh. Have I? I'm fine. Thank you. Probably just a little tired."

Although Jean nodded, she was frowning too. "It's certainly been a long day for you, a day out of the ordinary, and all this, it'll take some getting used to."

"Yes." Kenna smiled, grateful for Jean's understanding. It would indeed, plus rogue thoughts such as entering another dimension were bound to enter her head on occasion. There was just so much history here, as both Charlotte and Jean had said. History that was palpable.

In the first bedroom they came to, there was enough room for a single bed and a small wardrobe. Close to that was a bathroom, which, like the kitchen, was a good size, the walls painted a deep red, and boasting a modern shower big enough for two.

"Beautiful," Kenna declared.

Rather than go into the room immediately along from that, Jean led her to another bedroom straight ahead, one with twin beds and a table with a lamp between them. There was so much room, so much space, her head began to spin.

"This is the last room," Jean said, leading her to the room they'd bypassed. "*Your* room."

Jean had stood aside to allow her full sight whilst simultaneously turning on the light, not just any light either but a crystal chandelier that hung from the centre of the ceiling.

"This…this is mine?"

"It is." Jean's voice was reverential.

The room was like something from a book of fairy tales, from the soaring imagination of any young girl who'd ever dreamed herself to be a princess. Huge and just so grand – bigger than the whole flat she'd left behind in London. At the far end, three sets of windows ran from floor to ceiling, another floor-to-ceiling window at the side too, both with heavy drapes at them, sage green in colour. There was a dressing table, a chest of drawers that matched her in height, the biggest wardrobe ever, a sofa, two armchairs and a coffee table and something else – the bed, of course, complete with four posts and canopy, the latter matching the green of the curtains.

"Oh God, no, I couldn't," Kenna said. "I'll take one of the other rooms. This room, it's like…it's too stately for me, just…too much."

What was wrong with her? She couldn't stop babbling nor stem the tears that were filling her eyes, beginning to burst from them. With one hand, she reached out to steady herself, found the back of the sofa and headed closer to it so she could sit there.

"I'm sorry, so sorry…"

As her voice trailed off, Jean drew near.

"It's all right," she said. "Let the feelings come, let them wash over you. I was the same when I first came here so many years ago. I just…couldn't believe it. This is your room. *You're* the custodian of Drumlin now. You deserve this. This is your rightful place."

Jean's comforting words didn't stop the flow. If Adam were here, this would have all been so different. She would have been excited instead of bewildered, happy instead of sad. Tonight, their first night, they would have lain in that canopied four-poster bed and giggled, as much as they had in their early days together, like little kids rather than adults. When had it all changed? Why had they let it? And yet this was supposed to fix all that, the magic of Drumlin bringing back the magic between them.

She lifted her head and looked around at the room she'd thought of as so stately. It was exactly that, and it was hers and hers alone.

Jean reached out a hand to touch Kenna's hair, taking a few strands of it between her fingers. Kenna adjusted her gaze to look at her instead, saw the depth of her compassion and something else too, akin to wonder.

"Why are you here?" the woman asked, and her wonder only seemed to increase.

"Why?" Kenna answered. "Because of the job—"

"No," Jean said. "Why are you *really* here?"

Chapter Three

A stirring, a murmur, an echo. Tears falling, soft tears, like the rain in summer. Whose? Not mine, for that well is empty. Such a strange sound for someone who has heard nothing for so long. I exist in silence, a hollow, a void, a vessel as empty as I am myself. And yet another echo hovers, a reminder of all that existed before the silence. Not gentle as this new sound is, raw instead, brutal, able to tear your heart and your soul in two. I can't, I mustn't focus on it or it will grow louder, the shrillness of those screams, the jeering that greeted them. So much easier to drift, just drift, and not remember anything.

Or anyone.

My story, such as it was, can be forgotten.

As I try to forget.

As I lie here, just lie here, in a room once golden with the glow of love, now mired in perpetual darkness, covering me like the thickest of woollen blankets.

And yet, despite this, life has found me, voices have, a sadness and a bewilderment that is not my own, my eyelids beginning to flutter like the wings of a wild bird, to open.

No! No need to listen. It isn't him, the one I long for. It's a woman I sense. Who is she? What is she doing here? This is my home. A place I wanted to be forevermore. Once.

Loneliness. I ache with it. There is no real respite, not even in sleep. I fool myself regarding that too. I miss him, always. I want him back. 'I am nothing without you.' He said that to me once, the walls of a tunnel enclosing us. But the opposite is also true!

Why am I waking? Let me slumber. Please!

Whom I am begging, I do not know.

Certainly not God.

The sound that woke me has quieted. I strain to listen, but it has gone. And the memories begin. Good memories, only good. I beg for it to be so! If I must hear laughter, let it be his laughter and mine, such delight in it, such wonder. It is an echo I can bear.

That he loved me was like a miracle. He was the first man. The only man.

The forest was my home before the castle ever was, that which surrounds Drumlin. There I lived, first with my mother and a brother, then only me. I missed them, longed for them too, but I could not leave and venture towards the town to ease my loneliness. The smell of the pine, the herbs, the flowers that grow there, the ferns and the wild roses, they were what comforted me. Of course, I knew of Alexander before he knew of me. I would spy him hunting on horseback and on foot. And then he spied me – at last – as I peered out from behind one of the tall trees. How he gasped with surprise!

Men can be cruel; Mother had told me that. She had warned me to stay away from them, even with her dying breath. 'This is your world,' she had said, her bony hands clutching at mine. 'Tend to the animals. Make your tinctures. Live as we have always lived. A simple life is a good life, Rohaise. You belong to the forest. The forest is in your blood. Stay.'

And I did as she had asked, burying her and then my brother, who was younger than me by two summers. I stayed alone. But he had seen me, and once he had, he didn't forget me. He hunted me down too.

I was alone in my dwelling when he came. My senses, always keen, froze on hearing something other. So few ventured that far into the trees, yet there he was, calling out.

"Girl? Girl, are you there? Is it here that you live? Girl, answer me!"

I sat there, hunkered around the fire I had built, my heart something rabid, beating faster and faster. I was trapped, just like the deer of the forest are so often trapped, the rabbits and the boar. Could I burst through the door, flimsy though it was, fashioned from nothing but skins, and outrun him? Men are cruel, and yet this one I'd dreamed of, the height and the breadth of him, the darkness of his hair. Surely, he wouldn't send a spear hurtling through the air after me! But if he entered the dwelling, what then?

I rose at last and took a step forward, then rushed into the open, heading straight towards him, his eyes once again wide with surprise. He'd come alone. Quickly I saw that.

Finally, just before colliding, I swerved, continued past him, flying over the forest floor with all its obstacles, knowing exactly where each stone, each branch, lay.

He shouted again, gave chase, the sound of his feet like thunder.

Brave. He was certainly that.

The forest is fearful for some. Tales abound concerning what lies within, at the very heart of it. It is black as pitch, they say, no sunlight able to penetrate nor daring to. A realm like no other, unnatural even, the domain of the faerie.

I ran deeper into it, waiting to hear his footsteps falter, expecting it.

They grew faster instead.

I looked over my shoulder. That was my undoing.

ROHAISE

I couldn't believe he was still at my heels. Men simply didn't give chase here.

But he was different. As deep down I knew he would be.

The Laird of Drumlin. Alexander Buchannan.

My foot snagged in a root, and I tumbled to the ground, felled by my ally, the forest. And he was upon me just as suddenly, turning me round to face him.

I fought. Of course I fought. My mother had taught me how to. I was no match for him, though. Easily, he pinned my hands above me and stilled my body with his.

"Don't be afraid," he said. "I will not harm you."

"I am not afraid! Get off me! Get off!"

"No," he replied. "I will not."

I'd been tossing my head from side to side, red hair like blood gathering leaves and twigs, but I stopped. I had no choice, had to look into his eyes. And there I saw it, something he knew as well as I did, that I'd let myself be captured.

That I was ready…

So many memories, but that one of the first time our bodies touched, albeit fully clothed, there's just so much hope in it.

No more! I cannot bear it. For hope fled and too soon. Why do I persist? Torture myself when I have been tortured enough? Oh, the torture! Flesh that was used, was mutilated, limbs that were broken and burnt. Bones left to rot in the dirt.

Sleep.

I must sleep. Force shut my eyes.

Please let me sleep.

No dreams.

No echoes.

Just sleep.

Just nothing.

Emptiness.

Chapter Four

The day dawned and so brightly. Kenna hadn't expected to pass a dreamless night, hadn't expected to sleep at all but toss and turn instead, her mind raging with thoughts about the real reason Adam wasn't with her, but that hadn't happened. Instead, Jean had left, and, alone in the flat, she'd unpacked, showered, then eaten some toast, grateful the cupboards and fridge had been left well stocked. Afterwards, she'd climbed beneath the sheets of the canopied bed, leaving a side lamp on, thankful for its soft glow. Rather than Adam, she'd thought about Jean's words, spoken as the woman had stroked her hair: *Why are you* really *here?*

Jean hadn't explained what she'd meant by them and neither had Kenna probed, but they continued to repeat inside her head, over and over like a chant but one that increasingly soothed her, lulled her further into sleep. Perhaps this morning she could ask, although…the moment had passed. Was it right to resurrect it?

As she stood staring at the mirror above the dressing table in her room – grand too, with its gilt frame and glass only slightly mottled – her cheeks burned red, matching the hair that fell around her shoulders. Why cry in front of Jean like that? It wasn't like her, not in the least. She wasn't a hard person, but she wasn't as soft as mush either. She trod the middle ground. Just an ordinary girl who'd experienced an ordinary upbringing and an ordinary life since leaving home. Perhaps *that* was why she was here, why she'd jacked in her life in London because of a mere suggestion from someone she barely knew. Her life was *too* ordinary. Even her love affair with Adam, from such glorious beginnings – what she'd thought of as glorious, at any rate – had become…humdrum. And they both knew it. Hence, why he'd encouraged her to apply for this job, why he wanted to come with her, because they needed an injection of something different, something *extra*ordinary.

Yes, that was it. It all made sense now. But how to explain this to Jean? Not only was it too personal but also – again – too ordinary. *I came here because I wanted a change; we did, my boyfriend and I.* It wasn't passion that prompted the move, not for the castle or for history, just different scenery and a less hectic pace to the one she was used to.

With a shake of her head, she turned from the mirror and grabbed her bag, her destination the castle entrance, where she was due to meet Jean. If the former custodian asked such a strange and pertinent question again, she'd tell the truth, ordinary or not.

As she moved through the flat, she felt it again – such heaviness in the atmosphere, and that was just here in what was basically staff quarters. How would it be once she entered the castle proper? Like wading through treacle? She wondered what stories had played out at Drumlin over the centuries. And now it was her turn, her story…

Enough musings. She had to get on, not keep Jean waiting. Hurrying down the curved staircase to what was now her front door, she opened it and stepped outside. As she did, her jaw dropped. It was beautiful, breathtaking, early morning dew rather than the frost she'd expected clinging to bushes and trees. It was green as far as the eye could see, just like Charlotte had described it, the castle lawns giving way to the pines of the forest that surrounded them, all of which stood as warriors might, shoulder to shoulder. This was hers, all hers. Not technically – she supposed the Buchannan family might have something to say about that – but she was the keeper, a role that suddenly seemed as magnificent as the vista she was looking at. *Ragged* lawns, she realised, not manicured; nothing about the garden was. It verged on wild with overgrown hedges and thick brambles. There was much work to be done here. The weight of that impressed itself upon her too, but again she resolved to give it her best shot.

Finally, she crunched over the gravel pathway, still awestruck as she took in the ruin of what looked like a small chapel attached to the main body of the castle, an equally ancient dovecote beside it. Rounding the corner, she was greeted next by the front of the castle, the main entrance for visitors. There were several windows here, just like at the side and the back of the castle, including a grand stonework bay window on the first floor, jutting out. That wasn't where her eyes lingered, however; rather, they were drawn upwards and to the right of it to another window, likely that of a bedroom, drapes hanging on either side and the shadow of something within – another bed like hers? Canopied? Whose room was it? she wondered. Who had occupied any and all of them? Oh, there was so much to find out, to learn, to immerse herself in, that spark of excitement really catching light.

"There you are!"

Jean's voice infiltrated her thoughts, but it still took a few seconds for Kenna to avert her eyes, to acknowledge her, something that clearly didn't go unnoticed.

"What's caught your fancy?" Jean said, approaching her.

"Oh…I… Nothing. Nothing. It's just…in daylight…"

Jean's smile was indulgent. "Aye, it's even more impressive in daylight, isn't it? Although…" She paused. "Night lends it a certain something."

"A certain something? Yes, I suppose it does. Even more atmosphere."

"That it does. That it does. Ready for the grand tour?"

"Absolutely. I can't wait to get started."

After another approving smile, Jean turned her back, indicating for Kenna to follow. It was barely 8.00 a.m., and the castle was open to the public from ten till four each day, with kitchen staff arriving around 9.30 a.m. This meant they had the castle to themselves for a while, she and Jean, a time she hoped would be as magical as her first glimpse of the gardens and forest in daylight – seeing it all with fresh eyes, taking in the sheer majesty of it.

Jean extracted some keys from the deep pocket of her coat and opened the largest studded oak door Kenna had ever seen, grunting a little as she pushed against it.

"Darn thing gets stuck on occasion, particularly after a burst of rain. It tries to resist you, but brook no nonsense. Be firm with it," the older woman advised.

Once it had yielded, they entered through the dark stone outer porch and into the entrance hall, Jean groaning again, this time as she pushed the door shut. The thud it made as it settled into place was ominous, as if it had locked them in, imprisoned them.

"You all right?"

Kenna looked at Jean. How perceptive she was!

"Fine, it's just…"

"You're overwhelmed again?"

Kenna laughed. She was, completely. It was like she hadn't been able to think straight since arriving. "No tears this time, though, I promise."

"Doesn't matter if there are," Jean told her. "I'd understand."

"No, I..." Should she do it, ask her what she'd meant last night, the words she'd spoken? *I'm here because...because...* She'd formed a reason in the flat, but now it deserted her. Just as well, as Jean brought her hands together in a clap, then started delivering what Kenna presumed was the castle spiel, something she'd have to learn too.

"Dating from around 1030, Drumlin is a castle – or 'tower house', you could call it – of tremendous character and with a distinct sense of history. For the last seven hundred years, give or take a decade, it has for the main part belonged to the Buchannan family, given to Sir Gilbert Buchannan of Erroll in 1308 by none other than King Robert the Bruce."

Leading her further into the entrance hall to where a coat of arms, stag's head, battle armour and several swords graced the walls – the usual props, Kenna supposed – Jean continued with the history lesson.

"In the early 1900s, however, I'm sad to say, Drumlin Castle fell into ruin, only to be rescued again by Captain John Buchannan in the 1960s. Infested with dry rot, he had quite the task on his hands, but he was determined it should return to the Buchannans, as it had been so much a part of their history. He and his wife Arabella restored it to what you see now, a comfortable family home." Here Jean paused before adding, "*Very* comfortable, I'd say. And it's remained in the Buchannan family ever since. Of course, John and

Arabella have since died, and their offspring, two sons and a daughter, have chosen to live elsewhere in the world. It's the grandson who mainly keeps in touch, Duncan, rather than the rest of the clan. Still, can't blame them and no hard feelings, oh no, because somewhere deep-rooted in them is their love of ancestry. Although we're largely funded by the income the castle makes and receive generous donations from the Rotary Club, who organise several events for us, they often make up any shortfall."

Kenna was nodding avidly, determined to grasp every word when Jean burst out laughing. "Oh dear!" she said. "Oh my! I can see I've quite blinded you with science."

"No," Kenna protested. "It's…fascinating."

"Aye, well, there's much to learn, but you've time, plenty of time. Right now, it'll do to only know the bare bones of it. And to be honest, there's so much we *don't* know regarding what happened here. Although a castle in Scotland, it's not one of the biggies." At the word 'biggie' Jean lifted both hands and bent the two forefingers on each hand. "We're not National Trust for Scotland. We have to work hard to get any sort of attention, any visitors, even. Here, in the midst of this pine forest, people don't know about us, not really, despite the signs I've had erected and our website, and we don't have the funds to advertise more heavily than we do, not when they're needed elsewhere. We rely on word of mouth. But despite this or even because of it, what we are is one of Scotland's hidden gems, and those that do find their way to us, they don't regret it, put it that way."

With that said, Jean passed beneath an archway, heading towards a staircase – a central 'turnpike' staircase, she described it as – from which all rooms led off, Drumlin the only castle in Scotland to boast this feature. There were eight floors altogether, and the first room they entered on the first floor was the one with the bay window, plus the biggest stone fireplace Kenna had ever seen.

"John and Arabella used to host parties in here, the main hall," Jean explained, her foot tapping against the wooden flooring. "It's quite the events room."

Kenna raised an eyebrow as she looked around, wondering about that and whether Jean had deliberately said it, was planting a seed in her mind.

Back on the staircase, each tread was impressively wide, and there were alcoves with narrow windows in which had been placed various vases and statues. On the curving walls, tapestries of ancient battle scenes gave you something else to admire.

Kenna took it all in, listening to Jean although her voice was becoming more and more distant, as if she were fading somehow, as if the castle were absorbing her, doing exactly the same thing to Kenna, soaking them right up. Beautiful. It was certainly that, as she'd expected and seen from photographs on the website, but photographs could not convey the atmosphere. Only in being here could you experience that, and, as she'd surmised, it was even more intense than in the flat – as though it seeped through her clothing to her skin and entered the bones there.

In another room, the solar, there was another impressive fireplace, with an inscription carved upon it that Kenna ran her hands along, fingers sinking into the groove of each word. 'My hope is in ye, Lord,' it read and dated from the mid-1500s, Jean told her. Portraits in gilt frames also hung on the walls, depicting those that had occupied such hallowed ground previously, proud men and women, most with hair that was jet black and eyes that followed you.

Jean picked up something, which she waved at Kenna. "These information sheets were typed by none other than Captain John himself. They give you the history of each room as far as he knew it and detail the paintings and furniture, all brought back from his travels abroad to reside here at Drumlin. A fairly eclectic collection, I think you'll agree."

There were some rather exotic pieces, including a Buddha statue and other items that were more Indian in style. It didn't matter, though, or look out of place; all were antiquated and of good quality, adding to the ambience, Kenna reminding herself that this had become a family home and what a privilege it must have been to retire here.

In the formal dining room, there was service laid out on a linen-covered table. Again, not grand but quaint, white china with a gold pattern upon the rim. Manageable, that's what Drumlin was. A castle, yes, but a home too and not just for John and Arabella.

A place that had been loved. Definitely.

It was onto the bedrooms next, or so she thought.

"Actually, there's a library on this floor too," Jean said, her voice lower now, almost conspiratorial. "A library with a…rather interesting story."

Kenna raised an eyebrow; it was *all* interesting as far as she was concerned.

Again following Jean, they entered a room where the walls were deep green, two of them lined with books. A Persian rug covered the floorboards, plus there was a writing desk and chair, a pianoforte and a chandelier. Another stunning room, one with a deep alcove in which there was a window. It was here Jean walked towards.

"There was a monk buried right here in these walls," she said.

If her eyebrow had risen before, now Kenna's mouth fell open.

"A monk? Yes! I remember reading something about that on the website."

"Aye, yes, there's a mention of it, but we prefer to tell the whole story face-to-face. It was during the Reformation, when monasteries were being destroyed left, right and centre, that Joseph Buchannan, serving the Catholic faith, fled here to the ancestral home for sanctuary, which he found but only for a short while. He was ill, you see, at the end of his days. Members of his extended family, fearing what would become of his body, tore down this wall and buried him deep within it, endeavouring to keep him safe. Years later…" She laughed, bowed her head a little. "Och, *many* years later, a young local girl sensed something here, some…unrest. Captain John was informed but dismissed it. The girl wouldn't let up, though. There *was* unrest, and it was growing, manifesting itself in various ways."

"A ghost?" whispered Kenna.

Again, Jean laughed. "Every castle has ghosts, or so those that look after the castle will have you believe. But I'm talking about real unrest – noises, the slamming of doors in empty rooms, the wailing so distant you'd think it far off, but it wasn't. It emanated from right here in the library, Joseph growing increasingly tired of his burial place, trying to reach out."

"So what happened?"

"What happened? Och, well, Captain John could no longer deny it, and so, acting on the young girl's claims, he had the wall torn down, and, sure enough, there lay within it a skeleton, still dressed in black although the cloth was in rags, a Bible at his feet, inscribed with his name. He was liberated and laid to rest on consecrated ground."

"And that stuff that you mentioned, the slamming of doors, the wailing, did they stop?"

"Aye, lass, they did. All was quiet at Drumlin after that."

It was strange, Kenna thought, following Jean out of the room, that she didn't look triumphant about the peace that had subsequently reigned. She looked…saddened by it, maybe even confused. Wasn't it good that burial in a more fitting place had appeased the spirit of the monk? Ghosts were a part of castle culture. She understood that, but it was better, surely, that any phenomena occurring was the stuff of fiction rather than fact?

Such thoughts faded from her mind as they continued to explore the rooms, including Queen Mary's Bower, the castle's claim to fame being she stayed there once for a few days in 1562, en route home from the Battle of Corrichie. A surprisingly small room – despite 'bower' referring to a lady's private apartment in a medieval castle – it was also empty, kept as some sort of shrine, perhaps, never to have been slept in again, not once a woman of such high rank had laid her head there. Other bedrooms, however, were more sumptuous, boasting fireplaces with Delft tiles, as well as polished timber flooring covered by rugs and overlooked by oak beams, some of which were intricately carved or painted. Captain John had given them various names: the Tulip Room; the Royal Suite, so named because a member of the French Royal Family had stayed there once; the Trump Room, nothing to do with a former American President, Jean assured her; and Rowanfield, named after Captain John's boyhood home in Lerwick, Shetland.

On the sixth floor they came to the last room, those on the seventh floor being attic rooms used only for storage. Another four-poster bed graced it, at the foot of which was a chaise longue. There was also a table with a woman's hairbrush set laid out upon it, the casing a shimmering mother-of-pearl, over which presided a mirror even fancier than the one in her own room. On entering, Kenna had taken a breath. This was the room she'd looked at from outside, the pattern on the bed's canopy so much clearer now, that of red roses entwined. She moved closer to the bed, noticed too that the posts had carvings upon them. More roses, twisting around each other.

"Oh, this room," she whispered.

"You like it?"

"Like it? I love it!" There was something about it, even more so than in the other rooms, even Queen Mary's Bower. Drenched in atmosphere, it evoked feelings in Kenna she couldn't quite explain, a riot of them.

"Who did it belong to?" she asked when she could.

A small smile played about Jean's lips as she answered, some of the sadness fading that had clung to her since leaving the library where the monk had been buried.

"This, my dear, is Rohaise's room."

Chapter Five

"Pleased to meet you!"

"Pleased to meet you too! Welcome to Drumlin. I hope you love it as much as we do."

The staff had arrived, all two of them. Connor was tall, Laura the shorter of the pair, both in their early twenties, Kenna guessed, and brimming with life and enthusiasm. Connor's grey eyes sparkled as he held out his hand for Kenna to shake, and Laura, with her dark hair tied in a smooth bun, had the widest of smiles.

Back here at the rear end of the ground floor was a kitchen, a small café and the toilets, all converted sympathetically, none of the grandeur lost. It was in the kitchen that Connor worked, making teas and coffees and serving a small selection of hot food, cakes and sandwiches, with Laura helping him but sometimes having to cover reception too.

"It's a tight ship we run," Jean told Kenna. "It's only three of us at Drumlin, but we manage, even on the busiest of days. Actually, there's a fourth joining the ranks, just part-time, a gardener. Aye, he's new alongside you. You'll meet him soon."

Good. All good. *Manageable*, thought Kenna again. Of course it was. Jean had managed, clearly, the first official custodian of the castle, and therefore so could she.

"How many visitors per day do you expect to get?" she asked Jean.

"It can vary. As I've said, in late spring and summer, it's a steady stream. Sometimes organised coach tours include us, but the rest are made up of casual visitors."

"And in autumn and winter?"

Jean turned away at that point, distracted by something Connor was saying about an order that hadn't yet been delivered. She rushed off to the kitchen with him, Laura in pursuit, leaving Kenna alone for a moment in the café area, another portrait of an ancestor in full Highland regalia staring at her just as they'd done on various floors upstairs.

The Rohaise Room – or rather Rohaise's room, as Jean had called it – how her skin had tingled in there. Straightaway, the name intrigued her.

"What does it mean?" she'd asked, repeating it phonetically: *Row-haze*.

"*Rohaise* is Gaelic for 'rose'. Her name was Rose. As with most Gaelic names, if you say them quickly enough, they reveal themselves in the more Anglicised version."

"Was she a Buchannan?"

Jean had hesitated. "No. No, she wasn't. She was…a local girl, we think."

"A local girl? From Tulce?" That was the closest town.

"Maybe, maybe not. She was, for want of a better word, the mistress of Alexander Buchannan. They lived together for a while here at the castle."

"The mistress? But Alexander Buchannan's suite is on the second floor. How come she had her own room and why so high up? I'm not an authority on castles, not yet, anyway, but didn't it go that the lower in rank you were, the higher the floor you were placed on?"

"True, but…perhaps she requested this room. I mean look at the views!"

Jean was right; the views of the pine forest were spectacular.

"When was this?"

"Och, way back," Jean answered, flapping at the air with one hand – a trademark gesture, Kenna was coming to realise. "Alexander was the cousin of Francis Buchannan, a man charged with treason against James VI in 1594. Charged, then exiled. Alexander was given the castle after swearing loyalty. We're talking at the very end of the 1500s now. There isn't much known about Rohaise at all, to be honest; she remains something of an enigma. All that's been passed down is that she was Alexander Buchannan's lover and that, like yourself, she was a redhead, famed for her beauty and ultimately…her bravery."

"Bravery? In what way?"

"She died defending the castle, defending him, Alexander."

Kenna was incredulous. "What do you mean? Single-handedly or something?"

Jean nodded. "Aye, that's exactly what I mean. The Reformation may have come and gone, but there was still so much unrest. It was put about that along with the Gordons of Huntley, Alexander Buchannan had indeed followed in his cousin's footsteps, which actually is now thought to be untrue. Mud, however, sticks. The king's artillery was sent to nearby Huntley first and burnt the Gordons out, then proceeded to Drumlin, gun carriages in tow, brought up by sea from Edinburgh to nearby Banff, a cannon that would breach these walls. All at the castle fled; only Alexander and Rohaise stayed. Initially. Perhaps Alexander thought he could plead his case, reason with them. Then, finally, Alexander escaped too."

"How, with the troops closing in?"

"It's rumoured there's a tunnel. The story goes it's through there Alexander escaped."

"Why on earth didn't Rohaise leave too? Why didn't they just stick together?"

"Again, this can only be surmised, but the tunnel entrance would most likely have had to be covered up, and if all staff had gone, there was only Rohaise left to do it. She may well have gone with him, but at some point, she turned back, because when the troops arrived in their full, dubious glory, it was just her at the castle. Alone."

"What happened to her?"

How solemn Jean looked. "We don't know. Only that she died here."

"What about Alexander?"

"We don't know anything more about him either, whether he made it elsewhere, to England or even across the sea to France, and just…laid low. Of course, he could have been captured, but most likely we'd know if that were the case. The tunnel would have emerged into the forest, which troops would have been combing thoroughly. As I've said, his fate is a mystery. All we know is the king's men made an example of the Gordons, and they'd make an example of Alexander too, *especially* Alexander. No more half measures. They wouldn't have gone easy on him, and I doubt they went easy on Rohaise either."

Kenna gulped. "Where is this tunnel? Is it beneath the castle?"

"If it is, we haven't been able to find it. There's no actual cellar at the castle, but there are outbuildings – *ruins* of outbuildings, I should say. It could be anywhere."

"Wow," Kenna said, but as solemn as Jean. "I'm so sorry."

As she'd said it, the air around her had seemed to swirl, a cold draft responsible, perhaps, the day not so still anymore but a wind picking up and finding its way in.

Whilst now waiting for Jean to tend to the problem in the kitchen, Kenna wanted to gaze upwards at Drumlin, to take it all in again. Making her way to the entrance hall, she stepped outside, noticed the day was as still as it had been earlier, no breeze evident at all. A frown developing, she took a step back, as if shying away from the castle, her eyes on the upper floors, lost for a moment in a bubble of time in which she and she alone existed. When a voice managed to burst that bubble, she greeted it with a scream.

"Steady!" the voice urged. "I'm sorry, I didn't mean to startle you."

Kenna spun round, eyes as wide as if she'd heard – if not seen – something ghostly. There was a man before her who appeared in his mid to late twenties, a Scot, from his accent.

"Who are you?" she blurted out. "What are you doing here?"

"I'm Gregor," he announced, a smile on his face, an *amused* one. "The gardener."

"Oh! Oh yes, Jean said."

"Aye, I've just been appointed. Only a few hours a week, but still, it's a privilege to work here. A dream come true, really."

A dream come true? She'd thought the same not so long ago.

Kenna continued to survey him. He was tall, his dark hair curly and somewhat unkempt. He fit the look of a gardener, wearing a cream cable-knit jumper, black jeans and heavy boots. She laughed suddenly. What the hell did she mean, he fit the look? As if she'd know! She was a city girl through and through, now ensconced in the country, *entombed*.

All laughter abruptly stopped. She might even have staggered, because Gregor reached out a hand and laid it on her arm.

"Are you all right? I really am sorry to have startled you."

"I'm fine. I just… Where did you come from?"

It was his turn to look startled now. "Um…I'm local, a few miles outside of Tulce."

"No, no, I mean…you just appeared."

"I'm real," he said, catching on. "Honest."

She laughed again. Of course he was. He was as solid as they came. She introduced herself. "I'm Kenna Jackson. I'm taking over from Jean on the day-to-day running of things. As from today, that is."

"Pleased to meet you." Gregor enclosed her hand with his, lending some much-needed warmth. "I was just on my way to the kitchen to make a cup of coffee. If that's okay?"

"Of course! Please, help yourself."

"Aye, aye, I will. Well…I'd best get on. It's lovely to meet you. I expect we'll be seeing a lot of each other."

"I expect so," Kenna said as she stepped aside, and he walked past her, onwards to the kitchen, where Jean, Connor and Laura still were, Jean no doubt on her way back soon to complete the handover. For the moment, though, Kenna was still outside, still alone, watching him as he entered the castle. Just before he disappeared entirely, she called out.

"Roses," she said.

Gregor slowed, then turned. "Aye, what's that?"

"Roses." This time she spoke louder. "In the garden. Can we have plenty of roses?"

* * *

Jean stayed with Kenna for the rest of that first day before returning to her cottage on the edge of the forest, closer to the road – her 'retirement home', as she called it.

"So you'll be near," Kenna said, relieved.

Jean's laughter was throaty. "Aye. I'm still on the grounds, technically. It'll take you a good forty minutes to walk to mine or ten to fifteen minutes by car."

Close by. It really was. Something Kenna kept telling herself as the hours passed.

There were visitors, quite a few, the pleasant weather encouraging them, perhaps, and after touring the castle, almost all had tea and cake in the café. As for Gregor, Kenna didn't see him again that day, only the evidence of his handiwork on her way back to the flat that evening: overturned soil and a huge wheelbarrow piled high with weeds. Jean had returned home too after handing over the keys.

As she'd done so, her eyes had flitted upwards. Towards where? Kenna wondered. The Rohaise Room? Not necessarily, there were plenty of other rooms up there, and yet she couldn't shake that feeling, couldn't forget what she'd been told about the woman either – that she'd stayed at Drumlin and faced the king's men, alone, all to protect her lover, Alexander Buchannan. God, she must have loved him! Would Kenna die for Adam? For anyone? Had she ever felt that depth of feeling? Regarding Adam, she loved him but was also so angry with him. She'd called and texted several times today, but no reply.

She let herself into her flat, ravenous, she realised, having only had half a bowl of soup for lunch – leek and potato, as made by Connor, and delicious, a swirl of cream in it. They were nice, Connor and Laura. She liked their enthusiasm. They'd be a pleasure to work with. Gregor likely would be too, as long as he stopped sneaking up on her!

She prepared dinner, Adam on speed dial. Eventually, he answered.

"Kenna! Hi, how are you?"

"What the fuck, Adam," she said, stirring pasta. "Where have you been? I've been trying to reach you."

His voice, from being enthusiastic, became terse. "Working, Kenna. I've been busy."

"I'm busy too! I still found time to call you, though."

"I've been in back-to-back meetings. I answered as soon as I could."

"And last night? You didn't even check to see I'd arrived safely."

"Last night you didn't phone either. It's a two-way street, you know."

"A two-way street?"

Her hand no longer stirring, she had an urge to hurl the pan across the floor instead and rage some more. That strength of feeling she'd questioned earlier was certainly in evidence now. Stupid, though. And damaging, not least to her. She should breathe deep, collect herself, focus on telling him how brilliant it had been today. Tell him too about the history of the castle, about Rohaise. Still that woman dominated her mind, the fiery redhead. Rather than rail, she could use words to tempt him, make him say to hell with

London, that he was leaving immediately to start again, with her, in Scotland, like he'd appeared to want to do just a few short weeks back. Besides, he was right. She hadn't phoned him last night. It was true what she'd said to Jean about not thinking straight. Stubbornness might also have played a part.

Silence had erupted between them, but he was the first to break it.

"Look," he said, "just tell me how you're getting on. I really do want to know."

Her voice steady – the anger if not subdued, held in check, at least – she described the castle and the pine forest on the hills that surrounded it, the interior, the exterior, and plans she was forming to attract visitors not just in spring and summer but all through the year. Tea on the lawn, she said, would be a good idea when the weather was nice enough and Gregor had knocked the gardens into shape. She could also hire someone to play the bagpipes, the background music adding to the atmosphere as people wandered round the castle and grounds. And a ball! What about a ball? Held in the main hall, which was huge. All these ideas and more were running riot through her head, but grand ideas that would need financing. Ideas that were also beginning to peter out for reasons she couldn't quite fathom, as if the marauding hordes were an unpleasant thought. The charm of the castle lay in the fact it was off the beaten track – a gem, as Jean had described it – largely undiscovered, set so deep in the heart of the countryside as to be found only by stealth or chance. You had to be *determined* to come here.

She heard a yawn on the other side of the phone, followed by Adam declaring how tired he was. Immediately, he apologised. "Sorry, it's not you, it's work. I'm exhausted."

"Work you can do from here, though?" Kenna checked. *Eventually.*

"Yeah, yeah, of course, just not this particular project. Kenna, we've discussed this!"

How accusatory he sounded, as if she was the unreasonable one.

"We were supposed to come here together, Adam," she reminded him.

"And I will be coming up." Once more his voice was as tight as hers. "Just give me a week or two. Christ, Kenna, it's not that big a deal!"

"You've given notice on your flat, though?" She only had his word for it.

"You know I have."

"So it'll have to be soon."

"It will, yeah. Got a bit of an extension to cater for the change of plan, as I've told you, but then the landlord wants me gone. He already has the next people lined up, I think. Practically everything's packed. It's amazing, isn't it, how little you really own?"

She agreed with him but also pointed out how freeing it was. "After Drumlin, we can take off, literally go anywhere. And, Adam, there's a car here, a Volvo for our use. It's a bit beaten up but reliable, apparently. That's handy, isn't it?"

"Very handy," he replied, yawning again and eliciting some sympathy from her this time. He'd let her down, badly, but despite how upset she felt about that, she should end the conversation on a positive note, tell him she loved him, that she was looking forward to their life here. To kick-starting a relationship more strained than she'd previously realised.

ROHAISE

She was about to do that when Adam swore.

"Shit! Is that the time? Kenna, I've got to go, sorry. As tired as I am, I've got to be at The Anchor by eight, and I've still got to shower and everything."

"The Anchor?" It was a pub she knew well, on his side of town and one they'd visited together occasionally, all spit and sawdust and always crowded. "Who are you meeting?"

"Networking," was the answer he gave. "A complete bore, but it has to be done. I'll speak to you tomorrow, okay?"

The line went dead. No chance for her to respond further, certainly not enough time to offer any endearments, any reassurances. He didn't seem to need them, only she did. Returning to the pasta, she found a colander and drained it, intending to add some pesto and cheese. A simple supper, as it always was when she cooked for one. Adam was the one who liked cooking, not her, making it into something theatrical. That's what he was like, larger than life, a go-getter, ambitious. What if he hated it here, somewhere so quiet! And yet this had been his idea because, apparently, he hated it in London too.

The pesto coating the pasta, a pile of cheese on top, she took a seat at the table in the kitchen, lifted her fork and toyed with it rather than eating. Never satisfied. Not her, him. Two years they'd been together; she'd thought she knew him, that she wanted to be with him, long-term, forever. As the minutes passed, the clock on the wall busy counting them down – as the air seemed to close in on her, just as it had done earlier during the castle tour – Jean's words returned: *Why are you* really *here?*

Did she know Adam as well as she thought?

More than that, did she even know herself?

Chapter Six

"Are there any ghosts?"

It was Saturday, and Kenna had almost completed a working week at the castle. On Sunday Jean was taking over, as she'd do most Sundays to allow Kenna some time off. Not just a job, this was a way of life now – for the foreseeable future, at any rate – and the hours weren't that bad, nothing like she was used to. First thing on the agenda come Sunday was a walk in the pine forest, something she was looking forward to, breathing in air that was fresh and tangy, not underscored by fumes. She'd already been into Tulce early one morning. It called itself a town, and it had a few shops and a supermarket as well as a couple of takeaways and cafés, but it was tiny; half an hour and you'd walked around it. The people there had been friendly, though, as were those that turned up at Drumlin, numbering only between ten to fifteen per day plus a couple of coach tours, but then it was still so cold, so changeable, sunny one minute, raining the next, even sleeting. More would come with the warmer weather beyond Easter, she'd been assured.

This family was friendly, the ones standing before her in the entrance hall, a couple with a child who couldn't be more than seven or eight. He had asked the question: *Are there any ghosts?* A question not confined to the lips of a child; practically all those who entered here, young and old, said the same thing.

And she'd been briefed on what to say.

"Well, yes." Kenna adopted her widest smile. "There's Andrew at the door, a member of the Buchannan family from the seventeenth century. He likes to vet people as they come in, giving an approving nod to most, I have to say. There's also a maid in the kitchen, Netty. Sometimes she's seen mopping up long after the guests have gone home. She can't stand any mess. And last but not least, there's the monk, Joseph Buchannan. You'll find out all about him when you go upstairs. He's in the library. Or rather he was."

The boy began to look troubled, causing Kenna to rush on. "Don't worry, ghosts can't hurt you, and certainly not the ghosts at Drumlin. They're all friendly. It's just…it's so beautiful here, so peaceful, they can't bring themselves to leave. Can't blame them, eh?"

The boy started smiling again, tugging at his mother's hand, desperate to explore. That was the other thing with Drumlin – there were no guided tours. People could do as they wished, and some really lingered, soaking it all up, declaring later in the café how much they'd enjoyed their trip. 'Well worth it,' was often said. 'It's so unique. Charming.'

The day passed quickly, Kenna taking a walk outside between showers to check on Gregor, bringing him a coffee as he sheltered in one of the outbuildings.

"Sorry you're getting so wet," she said, handing him the Drumlin souvenir mug.

He shook his dark curls. "I'm used to it."

She looked around her. The old brick building, whilst only having three walls, had a roof, at least, albeit one with a few holes in.

"I'll get those patched up," said Gregor. "Then I think I'll use this as a log store."

"We have a log store," she said, having seen one to the side of the castle.

"This is bigger, and it'll be dryer, eventually."

"Ah, right, in that case, good idea. Wonder what this was once upon a time?"

"There would have been various barns and outhouses on the grounds, used for all manner of purposes. This would have been a thriving metropolis."

She laughed. "Hard to imagine."

"D'ya think?"

Intrigued by his response, she was about to ask him what he meant when she noticed he was shivering. "Look, come inside," she said instead. "I can drag the Calor Gas heater out from behind reception. Stand in front of that for a few minutes and warm up."

He shook his head again, a couple of droplets that clung to his hair flying. "It's nae bother. I've two more hours to go, and then I'll head off, sit by my own fire."

She raised an eyebrow. She'd heard the Scots were a hardy lot, and if Gregor was anything to go by, it was proving true.

Their coffee finished, she took the empty mugs and headed back inside to the kitchen, hearing Connor and Laura's laughter on her approach.

"What's going on here?" Kenna smiled as widely as them.

"Aw, nothing," Connor replied, flicking Laura gently with the tea towel he held in his hand. "It's just wee Laura here thinks I cannae make shortbread as well as she can, that her granny has the best recipe in all of Aberdeenshire, a *secret* recipe no less, but I've a secret recipe too, handed down from my granny, and so we'll see about that."

Quick as a flash, Laura flicked him with her own tea towel. "It won't compare, I'm telling you, and not so much of the 'wee' either, just because you're six feet tall!"

"I'm facing a shortbread competition from a shorty. You cannae make it up!" Connor continued to tease, the pair of them laughing still, eyes only for each other.

Kenna turned, left them to it, and headed back to reception, where a few local crafts were stacked on shelves behind the counter and on the desk for sale. Nine times out of ten, visitors bought something as a reminder of their visit, a Drumlin key ring or notepad; it was a good source of revenue that could easily be expanded on.

The family with the young boy came back about an hour later, enthusing about all they'd seen, especially Queen Mary's Bower and the library where the remains of the monk had been found. Foregoing tea and cake, they headed off, no more visitors for the day, sadly, Kenna idling away the remaining working hours reading a book and texting Adam. A week or two of delay had become two weeks for certain. As tempted as she was to moan about it, she didn't, held partly in check by his enthusiasm for when he did arrive.

Can't bloody wait, he'd texted. *This project is doing my head in. The client is outrageous, so demanding. I know I can't escape IT, not for a while, but at least I can escape London. I can be with you. That's all that's keeping me going right now.*

No kisses, but then he was busy, she reminded herself, and stressed. She texted back, saying how excited she was too, that it was quiet at the castle, but it'd get busier, and it would be so bloody exciting being here with him, so different to what they were used to, a better life for sure. It felt good to prop him up instead of berating him, a more positive thing to do. She didn't own him. Christ, in the last six months, she'd only really seen him at weekends, sometimes not even then because work had spilled over. Living together was something she longed for but also felt daunted by, another big change in the offing. It'd work, though; she'd pour all her effort into it as well as the castle.

With Connor and Laura clocking off and Gregor already gone, Kenna also left the castle, locking up behind her and hugging her arms against the cold as she hurried over gravel to her flat. It was only later when she'd showered and changed into tracksuit bottoms and a sweatshirt and was in the midst of making dinner, the radio blaring beside her, that she realised she'd have to head back to the castle. She'd left her phone charging there.

"Damn," she whispered beneath her breath. "Stupid thing to do."

Also strange that it had taken her this long to notice. When she'd first arrived, she'd kept her phone close, like a comfort blanket, she supposed. It was her contact to the outside world, to Adam, of course, but also her friends, Sal and the gang, some of whom – like Sal – were mystified at her decision to leave London, while others were envious, declaring they'd love to do something different too. She'd also phoned her parents: her mother, who lived in Brighton now by the sea, and her father, who lived in Cornwall. Both had been surprised, but as her mother had said, 'You're a big girl, perfectly able to forge your own path.'

A few days in, however, and she'd let the phone go, not held on to it so obsessively. It was both telling and surprising. Could she forego it for the entire night? Fetch it in the morning? She was tempted to try. After work, she tended to come straight back to the flat, not venturing outdoors again until the next day. No real reason, but no point in exploring in the dark either. When night fell in these parts, it fell completely.

She could leave it. She would. But what if Adam tried to call her? If she didn't answer, he'd worry. He was *unlikely* to call – they'd spoken on the phone already that afternoon, briefly before he'd headed into yet another meeting – but even so...

She should have it by her side. There was no landline at the flat, only at the castle in a small office – a cubbyhole, really – that lay off reception.

Kenna tried to forget about her phone, got on with preparing and eating dinner, settling in front of the TV whilst doing so, but found she couldn't rest, not entirely.

She was alone at the castle. Not even the ghosts for company, for there was no Andrew and no Netty, and now, thanks to being properly buried, no Joseph Buchannan either. They were all made up because customers, most of them, liked the idea of ghosts, *demanded* them.

Not just a phone, it was a lifeline, in case there was an emergency and she needed to contact someone. Or someone needed to contact her. She could picture Adam's texts even now: *Kenna? Where are you? Why aren't you answering? You haven't fallen down that turnpike staircase and broken your neck, have you? Kenna, text back!*

Her solitary dinner finished, she sighed heavily. She'd have to get it, be brave. *The castle's just a glorified home, nothing more.*

On her feet, she left the living room and trod carefully down her own set of stairs, it beginning to register how isolated she was, how vulnerable. She needed her phone, no doubt about it. Downstairs in the lobby, she tugged on her boots and flinched as she saw from the corner of her eye something scuttle along the flagstones.

She turned towards it. A beetle – large, shiny and black – disappeared into a crack in the wall. Not just flinching, Kenna swallowed. Although not insect-phobic, she was wary of them, especially of creatures like that, the kind she wasn't used to but which she bet lived in abundance here, hiding just out of sight. A few more days until Adam arrived, though, and a scenario such as this wouldn't happen again. If she forgot her phone a second time, she'd send Adam round to get it. Easy. Right now, however, it was far from that. She was nervous, no point in denying it. Grabbing the keys to the castle from a dish in the lobby, she'd hurry, get it over and done with.

A blast of cold air hit her as soon as she opened the door, making her wish she'd grabbed her jacket too. It was on the peg, just an arm's length away, but she had one foot out the door now and no wish to prolong the agony. She'd run to the entrance, head down and arms wrapped round herself, the same as earlier.

She stepped more fully into the night, the door as it banged shut sounding so final.

She shouldn't rush so much; she could trip, hurt herself, again feeling vulnerable as she imagined herself lying on the path with a broken ankle, any cries for help futile. She had to slow down, the coldness of the night making her lungs ache as she breathed in its rawness. It'd be April in a couple of days. Surely the weather would turn soon, become less…Scottish.

It was so quiet. With no owls hooting and no traffic, the intensity there in the day increased a thousandfold. *Intense* was definitely the right way to describe this place. History had made it so, filled with intrigue and tragedy and mystery. She'd planned on delving deep into Drumlin's past, becoming quite the expert, but now questioned the wisdom of that. Perhaps it was best to know just the bare bones of it, as Jean had said, whilst living here. Some events could play on your mind otherwise.

Still making progress, she rounded the corner by the ruined family chapel, aware of the castle to her left and how tall it was, *impossibly* tall, looming over her, blacker than the night and far more dramatic. The only light on this side was from her kitchen window, fading the further she walked. At the front, her gaze went upwards, towards windows like blind eyes. Foreboding, that's how Drumlin appeared. Hostile. No, she couldn't enter it alone, not at this hour.

Immediately, the voice of reason intervened: *It's just past nine, not late at all! Don't be such a coward; it's not haunted, not anymore, if it ever was. Ghosts don't exist, and the past can't hurt you. Get your phone. You* need *your phone. You have to have it.*

A lifeline.

A link to civilisation.

Damn! Damn! Damn! If only Adam were here!

From having come to a halt, she had to force her legs to move, and each time was a Herculean effort. Before long, however, Kenna was standing before that huge oak door, a grizzled old guard she could force into submission with a turn of the key. The reception was just off the entrance hall, the office behind that, not far at all, a few steps. No big deal.

Her hand reached out, and she inserted the key; rusty and heavy, it was another relic. There was no real security system either, she realised, perhaps because there was no need for it? Who'd come here at night anyway? Who'd be that mad? Leaning close, she had to squint to ensure the key fit properly, but it did, the levers scraping their way around the mechanism with painful slowness. At last the door opened, and Kenna shoved hard at it with her shoulder, groaning as she'd heard Jean groan when opening it that first time.

Inside it was as black as it was outside but with one difference: the air was thicker, as if it had somehow congealed. Negotiating it really would be like wading through treacle.

Still hesitating, if just for a moment, Kenna finally entered Drumlin, every nerve ending electrified, the hairs on her arms bristling as if charged with static.

Chapter Seven

Another sound, another echo. Again, my eyes open to stare into the gloom. Why must this happen? Sleep is all I have! The only thing left to desire. To sleep, to be left alone now.

Ah, here they come, the memories, relentless in their pursuit, tumbling in to fill every corner of my mind. I must not succumb! Not to all of them. I must fight, like I have fought before. Think only of the good. Of him, the reason I'm here, why I stayed.

Because I promised.

Just as he promised me.

He will find his way back. One day. And, like the first time he drew near, I will know who it is; there will be no mistaking. Only then will I wake more fully, wake gladly.

Memories, they're so like dreams. The ferny forest floor and the two of us lying on it, that first time and many times thereafter. The ground soft as a cushion, the branches of trees swaying softly overhead, closing in on us, protective, affording further sanctuary.

Alexander loved the forest as much as I did. It was there that he continued to visit me, talked to me, just talked at first. "Who are you? Are you alone? How have you survived?"

I laughed at the wonder in his voice and the awe in his eyes. I'd survived because I'd been taught to, because the forest, the deep, dark part of it that frightens so many, does not frighten me. I know every tree and every plant that grows, every animal that also calls it home. I know which fruit to pick, which mushrooms, all of which are plentiful. There is meat too. It is a bountiful land, I told him, noting how bright his eyes shone. There are herbs for medicines, foxgloves and dandelion, yarrow and vervain; the pine needles too will ease a stuffy nose or a fever. The forest not only harbours you, it will heal you if you let it.

He wanted to know all about my world; he hung on to every word I uttered. Of course, I knew about his world, the castle that the forest surrounds, a place for clansmen to gather, to plot and to plan. It was a world my mother had come from but which she had then forsaken. Always they plot, she had said, quarrels and fights the only thing to enliven them. This one, though, was different, as I had hoped he would be, as I had prayed.

When he touched me, properly touched me, I admit to being scared. Father had left us when I was young, but not so young I can't remember how he had treated Mother, how he would…strike her. Remember too that she fought back, refused to accept his brutish ways, driving him from our forest home, weakening him first with herbs, then cursing him as he staggered away, warning him not to return, ever. He was a man she thought she'd loved at first; she made sure to tell us that. 'I conceived you willingly, you and your brother.' But slowly, perhaps inevitably, he succumbed to the beast within him, failed to keep it tethered. And Mother could not – would not – bear it. 'For your sakes, for my children.'

Alexander saw I was afraid, this wild redheaded woman who had bewitched him. "Are you a witch?" *he murmured.* "Have you cast a spell on me?" *If a child of the forest and a witch is the same thing, then perhaps I was. I was also young and so very much in love.*

As my breath hitched, he came closer still, then stole it completely, his lips upon mine, his hands easing the skins I wore from my shoulders.

Afterwards, we continued to lie in each other's arms, and time passed, but it meant nothing, just as it means nothing now. We paid no mind to it. Often, he would visit me. Often, we would lie for hours, the sun warming our skin during those hazy days of summer. But summer is far too short. It must yield, make way for autumn, for cold blasts and endless rain. I loved all seasons despite how the wind can howl, how hard it laments, because each is still beautiful. I've even welcomed the snow and the ice, for the snow, when it is first laid, lends yet more magic to the forest, creates a true other world.

Was I lonely in the forest before Alexander? Several winters had passed since my mother and brother had died, no herb tincture I could concoct powerful enough to save them, not in the end. So, perhaps I was lonely. And perhaps it was this that sent me after him. If so, then I am thankful, for look what I gained! A heart that no longer yearned, was no longer heavy.

I could stand the cold, wrapped in furs and with the fire ever glowing. Alexander could not. He would shiver, his breath misting before him, his cheeks growing red, his lips sore.

"This is madness," he said. "Come back with me, to Drumlin. Stay with me there."

I shook my head. "We're alone here. At the castle, there are others."

He gripped me by the shoulders. "Servants, mainly. All right, others come and go, but it doesn't matter. Rohaise, if you're my woman, you've a right to be there."

"But one thing I'm not is noble."

Oh, how he denied it! "You are nobler than anyone! Braver, more beautiful. You are everything, Rohaise, my world, and I will bring you to the castle, and it will be your home too. This…this…" Words failed him as he gestured all around. *"I am not a beast. I cannot live like this. We cannot. At Drumlin, we have a warm hearth to sit by, as tall as a man and as wide as several. It's there, waiting for us."*

For a moment, I was angry but also confused. All during summer he had never once mentioned the castle. Living like a beast, as he'd put it, had been good enough for him. More than that, he'd enjoyed it, the freedom of the forest, the respite it offered from prying eyes. Then I had to remind myself, I was born to the elements. He wasn't. He didn't know how to endure in the open; very few do. There must be compromise.

"I will come with you," I told him. "But if it doesn't suit me, if I cannot bear it as much as you can no longer bear this, I will return."

"Leave me? You can think such a thing?"

"I am the forest," was my simple reply.

I did indeed leave it. I sat astride the horse he had brought with him, my legs flanking the animal's smooth dappled coat, my arms tight around the man who held the reins. I drew closer to the castle than I had ever been, a building almost impossibly tall, formed not of wood and skins but the hardness of stone. Here, the forest had been beaten back, but somehow, and graciously, it had accepted that defeat – it allowed the castle to be there. And that gave me hope.

Alexander climbed down from the horse, then helped me down too, tethering her to a post before taking my hand.

"Come," he said. "You have shared your home with me, let me share mine with you."

It was bitterly cold as we neared the entrance to the building, but it wasn't that which caused me to shiver. I was scared again. I might have spied upon the castle many times from the distant safety of the trees, just as I would spy upon Alexander, but never had I been in it or even dreamed such a notion. I had no desire to, no want. I had drawn Alexander to me, and I was content with that. Wished he could be too. But it was not the way of it. The way of it was this: to share his home as he had begged me. It was a world of men I'd be entering, Mother's words whispering in my ears: 'Stay away from them. Stay safe in the forest. Live, Rohaise, live long and live gently.'

But I could not live without Alexander.

I entered the hall, my hand still in his. Not once did he let me go, did he falter, and again my breath escaped me. Inside, it was something beyond imagination, beyond expectation, even. There was no lusty wind, barely a chill; there was comfort and shelter, there was Alexander, not just the man but his essence, etched into the very air that I breathed. Below my feet, the ground was as hard as the walls that surrounded me.

He drew me further in, helped me to climb upwards, stone step upon stone step rising higher, twisting and turning, cones of fire smoking against the walls. We left the staircase, although the treads continued on, and entered a room where a hearth was, the one he'd described, as tall as a man and as wide as three, logs piled onto it, belching out heat.

I have risen, I am on my feet now, thinking of it. After so long, I take a step forwards, approaching my own hearth, much smaller than in that room, and dormant. Lifting my arms, a sudden gesture, I thrust them outwards. It's been an age since I've done this, held my hands in front of the fire, felt not a chill but such warmth. Felt wonder and excitement too. This was new to me then, so new, but I was brave Rohaise; Alexander had said so. 'You are nobler than anyone. Braver, more beautiful.' I was his Rohaise, in his home.

"*Your home,*" *he'd whispered.* "*Rohaise, this is your home too."*

The castle...
Drumlin...
Where a queen had stayed.
Then me.
I came to love it. Dear God, I loved it! Our life here.
Was I wrong? Too arrogant? Just so certain it'd be different for me.
And if so, did I deserve the price I paid?
Such a terrible price...such terrible pain... The screaming...the laughter...and, worst of all, his absence. An absence as enduring as these walls.
I know what happened to me, but what happened to you, Alexander? What fate did you meet?
Another echo but so much closer, a howling, a keening, unbearable.
What is it? A memory? Those that refuse to fade, even though I wish them to.
Who is it?
It takes time to realise my hands are no longer in front of me but cupping the sides of my face, to understand it is my mouth that has opened.
That this isn't a memory at all.

Chapter Eight

What was that? A noise, not distant but close. Too close.

Kenna stood where she was, inside the entrance of the castle, trembling harder than before. Imagination was not to blame even though it had tried to break loose several times between the flat and here. She'd remained in control, however – just. Now, despite continuing to strive for logic, her body was betraying her, her legs shaking badly.

She didn't have to investigate. She could just do as she'd intended, grab her phone and go. Funny how she was frightened here, and yet in her flat – which was, after all, still a bona fide part of the castle – she was comfortable enough. Soon, she'd be back there, having bolted the door, on the phone to Adam and laughing about this. If he were here, *actually here*, they'd be laughing right now, spooking each other further.

But he wasn't. And she was alone. In an ancient castle, having heard a sound, an echo.

There was no one at Drumlin. All had gone home. She'd watched them go, Connor and Laura, at least – not Gregor, as he worked outside, but the pickup truck he drove was absent. As for Jean, she wasn't due in till the next day, Sunday. Funny, really, that Kenna hadn't seen her since Monday, that she'd trusted Kenna that much right from the off, handed over the keys to the castle, then just…left her to it. She should be flattered, she supposed. This was what she'd wanted, more responsibility.

Houses made strange noises at night, with pipes and bricks and wood settling as temperatures changed, and it seemed castles were no exception. Heading towards a panel to the left of the entrance, she flicked several switches, craving as much light as possible. The wrought-iron chandelier above her and the wall sconces duly obeyed, but they weren't as bright as she'd hoped. Rather than illuminate each corner, they just created deeper shadows. Still, it was better than nothing. Reception was her destination, the small office at the back of it. How many texts or calls had she missed from Adam? she wondered. Her stubborn silence must be causing him such worry.

Her eyes avoiding the accusing glare of the stag's head, she forced herself onwards until there was another sound, a…*shriek*. Was that it?

"What the fuck?"

An owl or some other bird was guilty of this. That made sense. Something had flown down a chimney and become caught there or had entered unnoticed via an open door during the day. It was clearly in pain, a broken wing, perhaps. Listening, Kenna stopped and turned towards the archway that led to the kitchen and cloakrooms on the left and the turnpike staircase on the right. If there was a bird trapped, she could deal with it in the morning. But then…what if it didn't make it till morning? Displaced and bewildered, it would fly into every wall, hurl itself at the window over and over, craving release. Could she leave it to such a terrible fate? Alternatively, she could find out which room it was trapped in, open the window and let it find its way out, back to where it belonged. If it had injured itself, it still mightn't survive, but at least she'd have done all she could for it. She'd have tried. She couldn't go to bed *not* trying. Wouldn't be able to sleep. There were no ghosts at Drumlin, just those invented for the visitors. Despite the real events that surrounded the monk, his story too was most likely vastly exaggerated. The shrieking had come from an animal. An animal she had to help.

Her eyes closing briefly with sheer frustration, she approached the archway. She'd been looking forward to a relaxing evening, but it was turning out to be anything but. Beneath the archway was another light panel, and again she flicked the switches, trying not to think of the gloom at her back. All was silent now, so quiet, like she'd entered a mausoleum rather than a former dwelling. Just a quick search of the floor above, where the sound must have come from. That's as much as she could do.

On reaching the first floor, she opened the door to the main hall, cavernous with its hearth, the inky night pouring through the bay window to occupy the room.

"Birdy," she called out, feeling utterly ridiculous but wanting to hear something again, even if it was just the sound of her own voice, because the silence was…*deafening*.

There was no squawking, no flapping of wings, no shrieking, just more silence and an emptiness so stark it leapt from the room and into her heart to bury itself there. Quickly, she shut the door, the deep breath that left her whilst doing so decidedly shaky.

Back on the staircase, she looked upwards, beyond the wall tapestries, what lights there were simply not adequate. Not just her breath, her entire body was shaking again, especially as she recalled what Jean had said to her on her first day at Drumlin: *Night lends it a certain something.*

Kenna had first seen the castle at night; a house it might be, but it had seemed like a monolith, and it seemed so again, a place as big as the history it housed, as the personalities that had lived there. *A woman died defending this castle!* And yet here she was, Kenna Jackson from the twenty-first century, too afraid to even enter.

"Pathetic," she muttered, her hand on the rope that constituted a handhold as she hauled herself further upwards, reaching various rooms on various levels, opening and closing doors, including just a quick peek in the library, the image her mind conjured of Joseph Buchannan's skeleton buried within the wall far too vivid. Even in Queen Mary's Bower she'd experienced a frisson of something, visualising the petite shape of the woman, her skirts so full and bodice so tight, staring out the window, just…staring. Had she ever wondered about her fate? Had she ever contemplated it? A dreadful end, the worst.

"Enough!" Kenna slammed the door shut on the bower and went back to the staircase. A couple more floors to check, or she could just return to reception and collect her phone. She'd done enough, surely? Her conscience was clear. Oh, how stupid she'd feel later when she returned Adam's calls. She could just imagine the teasing in his voice.

Her breath caught in her throat. Something had disturbed the silence again…not a shriek or a cry this time, something low, like a…murmuring. Yet still as wretched.

"Who's there?" she called out, certain now that someone was.

If only she had her phone on her! But what to do with it? Call the police? She didn't even know the number for the police, not here in Scotland. Was it the same the UK over? She didn't know, couldn't think. She could call Jean, of course, get her to hop in her car and come on over, but Jean's time at Drumlin was done. This was Kenna's job now, her castle.

"Shit! Shit! Shit!" she breathed, climbing higher and ignoring the fifth floor, for the murmuring, such as it was, was not coming from there but above. There was only one room on the sixth floor, before the staircase twisted round again towards the attic rooms and then out onto a narrow battlement walk, one which hadn't been trodden in years, according to Jean, only to clear leaves and twigs if the wind had blown them there. One room on the sixth floor and, oh, what a grand room it was: the Rohaise Room. Such a beautiful name, when she thought of it. Not an English rose but a Scottish one, blood red.

The sound came from there.

Rather than call out again, Kenna remained quiet, tossing her own hair behind her shoulders, determined to solve this puzzle, to quell any notions growing in her mind. *The castle is not haunted!* People had lived here, people had died, their spirits going elsewhere. Kenna wasn't particularly religious, had been brought up with only a nod to Catholicism, no more than that, but that a soul went to heaven, to rest eternal, was an idea she liked. The deceased didn't linger.

Be brave, like Rohaise was brave. Share more than the fact that you're redheads.

Adrenaline fuelling her, she flew up the last few steps, reached for the door handle and pushed it open. Immediately, she lifted her arms, expecting something to launch itself at her – the bird, the creature, anything. But there was nothing and no one. Kenna looked around. The sound *had* come from here, the murmuring, at least, and possibly the shrieks. She needed the light in here more than ever. She'd check every corner, every crevice. Make sure this room was as empty as all the others. *There is nothing here!*

Except there was. Not just the weight of history but of something else. There was despair in this room. Heartbreak. Kenna continued to stand there, her eyes not darting around anymore, as frantic as the bird she'd imagined, but fixed solely on the bed. The *original* bed, from the days of Rohaise and Alexander, a four-poster like the one she occupied in the flat but with roses, not just on the fabric that had faded from red to pink but carved into the very wood itself, on the posts – intricate, delicate, perfect, every one of them. Rohaise's room. A woman who perhaps had the most to tell of her time here, and yet she was known only as Rohaise, her story not written, only talked about and fading. Not a fairy tale, though, not in those days. This woman had died at the hands of an army. Had they been brutal, as Jean suspected? As brutal as armies could be, even today. Despair. Yes, there was definitely that. As Rohaise must have ached with it, so now did Kenna, hugging herself tight with her arms as if trying to impart some solace.

She was drawn to the mirror. How mottled the glass was in this half-light, the reflection hazy, no sharp lines, no real contrast; instead, everything about her was soft, vague. Rohaise must have stood like this and stared at herself, Alexander behind her with his arms around her waist. She would have worn a dress of emerald green or deepest burgundy, most likely velvet, would have smiled as he'd touched her, laid her head back against his shoulder, her eyes – green, they must have been, like Kenna's – sparkling with delight, with a happiness she had never known before, that she didn't know existed. Alexander would have bent his head, his lips tracing the delicate skin on the side of her neck, gently, always so gently, his featherlight touch sending shivers down her spine. She would close her eyes and revel in the moment, just as Kenna had closed her eyes and was revelling in it too. The woman had died not just protecting the castle but him. That's how intense their love was, a love so rare that some people never experienced it, that sense of wholeness when two halves meet. How lucky she was. How privileged…

Kenna opened her eyes, still dreamy from where her thoughts had led her, lost in romance this time rather than despair. *Hazy* was how she'd summed up her reflection, as something vague rather than defined. But as she looked again, as she peered, she saw something not soft nor vague nor hazy at all – her own face but hardened somehow, something glinting in eyes greener than hers, something…terrifying.

A shriek. This time it came from within, ringing in her ears, hitting the walls and rebounding. The reflection…it wasn't hers…it couldn't be. Galvanised, she threw herself towards the door, half expecting it to slam shut in front of her, to trap her there with so much despair, so much…anger. It didn't, though; it remained open, and she bolted through it, racing down the stairs, praying that she wouldn't trip, wouldn't stumble. That whatever she'd seen wouldn't step out of the mirror and follow her, tear her apart.

This place…it was haunted after all. By her. By Rohaise. For what else could explain it? There was no bird, no live intruder. Just the past, coming to life.

At last, she reached the bottom of the staircase. She'd head to the exit, she wanted to, but she also wanted her phone, to speak to Adam, have him calm her. *I know what I saw!*

Glancing only briefly behind her, relieved to see no phantom figure in pursuit, the staircase empty, quite empty, she'd do it, take a chance, prolong her stay in the castle but only by mere seconds – head to the office, grab the phone, then leave. Adam. Oh God, she wanted to hear his voice! To reassure him as much as she herself needed reassurance.

The office door yielded, and she switched on the light. There it was! Her phone, facedown on the desk, right beside the landline, not just one lifeline but two.

She grabbed it, ripping out the charging lead, not bothering to turn the lights off here or elsewhere. Let them blaze all night if they had to. Blaze? That was hardly the word for it, the darkness too ingrained to retreat so willingly. Retrieving the keys from her pocket, she headed across the entrance hall, certain, absolutely *certain* there was something standing in the archway besides the stag looking at her – a figure, tall and with red hair.

"NO!"

She would not look, give in to such ridiculous fancies. All she'd do was run into the blackness of the cold night, slamming the oak door behind her, locking in whatever was there. Confining it. Her hands trembled as she did so, the lock stiff, so hard to move!

"Come on, for fuck's sake!"

It rattled into place, finally.

Still sprinting, she retraced her route around the side of the castle, past the ruined chapel and back towards the flat, clutching at the phone, feeling how real it was, how solid. Just before reaching her door, she turned it over, desperate to see Adam's name on the screen, the words he had typed.

ROHAISE

Where are you, Kenna? Why are you not answering?
 There was nothing.

Chapter Nine

She had some explaining to do.

The night had disappeared and Sunday had dawned, and Kenna was back in the castle, trying to form an explanation – a *sane* explanation – for why Jean had arrived to find Drumlin with all the lights switched on, hiking up the already extortionate electricity bill.

"I…um…well, I left my phone here last night after work, had to come back and get it. And…um…what happened was, I thought I'd check the castle."

"Check it?" Jean said, one eyebrow arching.

"Yes. Just to make sure everything was all right."

"Why wouldn't it be?"

"Because…because…" Damn it, should she come out and tell her the truth? *About the shrieking, the face in the mirror that changed, that hardened…* If she did, Jean would think she'd employed someone hysterical. Lifting her hands into the air, Kenna brought them together again. "I just…forgot…about the lights." Lame. So lame. "It won't happen again. I know we're on a tight budget." Which was a lie. She knew no such thing, only that her salary was reasonable, being as it included accommodation – not comparable to her London wage, but then there wasn't so much to spend it on up here either, and so it *was* comparable, by degrees. "I won't need to come here again after dark, most likely," Kenna continued. "Not gonna forget my phone a second time, that's for sure."

Jean nodded. She didn't seem angry about what had happened, just…curious. Her eyes, always so intent, Kenna thought, scrutinising her as she talked as if *expecting* her to say more. And still Kenna was tempted to, wanting so much for someone to tell her not to be so silly, to point out that imagination will always dominate in a place like this.

There had been no texts from Adam and no missed calls. Last night, with the phone in her hand, she'd entered her flat, locked the door and then ran up the curved stairs to the living room. Once there, she'd sunk down on the sofa, clutching the phone still, willing there to be a message when she next looked at it, hating it for remaining clear.

She needed to speak to Adam, to someone. The silence was claustrophobic. Glancing to the left, to where only a wall separated her from the main body of the castle, she'd shivered, freezing cold suddenly. Whose face had been in the mirror? A face so like her own. Rohaise's? It was her room she'd been standing in, fantasising about her, about Alexander too, her lover, and how they'd embrace. A hardened look, a look of fury. That's what had replaced Kenna's otherwise beatific expression. She *must* have imagined it.

"Adam! Where are you?"

Her own furious words had broken the silence. She'd call him, just as she'd done earlier in the day, as she'd done yesterday and the day before. It was always her! Had it been like that in London? Had she done all the running? No! Not at first, anyway.

Disposed of. She'd thought that previously on the train coming here, that he'd encouraged her to leave, never intending to go with her. Get her out of the way. Why?

Selecting the Favourites screen on the phone app, tense fingers hovered over his name.

No. She wouldn't call him. As desperate as she was. She'd wait for him to call her this time. See how long it took. Willing that it wouldn't take any time at all.

Her decision made, she'd risen and returned to the kitchen to eat some of the food she'd made earlier. It had stuck in her throat, almost choked her. Admitting defeat, she'd headed to the bedroom, there to lose herself in a good book – not romance, the last thing she wanted was to read bloody romance! – but a cosy crime, nothing that would make her heart beat faster than it already had tonight. And for all the wrong reasons.

She'd fallen asleep, miraculously, woken as daylight penetrated the room, and the first thing she'd done was reach for her phone. Again, the screen was blank. She'd give Adam just a few more hours, persuading herself to be patient, that he'd call her, he would, complain about another meeting or the client he was working for. How tired he was.

And now she was standing in the entrance hall of the castle with Jean, explaining, feeling wretched, actually, and trying to hide it, her upset about Adam, her confusion about what had happened here last night and the prospect of more nights alone at the castle.

"Ach!" Jean declared at last. "It's not a worry about the lights. Maybe…maybe it's a good thing."

Now it was Kenna who scrutinised her. "Why?"

"It's just…it must look nice at night from outside, the castle lit up."

Kenna supposed so, although certainly she hadn't

stopped to admire it.

"Don't know why I never thought about it before, leaving a light on. I *should* have." Still, Jean was talking, but this time almost to herself, a frown upon her face. "It might just help."

"Jean?" Kenna said, growing more confused.

Jean didn't answer straightaway; instead, she gazed past Kenna, towards the archway where the staircase was. Kenna was just about to prompt her again when Jean smiled.

"Leave a light on, why not? Too much darkness is never a good thing."

"A light on where?"

"Rohaise's room? It's on the highest floor, and so a light that can be seen for miles."

"Oh. Okay. If you think so."

"I do, I do. Not the chandelier, just a lamp in the window. It could be on auto timer so you don't need to haul yourself up there before locking up. I'll sort it."

"Well…great," Kenna replied, shrugging.

"Anyway, I'd best away to the kitchen, see what Connor and Laura are up to. A warring pair, but something in me thinks that, regarding Laura, she protests too much, d'ya ken?"

Jean winked at Kenna just before she headed off, calling one last thing over her shoulder. "And away with you too! It's your day off. Head into town or the pine forest. Aye, it's a lovely day for a walk in the pine forest."

As Kenna watched her disappear, she shrugged again. She could head into town, she supposed, not Tulce – there was barely anything to keep her amused there – but into Aberdeen itself, a forty-mile trip via winding roads. The Volvo that came with the job might look knackered, but it was proving reliable enough. Like the castle, it just went on and on. Back in London she didn't have a car; she'd catch the bus or tube everywhere. Her parents, however, had paid for driving lessons when she was eighteen, and she'd passed the first time. Something she was now extremely glad about. Also, that she had relatively quiet roads around Drumlin to nurture her reintroduction to driving. On her day off, she could indeed escape, find civilisation, look at a different set of faces. But…maybe she didn't want to. Jean was right. It was a lovely day for a walk – more warmth in the air, the spring sun not as shy as it had been. She would indeed go to the forest as she'd originally planned to, but first she needed to check something. She wouldn't last another day at Drumlin otherwise.

Kenna approached the archway but, unlike Jean, turned right instead of left, hearing the drift of laughter from behind her – Connor, Laura and Jean sharing a joke. A sound that brought a smile to her own lips. Almost.

On a deep breath, she climbed the stairs just as she'd done the night before, as she'd done dozens of times since being here. So many stairs, so many rooms leading off them. Higher and higher she went. To her room. Rohaise's. The door wide open, just as she'd left it, the air even heavier, closing in on her as the silence tended to. And yet it was what had *pierced* the silence that had brought her here before.

She walked in. *Boldly* walked in. The castle had once been Rohaise's home, but now it was hers – for a year, at least. She had to dispel any crazy notions, nip them in the bud.

She went to the mirror, her shoulders back and head held high. The daylight wasn't all that gave her courage. Like

Rohaise, she was no pushover either. Christ, Sal couldn't do this! Live alone at a castle, surrounded by nothing but trees. She'd said so, not just once but dozens of times. She, Kenna Jackson, was unafraid, and what she'd seen in the mirror was her mind playing tricks on her, having wandered precariously.

There was her reflection again, her head inclined slightly, red hair at her shoulders, a defiance in her eyes, in the set of her jaw... *My reflection, just mine!* Nothing to do with a woman from a bygone age. That woman was dead. Buried. Gone to bones. But buried where? In the grounds? The forest? Where had the king's men left her?

So hard she stared, almost daring the reflection to change. *If you can do it by night, why not by day? Think you can frighten me now, do you? That I'll take the bait?*

Kenna laughed, quite suddenly and quite hard.

What on earth was she talking about? What bait?

"Enough!" She stopped laughing and spoke instead, her voice sounding firm even to her own ears, like a schoolma'am.

She needed to clear her head and get some fresh air. The whole day stretched ahead of her, and with it the freedom to live it exactly as she pleased.

Chapter Ten

The woods are lovely, dark and deep. A line from a favourite poem by Robert Frost. *These* woods were lovely, the trail she was on seemingly endless. God, it was so easy to leave the world behind in a place like this! To forget it existed. Easier than at the castle, where it too seemed as if civilisation were the myth. She could even forget about Adam, immersing herself in nature and nothing more, the verdant majesty of it.

Tall pines towered above her, such bright shades of green, the smell of pine needles drifting on a gentle breeze, causing her to inhale, clearing her lungs as well as her mind. What a difference in the air quality! It felt so clean.

Lovely and dark, and deep too, the call of birds resounding every now and again, a ferny carpet on either side. She'd wandered from the main track, following a less designated path, relishing this time alone when she'd thought she'd hate it. Serene, as opposed to a myriad of other emotions that had plagued her this week. In amongst the trees and the ferns, she didn't just feel at peace, she felt at home. Odd, really, as she wasn't given to walking in woods in London, because there *were* woods you could travel to if your heart desired. But hers hadn't; it never usually crossed her mind.

She *loved* it here in the forest. Wanted to keep on

walking, for the trees to swallow her up entirely. Perhaps she'd never leave, never find her way out. Would that be such a bad thing? If she got lost, she'd simply lie down, let the softness of the fern swallow her up, close her eyes and escape from the disappointment of the twenty-first century and the pain of an absent boyfriend. The world as she knew it something different now.

Time passed. She didn't know how much. She hadn't brought her phone with her, the comfort blanket discarded, nor worn a watch. *You really wanted to lose yourself!* Maybe.

How had it come to this? A conversation with someone and everything could change, and so drastically. Should a person be afraid of change, though? Kenna wondered. Wasn't that what life was about? The true challenge. Keeping things fresh.

This was supposed to keep her relationship with Adam fresh. The move to Scotland. What a joke! No chance of that if he couldn't even put in an appearance. Was the change to be more all-encompassing than she'd realised? Would he ever show up?

Questions, questions, when all she wanted was to discard them. She focused on the landscape. What were these plants all around her? So many species, so much variety.

She kept on walking, the woodland thickening, her hands stuffed in the pockets of her coat and her head down, breathing deeply and evenly. Time continued to dissolve, Kenna paying it no mind because in the woods what did time mean anyway? It was counted by the seasons and the passages of the sun, nothing as regimented as Babylonian hours, minutes and seconds. Here, only the natural order of things existed.

She must have walked an hour, maybe longer, and in one

direction only, into the heart of the forest if such a heart existed.

So dark here, with no sense of where the sun was in the sky, the light deeply filtered and muted by the trees. Everything so...silent.

Her head having been bowed to watch her footing amongst the stones and ruts, she raised it and looked around, spun too on her heel. There was nothing and no one, only her, so small against such tall, tall trees, and yet she felt *connected* to the whole, offering some significance after all.

For no reason, or for every reason, she broke into a run, exhilaration flooding her, the full realisation of what she'd done finally hitting home. It had taken an entire week of being here to accept her change of fate, a change that Adam had prompted but which, in truth, she'd grabbed at more than him. After all, she'd been the one to contact Jean. She'd had the interview and had said, 'Yes, I'll take the job. Thank you, thank you so much.' There wasn't anyone else to blame, not really. Adam might have been the prompt, but he hadn't forced it. He didn't have that kind of power. Strange how easily she'd got the job. Did so few want to live like this, in a castle surrounded by a pine forest, free, truly free, having broken the restraints of life in the fast lane? *Like being on a permanent holiday.*

The smell of the pine really was pungent, so heady, a drug in itself.

There was a clearing up ahead that she headed towards, drawn there, the curiosity of it. The trees seemed to give way, to respect it. A bare patch of land, but, even so, she felt a frisson as she came to a standstill in the centre of it, as if something *had* been there long, long ago, maybe even a dwelling of some sort, and it had looked quite different. A sound startled her, pulled her back to the moment, and she looked up to see a bird on the branch of a tree, trilling as it eyed her. She gazed back, her eyes locked with those that were more like polished black jewels, bright and shiny. The bird stopped singing and inclined its head to the right although it continued to hold her gaze, a surreal moment, bizarre, and yet…aside from birdsong and her own breathing, she could hear something else now too, a whisper of sorts. Was it the trees? She'd heard they could do that, speak a language of their own. But this whispering was growing louder.

She could make out words.

Actual words.

My love…my life…

Always…

Forever…

It wasn't the trees; rather, someone was in the woods with her, teasing her.

Once again, she spun round. "Who is it? Who's there? What are you saying?"

No answer, and the whisperings were low again, barely audible. Except one word.

Always. Always. Always.

Finally, the pound of her heart was the only sound to fill her ears as she scrutinised the trees and the space between them that was saturated with darkness. She'd lost track of the day, hadn't worried about it, but now she wanted to know how long she'd been out here, *desperately* wanted to know. It was nowhere near dusk, was it? All right, okay, she hadn't left for the woods straight after revisiting Rohaise's room, granted, had gone to the flat and pottered. But she hadn't left it that late either. If it was approaching dusk, if time truly had disappeared, it would get darker still…trap her. The freedom she'd prized an illusion.

If anyone had followed her, they refused to make themselves known, were perhaps hiding there in the trees, waiting to pounce. *This isn't London!* Even so, she was shivering and not just because the temperature had dropped as the day had waned. She had to return to Drumlin. The sanctuary of it.

Always! Always! Always!

Words she thought had become subdued now returned, a strength behind each one, an insistence. Whoever was responsible, what did they mean by it?

She glanced upwards again at the bird, who was still looking at her, not a feather ruffled upon its back, coppery brown with a small bill. Beautiful, really quite beautiful, as the rest of the forest was beautiful. Or had been. Now both the scenery and its inhabitants seemed menacing, the trees around the clearing not something static or respectful but inching forwards, encroaching, ready to crush the life from her. From which direction had she entered? She couldn't tell. Every exit looked identical.

A city dweller, unused to the country, to this…wilderness. For that's what it was. Truly. No way she was connected. She was used to structures of steel and concrete, familiar streets. Those she understood, not this. There was having an adventure and there was stupidity. *She'd* been stupid, venturing so deep into a vast woodland, paying no mind to the path she'd taken, veering off it, deliberately losing herself as if playing a game. She looked upwards at a patch of sky, the sunlight weaker than ever, the blue deepening.

ROHAISE

Trapped in the clearing with the whispers.

As she'd done the previous night, she did so again. She ran. This time into the trees. There were paths, several, barely carved out, hardly traversed. Because most people were sensible, most *would* stick to the main trails, weren't as arrogant as her, as ignorant.

The ground was littered with roots that threatened to snag her. She had to slow down. Falling was a very real prospect, and who'd find her? The person who was whispering?

The trees up ahead were thinning. They had to be! More daylight able to penetrate. Maybe not as late as she thought, midafternoon, that realisation bringing a sense of relief but not enough to slow her. Not enough because another thought surfaced: What if the path she was on was incorrect? It wouldn't lead her home but elsewhere. And if that was the case, it could take hours to find the right path, and night would indeed come.

"Aargh!"

Tears as well as fear blinding her, she had no clue what she'd barged into. A tree? It couldn't be, was softer than that although still solid, still tall and imposing.

"Whoa! Calm down. I've got you. I'm here now. You're okay. You're safe."

Chapter Eleven

She felt even more of an idiot than she had with Jean.

Gregor had caught her, Gregor Lockart, to give him his full name, holding her as her body shook, relief at last overriding fear as she clung to him. It took a good few minutes before she could let him go, and when she did, she noted concern in his eyes alongside something else, a gentle amusement?

"Are you laughing at me?"

"Of course not. But…what happened to you? You look…"

His voice fell away, perhaps out of kindness. What did she look? A wreck? Absolutely. A terrified, pathetic wreck. Once again, she had some explaining to do.

"I was in there, deep in there, in some kind of clearing. There was a bird…I was looking at him, and he was singing." The song had been more than simple trilling, she now realised; there'd been a melancholy to it, an ache. "And then…and then…the bird fell silent, and there was the sound of whispering close by, one voice, maybe two. It wasn't the leaves rustling in the trees or that kind of thing. There were words, actual words. One word in particular: 'always'."

"Always?"

"Yeah! Repeated over and over, growing more insistent."

"Kenna, I…"

An idea occurred. "It wasn't you, was it? Fooling with me?"

"No! I'd never do such a thing."

How indignant he was but also hurt. Of course it wasn't him. Why would he tease her? Besides, the voice had been so much softer than his, at first, anyway. A female?

"Sorry," she said. "I just… God, it was weird. I didn't imagine it, though, not this time."

She clamped her mouth shut. He didn't know what had happened in the castle the night before; no one did. She was *not* hysterical. Never before now, at least. She was levelheaded Kenna, sensible. She had to stay that way.

"Sorry," she repeated before adding, "Could you…would you…hold me again?"

As he put his arms round her a second time, she breathed him in. He smelt of pine too, of fresh air and something else, wood smoke, a musky scent she liked, that made her feel further comforted. It was the total opposite of Adam, who drenched himself in expensive aftershave. Gregor was as natural as the landscape that surrounded him.

Eventually she stood alone again, her lips forming another apology, but he spoke first.

"You just went a little too far off the beaten track today, that's all. And…well…if you're not used to it, it can be daunting."

Daunting? That barely described it, but she let it go.

"Here, walk with me," Gregor continued. "I trust it's the castle you're heading to?"

"Yes," Kenna replied. "If you could show me the way I'd really appreciate it."

"Of course."

For a few moments, they walked in silence, and then Kenna had to ask.

"Does anyone ever come here?"

"Into the woods?"

"Yes."

"Besides me?"

She laughed. "Well, yeah, besides you."

"People from the local area do, to walk their dogs or just to get some exercise. There are other woods around, though – plenty, in fact. You see, these are private woods, belonging to the Drumlin Castle estate, so, technically, if you're not visiting the castle, if you haven't paid your entrance fee, you're trespassing."

"Really? All this is…private?"

"It is, but it's never enforced, not in recent history. So, aye, people come here just like I do, but perhaps they don't go as deep as you went."

Kenna shuddered as she looked back over her shoulder at woodland that still seemed ominous. "The whispering I heard, I wonder if someone followed me."

"In there? Why would they?"

"Because…because…" *I'm from London.* That's what she wanted to say. *A place that's not particularly safe, that gets scarier by the minute, that can make you paranoid.* But there was no need to be paranoid here. "Look, I was just a bit unnerved, you know? Lost my way, got disorientated, carried away, I suppose."

"Not by the faerie, at least."

She shivered again. "The faerie?"

"Aye," Gregor replied, a smile back on his face. "In Scottish folklore there are two types of faerie, the Seelie Court and the Unseelie Court. The Seelie are friendlier but can still be dangerous. The latter, the Unseelie Court, well, they're downright malicious. They don't like humans, play pranks on them, and the forest, *the deep forest*, that's their domain."

"What the…? Gregor!" As he burst out laughing, she thumped him in the side, albeit playfully. "Are you saying it was the faeries taunting me?"

"Aye…no…I don't know. Of course not."

"You can't seem to decide!"

"Just tales, that's all," he told her. "And the reason most people stick to the path, even in this day and age. Myths and legends are very important to our cultural identity, and Scots are patriotic, mostly, so we hold on to everything that identifies us, even folklore."

"Yeah, I get it, although I don't know much of anything to do with myth and legend. Or with the countryside and castles, for that matter. God," she said, sighing, "I'm a proper townie!"

"And yet here you are."

"That's right," she said as they continued to walk, no end in sight, the forest still stretching in every direction, "here I am."

He slowed down a bit. "So, what brings you here, exactly? If you're such a townie."

"A change of scene, I suppose. Something new."

"What were you doing before?"

"Working in the editorial department of a publishing company."

He frowned slightly. "You didn't like the job?"

"It was all right. I had some issues with the boss. She basically ignored me, overlooked me for promotion a couple of times, which was hard because I know I'm a good editor.

I love words, I really do, but...I was beginning to love them less. I did the job for five years. Could see myself doing it for another five, *twenty*-five. I think that's what scared me!"

Only as she said it did she realise the full truth of that statement. She'd have remained in that office for as long as she was able to, bored but accustomed to it.

Gregor had stopped completely now and was looking at her, his eyes as intent as the bird's had been – as dark, she realised, consuming her.

His words, though, when he spoke, were innocent enough.

"So you've completed your first week, as have I. Odd that we started at the same time. What do you think of it?"

"I..." She bit her lip, wondered how to answer. Truthfully, she supposed, or as near as damn it. "It's interesting. It's keeping me on my toes." Dragging her eyes from his, she pointed to a tree. "There! I saw a bird like that in the clearing."

"That? Ah, that's a Scottish crossbill, a type of finch and unique to the pine forests of Scotland."

"Really? Wow. And those," she continued, pointing to the ground, "that clump of mushrooms—"

"Are poisonous," he said. "They're known as the death cap. They come in various shapes and colours, but don't go near them or any mushroom unless you have a guide with you, someone knowledgeable. Even just touching them can be toxic. I had a schoolfriend who got really sick once when he did that, thought he was going to die."

"The woods are full of danger," she said, her voice low again.

"They can be, but they're full of magnificence too. Just over here – come on, I'll show you – the narcissi are in bloom."

He led her a few metres onwards, and, sure enough, bursts of yellow were everywhere.

"They're gorgeous!"

"They are. There're still a few clumps of snowdrops left, and campion. Bluebells are also emerging. They'll be glorious in May, as will the wood anemones, and here, you'll like this one." Again, he moved a short distance from her, then bent down. "This is the twinflower, so called because there are two flowers to each stalk. They smell of vanilla. Here." He picked one and handed it to Kenna.

She took it, enjoying the nature lesson. The flower did indeed smell gorgeous, as heady a scent as the pine of the trees.

She asked him what flowers he intended to plant at Drumlin.

"Oh, a good variety. Heathers and thistles, of course, primroses, dahlias, lilies, some wildflowers for the bees, and roses. You wanted roses, didn't you?"

"Will they bloom in Scotland?"

"Aye, roses may look delicate, but they're tougher than you think. They grow wild out here too in the forest. Again, it'll be in May you'll see them."

"Wild roses? What colour?"

"Pink, usually."

"It's red roses I want at the castle."

He smiled. "Okay then, red roses you shall have."

"Who funds the planting, Gregor? Is it the Buchannan family?"

"Them, and the local Rotary Club. You see, the locals love the castle. It's part of their history too, so they want to do right by it."

"Of course," replied Kenna as they resumed walking. "You know so much about the forest."

"Aye, acquired knowledge, though. I wasn't born to it. My interest in horticulture and…other things came much later."

"Other things?"

"I study history too."

"So the job at Drumlin really is your dream job."

He nodded. "It is."

"What did you do before?"

"Before?" He looked at her, but only briefly. "Before I…drifted, I suppose. That's the only way to describe it. And not always in the right direction."

"Oh. Sorry, I didn't mean to pry."

"It's fine. My past is what it is. I've learnt from my mistakes, moved on."

"When you say not in the right direction—"

"I was in prison."

Kenna gasped, couldn't help herself. "Prison?"

He kept gazing straight ahead. "For stupid stuff – theft, handling of stolen goods, that kind of thing. Things I regret now, bitterly, but I'm on a different trajectory, as I've said. It was in prison I discovered I liked gardening. That was my job. It got me out into the open air, gave me a lifeline, and in the evenings, I would read, history books mainly, nonfiction. I became fascinated by the Romans, the Greeks, and the Scots, of course."

"Something good came of it, then," Kenna said, "which is great, really great." She caught his eye again, noting pride in his expression but that shame also lingered. "How old are you?" she asked, surprising herself further by how forthright she was being.

"Twenty-six."

"Oh, the same as me!" she declared. "What month were you born?"

"January."

"Same again!"

"What date?"

"The tenth."

"Ah, I'm the twenty-ninth."

"You're younger than me."

"Just a wee bit."

And yet how different their lives had been, his less ordinary than hers by far.

"It must have been tough," she said.

"It was, and it should be. It's meant to deter."

"I'm sorry."

"What for this time?" He stopped, as did she, the pair of them facing each other again.

"That you had to endure that."

His grin was really quite endearing, making him indeed look younger than her, whereas straight-faced he seemed older, more careworn. "You've nothing to be sorry for, but…thanks. Thanks a lot. I hope it hasn't made you wary of me. I'm a changed man, I promise. History is fascinating, it defines so much, but I won't let my own history define me. All I want is a good life, honest, clean and simple. Jean understood that, and I'm grateful to her for taking me on, for giving me the chance I needed. She's a good woman. The cottage where I live is down to her too. A friend of a friend of hers has gone travelling, for a year at least, and just wanted someone to look after the place, do some minor repairs, more gardening, that kind of thing. The rent is next to nothing. It's piecemeal."

Kenna pushed a few strands of hair from her eyes. "Jean *is* a good woman. She gave us both a chance. And I'm not wary of you at all."

On the move again, Gregor assured her it wouldn't be long until they reached the castle. It was growing colder still, and she was looking forward to settling in front of the log fire with the TV on or a good book to hand. Just being safe.

He told her he was studying for a degree in history, part-time via the Open University, that the modules encompassed a broad spectrum, but he was also reading more and more about his own land, the clearances, the Reformation, the warring clansmen. For him, Drumlin and the family that had lived there on and off for centuries was particularly intriguing.

Kenna listened intently as he spoke, enjoying the lilt of his voice as much as the subject. Before she knew it, they'd reached the outer ring of the forest and were trudging up the long, looped driveway to the castle itself, where Gregor had left his truck, having dropped off some tools this afternoon before his walk in the woods. The day was fading fast, past four o'clock, it had to be, more likely five or six; she wasn't yet accustomed to the hours of daylight, having been mostly within the castle during working hours. She'd be alone again this evening, but she was fine with that, getting used to the solitude.

"That's different." It was Gregor who saw it first as they rounded the corner.

"Oh wow," added Kenna. "She's done it already."

A light was on in Rohaise's room, weak, but it'd grow stronger as the night settled in.

"Has it been left on by mistake?" checked Gregor. "Do you need to turn it off? I'll come in with you if you like."

"No!" Her answer, more like a startled cry, clearly surprised him.

"Oh, I didn't mean—"

"No, it's all right," she flapped. "It's meant to stay on, you see. It was something Jean and I discussed, that we'd leave a light on in the Rohaise Room, sort of brighten up the castle a bit, provide a beacon shining as far as the eye can see."

"Ah," said Gregor, nodding. "Now, Rohaise, there's an interesting story."

She turned to him. "It is, the woman who died defending the castle and protecting her lover. But that's it, that's all I know. As a history buff, do you know more?"

He shook his head, his gaze returning to the lit window. "That's all that's known in general, I think. There's nothing written down, not as far as I can find out. Just information passed down through the ages the old-fashioned way, via word of mouth."

"Myth and legend," said Kenna, crestfallen.

"Myth and legend is often the most accurate truth. Have you thought of that?"

"Even the faerie you were talking about?"

"Especially them."

He laughed and so did she, but they soon quieted.

"I want to know more about her," she said after a few moments. "Can you help?"

"I can try," Gregor promised. "If you'd like me to."

"I would, very much."

They'd all found their way to Drumlin – she, Gregor and, before them, Rohaise, a woman with long red hair like herself but who, if that reflection in the mirror was anything to go by, had an anger that could burn you alive.

Chapter Twelve

Not complete darkness. Not anymore. The light, though I shun it, insists on encroaching. Here in this room, on a table by the window, is an orb that glows. Why? What purpose does it serve? Such a strange light, not like the light I am used to, the fire…

Fire. Once it would save me. When winter gritted its gnarly teeth, it was fire that prevented our bodies from freezing, that made the days and the nights something to be borne. Such bright flames that leapt high, that drew other creatures closer, also seeking comfort, and they were welcome, every one of them. The forest gave us plenty to burn, a bounty to be shared amongst those that needed it, that could not burrow deep. Fire kept us warm in the castle too, as did the castle walls. Such thick walls! Walls I would run my hands along, that I grew used to as those within the castle, the others that inhabited it, grew used to me.

It took time for them to do so, for bitterness and resentment to fade from their faces, anger that this girl, this wild thing, uncouth and uncivilised, should be brought within, just as I had brought Alexander deep within the forest. He had loved it there, as I did, but he loved it at the castle more. And because he did, I must love it too. I admired the might of it, certainly; it had held strong summer after summer, winter after winter, for longer than I was able to imagine. And it would continue to do so, after Alexander and I both turned to dust. That was the wonder of it, the glory, that this structure, forged by the hands of men, might outlive the trees in the forest, even, wouldn't wither or die. A fortress for our love.

Such sweet days and nights spent by the fire. His skin was beautiful in the glow of it, golden, mine so pale in contrast, 'pure', he'd said, without a blemish on it. Sweet days indeed, but how I agonised about the attitudes of others. Alexander, though, only laughed.

"I rule here. They bow to me. You are by my side, and there you will stay."

Any that came to our door, that disapproved of our union, he sent on their way. On seeing this, the servants remained quiet, for they too would be cast out if they insisted on wearing that same sullen look when tending to me. No more warm bed for them by the fire at sundown; they'd be banished into other towns and other cities instead, far, far away. But…as brusque as he could be towards them, as threatening, I never was. I never saw myself as superior just because I was his lover, his…'mistress', I'd heard it said, a word I wasn't familiar with, could only guess at its meaning. I wasn't superior to anyone or anything, but neither was I inferior. Alexander told me that and Mother before him: 'Never accept you are less, for I have not raised you that way. A thousand men could not survive the forest as you survive it. You're special, Rohaise, my winter rose, my summer bloom.'

If anyone upset me, I was to tell Alexander. But I never did. They began to realise that, even appreciate it. A wild thing in the castle, but not something that would destroy them.

They would come to my room, a room that was mine, all mine, that I'd requested, near the very top, because from there I could see the forest in all its glory, remind myself just how close it was. They would light the fire when it had burnt to nothing, even when I hadn't asked them, and they would keep me warm, bestow on me a smile as they retreated from the room, just a hint of one, but it was enough. And in return, if they complained of an ailment, I would tend to them by the fire, using salves and tinctures made from herbs I'd accumulated that soon worked their magic, made them feel well again, better than ever.

Fire. Always the flames would mesmerise me, the grace of them, performing the most intricate of dances. A miracle. The saviour of lives. Until they are turned against you.

Then, oh then, the havoc they can wreak, the pain! Flames that no longer dance but devour you, greedy flames, their appetite immense. No one should feel the flames upon them, no one! For their bite is as cruel and as vicious and merciless as men. There is no respite, not even a moment to catch your breath. Rather, your breath is devoured too, alongside the screams and the pleas that form dying on your lips. Hair as red as fire becomes fire also, billowing all around, shooting sparks into the sky, golden embers. A beauty in it, but a terrible one. And then all beauty fades, becomes unrecognisable.

And that is what the orb reminds me of! Why I shun it! And yet still it burns.

The light, I want to dash it to the floor, snuff it out, snuff out these memories too, these echoes. I don't want them to fill my head as they do. It is peace I seek, only peace, to lie in my bed in my castle, my home, surrounded by the forest, the trees, and wait. And yet peace is but an echo too, swallowed by the memory of fire.

The fire stole everything from me. My life.

But what came before it was worse.

Chapter Thirteen

What was this? Some kind of joke? Was Adam teasing her, testing her, even?

With the phone held out before her, her hand shaking, her entire body too, Kenna read the email again.

I'm so sorry, but I won't be coming to Scotland, not in the foreseeable future, anyway. Work keeps piling up, and I need to be here in London. I don't know where it's all coming from, but I can't turn it down. I have to take it while I can. Kenna, I really am sorry, but now just isn't the right time for me. I thought it was, but I was wrong. It's like, I don't know, Scotland seems so far away suddenly. I've never even been there! What if I don't like it? I still love you. I want to be with you, one day, but I can't leave, give this all up. I'm staying on at my flat. The new tenants chose elsewhere in the end, which was a stroke of luck. Look, I'll call you soon, try to explain more. Don't hate me, please. Whatever you do, don't hate me. I need time, that's all. Time and space to reach a decision.

It had to be a joke, Kenna decided. This was his idea to come here, and there were reasons for it, *sound* reasons. The more she read his email, the less sense it made. She'd call him. Right now. Maybe he was having some sort of breakdown because of the pressure of work – another reason he'd wanted to escape, to be free of all that, to go at his own pace. In London, in situ, it was too easy to become embroiled. She'd been like that herself too, suffered a workload that could break anyone's back.

Words. Her life had always revolved around them. First in the form of books, reading anything and everything as soon as she was capable, then studying literature at Sheffield University before returning to London to edit the words of others. She *still* wanted her life to be about them, despite working at Drumlin, but her own this time, something she was excited about, various ideas already emerging. Today, though, words were killing her.

She was being dumped, because, no matter how Adam dressed it up, he was ending it. *I still love you.* Really? You'd lead someone on – *spectacularly* lead them on – get them to change location, to wait for you in a distant place and then what? Just not show up? Was that loving someone? Did he even know what love was? Did she? Because how could she love a man who was capable of this? Such betrayal.

She had to speak to him, get to the bottom of it, the *real* reason he wasn't coming. Persuade him to see sense. He had to honour his promise! A year of lonely nights at the castle were all that stretched ahead of her otherwise.

Her hands barely able to navigate the screen, jumping as though tiny little repetitive shocks were being administered, she finally heard the dial tone.

"Pick up, Adam. Come on."

He didn't. It went straight to voicemail. She listened to him speak, his voice infused with energy but a ghost of a voice nonetheless. "Hey, thanks for calling! Can't answer, though, not at the moment, but leave a message and I'll get back to you."

She called again and again, left several messages, all of them similar.

"Adam, I've got your email, and I don't understand it. Call me back as soon as you can, okay? Adam, where are you? We have to speak, we have to sort this…mess out."

A mess. That's exactly what she'd got herself into. Stuck in Scotland, of all places, the wilds, the boondocks, unable to just hop on a tube to his flat and bang on the door.

Quickly, she put it in perspective. Yes, she was a long way away, but not a million miles. She could still take the train, see him in person, thrash this out face-to-face – but for the castle. She was in charge of the day-to-day running and couldn't just leave.

"Pick up, you bastard!"

He wasn't going to answer. If he was seeing her calls, then he was ignoring them, and time was marching on. Soon she had to open the castle, greet what visitors there were, organise Connor and Laura, love's young dream – only it seemed they didn't know it yet – whilst she…she was caught on the flip side of love, in a nightmare.

As much as she wanted to hurl the phone at the wall, she refrained.

I need time, that's all, he'd said. *Time and space.*

Maybe she did too. Just as well because right now, time and space were all she had.

* * *

Strange how time passed at the castle. Some days it hung around, minutes dragging as she waited for visitors to arrive, and then when they came, turning up all pink-cheeked and eager, often with children in tow, the flurry of excitement was almost too much, and the day whizzed by. Some visits lasted hours as people asked question after question and took advantage of the grounds too, even picnicked there. Kids would thunder up and down the staircase, dart into every room, Kenna wanting to yell after them, to request they be careful. The treads were wide, but even so, what if someone tripped and fell? She didn't want any accidents, but she kept quiet, let them have their fun, because...well, because this place needed frivolity to chip away at the weight of what already existed, to try to, if not replace it, balance it. Because when the guests were gone, when Connor, Laura and Gregor returned home, Drumlin was a different beast. It was sombre, it brooded, the memories it housed a burden.

Gregor was true to his word. Aside from his job and his studies, he'd been trying to find out more about Drumlin, or rather Rohaise. They didn't even know her surname – if she had one – only the barest of details. And yet it was Rohaise's bedroom where people lingered most; Kenna had noticed that. Even the kids simmered down, everyone just standing there silently as if trying to sense something, intrigued by this mysterious lady.

There was snowfall in spring, right at the end of April, a heavy blizzard that had stunned Kenna, the sheer quantity of it. It never fell like that in London. Here it covered everything, was feet deep, making it all look so brand new, this relic from the past and the grounds in which it stood. It even brightened the night, which was a good thing, lending her the courage to venture outside once the sun had set, just round to the front of the castle, her eye always drawn to the room on the sixth floor and the light that now shone there.

Kenna never managed to speak to Adam. Every call, every text, every drunken plea at midnight fell on deaf ears. She was angry, of course, but strangely not as much as she'd thought she might be. He hadn't forced her to come to

Scotland; she continued to remind herself of that. She could have said no, laughed at him, binned the idea, but she hadn't. Moreover, she was *glad* she'd come, her old life a dream, even him, even Adam, gone up in smoke.

This was her life, she was certain of that, in a castle in the deep snow in Scotland. And although Jean kept largely in the background, taking over from her on Sundays still and dealing with the finances, Kenna enjoyed spending time with her new colleagues, Connor, Laura and Gregor, and how different they were to the people she used to know. Driven but not in a dog-eat-dog manner, far gentler than that. Life in Scotland didn't drain you the way life in London often did, London friends too, much as she missed them. She missed Sal especially, who'd promised to visit soon, no doubt eager to tear strips off Adam, her hunch about him proving right. If only Kenna had listened, been more careful, but she'd thrown herself headlong into the relationship, a relationship of air, it seemed.

First, though, Gregor was coming to visit – this evening, sitting with her by the log burner after ensuring her stock of firewood was larger than ever during this cold snap. She was cooking for them a simple dinner of spaghetti and meatballs, to be washed down with a glass or two of Chianti.

The sauce simmering nicely away, she left it so she could tend to herself, grabbing a quick shower and then towelling off in her bedroom. Slipping into some comfortable clothes – jeans, a tee shirt and a jumper, woolly socks on her feet – she wondered what Gregor would wear, his everyday work clothes not too dissimilar to what she was wearing now. She looked forward to his company, the easy chat between them, because it *was* easy. There was always something to say. When he'd confided in her about his past, it seemed to have created a bond, that of friendship and trust. Whilst Connor and Laura were good fun too, with Gregor there was more depth to their relationship, although strictly no romance. After Adam and the way he'd let her down so badly, she was done with men for a long while. Did she hate Adam? No, she didn't. But she was sad, definitely that. Bruised and wounded too.

Still deep in thought, she crossed over to the dressing table and began to brush her hair whilst studying her reflection. In the electric glare of the chandelier's numerous lightbulbs, it looked redder than ever, a bloom to her cheeks and her lips red too, though she wore no lipstick. She seemed different, somehow, the country air suiting her.

Her hair gleaming, she replaced the brush on the table, eyes then returning to the mirror. She moved her head, first one way and then the other, a woman of her time, modern enough, but there was something else about her too, again courtesy of the light, which was playing tricks, perhaps. She could imagine, if not see this time, a woman from another age. How she would look if the centuries fell away.

This was a game she played quite often lately, her curiosity piqued by her surrounds. *What would it have been like? What would I have been like?* A tough time, brutal, and women the playthings of men, with no real rights. Subject to their laws, their control. But there was power in beauty. Men succumbed to it, over and over. Were bewitched by it.

Bewitched?

Why did her heart beat faster at that word, become something wild? Her eyes were on her own face, solely that, the green of them so vivid. Kenna was modest, laid as much emphasis on a good personality as a pretty face, but right now, she thought herself beautiful. Breathtaking, even. And yet she had bewitched no one. Least of all Adam. But someone had, another redhead – Rohaise, of course, ensnaring a laird. She was not of noble birth; certainty of that struck like an arrow. She would have been recorded in history if she were a wife and not a mistress. Gregor had agreed when Kenna had voiced that opinion.

"Aye," he'd said. "Highborn and Alexander Buchannan would likely have married her."

But he'd defied convention, as men had carte blanche to do, and in turn so had she.

"Is that what you were, Rohaise? A witch?"

Still she stared at herself, unable to drag her eyes away. Not evil, as witches were so often portrayed, in league with the devil, but *regarded* as a witch, a woman living by her own rules, a beauty… "A child of the forest."

Kenna gasped. Where had those words come from? She'd spoken them before her brain could comprehend.

Imagination really was kicking in. This time, she'd let it. It was part of the reason for being here, to find something to inspire her, that would get her own fingers tapping away on her laptop, weaving a story of her own.

If Rohaise had no history, perhaps Kenna could create one for her.

A child of the forest. A witch.

"So beautiful she outshone the sun." Her lips were working still, as if she was indeed under a spell. "Not a plaything, an equal, treated with love and respect by the man who adored her, who brought her here out of the forest, to Drumlin, his home becoming hers, the two of them enraptured, days passing that were permeated with bliss. Yes! That's how it was exactly. A child of nature, but you loved it here, marvelled at what was man-made too, a place that had existed for centuries before you and would continue to exist for centuries more. Something so enduring. But…" Did the lights just flicker as she continued to ruminate? "What end did you meet? There were lies and a betrayal." Jean had touched on this, and Gregor had elaborated. Rumours had spread that, like his cousin before him, Alexander Buchannan was no Royalist. Had his family been responsible for that? Those that vied for his title and his lands, knowing what to say and whom to say it to. "But were there other rumours as well, equally damaging?" This was her own embellishment. "After all, if you consort with a witch, you're not just against the king, you're against God."

Kenna paused, her heart hammering, her breath coming in short, sharp gasps, waves of hot and cold washing over her, then no longer cold but hot, just hot.

Everyone knows what happens to witches!

Not her words. Not that time. She'd been staring at herself, and her lips hadn't moved. But someone, *something*, had said them. A deep voice that rasped.

Kenna did know what happened to witches, and it could answer why there was no burial ground for Rohaise. Because her body had been burnt and what remained of it, brittle bones, torn apart and scattered. No burial and no ceremony, just hard rain beating down upon them, pushing them deep into the earth, the leaves and twigs of autumn hiding them further.

"Everyone knows." Her voice repeated the words, her eyes full of tears, her body rigid, still hot as if she were burning too.

Feeling Rohaise's pain, her agony, her anger…

"No! No! No!"

No way she could bear it or her reflection either, her face

not beautiful but a hideous thing, her mouth wide open and screaming, revealing a chasm as black as the depths of hell, a sound emitting – a wailing – not an echo nor something distant, as it had been before, but dredged up from deep inside, and it continued, went on and on, was endless because agony was endless. It was timeless, eternal.

"NO!"

Chapter Fourteen

"I'm fine, really. I'll be okay in a few minutes."

"Take some more wine."

"Yes, good idea. Thanks, and…sorry, you know. What must you think of me?"

Kenna and Gregor were sitting in the kitchen of her flat, a blanket around Kenna's shoulders that he had placed there, trying to calm the shivers that wracked her. She had screamed, and he had come running in – thankfully, she'd left the door on the latch, the lack of a doorbell meaning she wouldn't hear him knock if she was in the kitchen or bedroom. He had rushed up to her and once again taken her in his arms. She had fought him at first – something else she was embarrassed about – pummelled her fists against the width of his chest, screaming, this time for him to let her go, 'to unhand her', as she'd put it, peculiar words that didn't seem her own either, that she would never ordinarily use.

She had calmed, though, eventually. And then she had sobbed, confused and frightened still. After a few minutes, he had led her out of the bedroom, down the hallway, into the living room and beyond it to the kitchen, where he'd sat her down and poured the wine. She'd taken the glass from him and not sipped but gulped at it.

"What happened?" he wanted to know.

"I… You know what? I'm not sure." Quickly, she refuted

that. "Of course I know what happened. I got carried away again, that's all."

"Carried away?"

"Not by the Un...seelie Court, is that what they're called?"

"Aye, they are."

"No, nothing as sinister. Just my imagination at work. I was staring in the mirror, having just brushed my hair, and I was thinking about Rohaise. What she was like, the power she wielded over Alexander, the life she lived." Her voice lowering, she added, "Her death."

"Her death?"

Sure her cheeks matched her hair in colour, she wondered whether to stop whilst the going was good or continue.

"Kenna," Gregor prompted. "It's okay, you can tell me."

She laughed shakily. "And you won't judge?"

"Did you judge me?"

"Sorry?" she said, frowning.

"When I told you about my past. Did you judge me?"

"No! Of course not. I believed you when you said all that was behind you."

"You did, and I appreciate it. And I'll believe you, whatever you tell me."

Such sincere words were greeted by a silence that seemed to hang in the air between them. That made her shiver again, but for entirely different reasons.

She took a deep breath, placed her glass on the table and clasped her hands together. "I was thinking about her, and suddenly, strangely, it felt like I got an insight, you know, a flash of something."

"Go on," he replied.

"We've sort of guessed she wasn't a lady of nobility or there'd likely be a record of her somewhere in history. With that in mind, the notion entered my head that she was a child of the forest, *this* forest, the one that surrounds us. The words burst from me, actually, those very words. *A child of the forest.* Is that likely? Did people live in the forest then?"

His cheeks creased with slight laughter. "They did, and not just in Scotland, all over."

Exasperated with herself, she shook her head. "Of course they did. I know that; I took history at school. To GCSE level, anyway. Well, that's what she was in my imagination, somebody who lived in the forest, and somehow, maybe whilst out hunting, Alexander Buchannan discovered her, was dazzled by her. He fell in love with her."

Gregor was nodding, dark curls falling forwards, which he tamed with his hand. "Yep, that could be the way of it. It's feasible, certainly."

"No way Alexander could live in the forest with her, not when he had a castle to call his own, so he brought her here instead, to Drumlin, and here she stayed as his lover, his mistress." She flushed saying those words, feeling them to be a little personal somehow. "And then Alexander had to flee because of lies spread about him, not just that he was anti-Royalist but something else too."

Gregor frowned, picked up his own glass of wine and drank from it. "What else?"

"That he was consorting with a witch."

He almost spat the wine out. "A witch? You're saying Rohaise was a witch?"

"No!" Kenna said, glancing over at the wall, hoping, praying, that her words hadn't carried into the main body of the building. "*I'm* not saying that, but those wanting to overthrow him, they'd resort to all kinds of measures, surely?"

"Yeah, yeah, I suppose. Politics doesn't change, it seems."

She smiled at that, albeit weakly. "So there I was, taking my imagination, or rather that theory, one step further and thinking something else too. The punishment meted out to her, when finally she was dragged from the castle, when she fell into the hands of the king's men. I remember reading somewhere once that they didn't tend to burn witches in England. They hanged them, but in Scotland, it was a different matter, wasn't it?"

Gregor paused for a moment before answering, as if having to collect himself. "Yes, that's right, with regard to that, Scotland's track record is shameful. They burnt them after first strangling them, but strangling them to death? Who knows? I've read suggestions that sometimes they were deliberately left alive, that they—" he lowered his head "—the so-called men of justice, the spectators, even, wanted to witness their agony."

Kenna sighed. "Poor Rohaise."

"But we don't know that's what happened to her," Gregor said, gently rubbing at her arm. "She died certainly, here at Drumlin."

"At the hands of the king's men."

Gregor nodded.

"Would they have gone gently on her?"

"Gently? Well…"

"It wasn't a gentle time, Gregor! You know they wouldn't have done. Christ, she probably knew it, and yet still she stayed. She sacrificed herself."

"As fascinating as history is, sometimes it's best not to dwell on details."

Kenna mulled this over before admitting something else. "There was a voice," she said. "Not mine. I know it wasn't. It was as different to my voice as night is to day."

"What did it say?" he asked, and she smiled again, thankful he wasn't dismissing this latest detail. Adam would. Adam would be appalled by her behaviour, think she was going nuts. Most likely he'd laugh at her, but not Gregor. There was no smile on his face at all now; it was intent instead, this man who loved history, who *believed* in it.

"It just said, 'Everyone knows what happens to witches,' and it was a...nasty voice, rasping, mocking." She trembled to recall it. "There was laughter in it, cruel laughter." She closed her eyes briefly. When she opened them, he was still looking at her, no air of judgement about him at all. "I'm not mad."

This time his smile was wide. "I know you're not. Far from it. You're sane, you're brave and you're..." His voice trailed off, but then he added, "Whatever happened, it's over. You were caught in a moment, that's all."

"Yeah, yeah, I suppose so."

"And in a place like this, that's easy enough. Look, if it helps, shall we go back to your bedroom and check it?"

"Look under the bed, that sort of thing?"

"And in the wardrobe," he replied, playing along. "There's nothing here, Kenna, not now. Like I said, it was a moment, an emotion, a feeling from long ago that you perhaps tuned in to. You know there's a saying, 'history is alive.' It's alive because it's everywhere, all around us, and nowhere more so than at Drumlin. We can learn from the past, we *should*, but it can't hurt us, not again, because as alive as it is, it's done and dusted."

Fey, that's what Gregor Lockart was, she decided, like

she'd heard the Scottish were, the Irish and the Welsh too, nations more inclined to believe in the otherworldly because their own history was so entrenched in it, the old ways, the magic.

She stood up, an abrupt gesture. She had to stop these flights of fancy, stay grounded.

Instead of walking to the bedroom, however, she headed towards the counter and the bottle of wine. Bringing it back to the table, she began refilling their glasses.

"I'm driving," he said, staying her hand.

"Do you have to?"

"It's too far to walk!"

"Don't, then. Stay here. Just for tonight."

"Here?"

His amazement caused laughter to burst from her. "There are two spare bedrooms, you know! Look, I don't want to check anything. Of course there's nothing here. It's just…I've had a really crap few weeks. I haven't told you, told anyone, not even Jean knows all the details, but my boyfriend was supposed to come and join me at Drumlin, not to work, just to live. He's in the IT industry, and as long as he's got a computer, he can work anywhere, you see." She not so much sat back in her chair as slumped in it. "It was his idea to come to Scotland. He was gung ho about it, but then work got in the way. He couldn't come up, not initially, and then…he decided not to come at all. He emailed me to tell me and hasn't been picking up the phone since. So, yeah, I could use a drinking partner."

Gregor drank deep. "So this was his idea, eh? Any regrets, though?"

She also drank, considering his question. "Do you know something? I'm getting used to it." She glanced in the direction of the bedroom. "Perhaps *too* used to it."

"I'll stay," he said. "Of course I will. But you are safe."

He sounded so sure, and she should be as certain. She *was* certain. The more she drank, the more certain she became, later in the evening able to laugh at what had happened, to scamper down the passageway after all, with Gregor, the pair of them making light of it, howling as they went, even raising their hands and 'woo-wooing' on occasion. Bursting into her bedroom – a normal room, that's all it was. *Splendidly* normal.

Whilst in her room, she stepped closer to the mirror, still emboldened by the wine.

A mirror that was also normal, the reflection in it none but her own.

Gregor came to stand behind her, just as she'd imagined Alexander had stood behind Rohaise in the Rohaise Room. But that's where the similarity ended. His arms didn't come out and encircle her waist, and she didn't lay her head back against his shoulder, his head lowering to kiss her neck, one hand moving her hair aside, hair that was like fire…

She shook her head, laughed again. Spinning on her heels, she faced Gregor.

"Thank you," she said.

"For what?"

"For being here. For staying."

He held her gaze. "The pleasure's all mine," he replied, that smile, the one that made him look so much younger, back on his face.

She swallowed before speaking further. "Because you're the only one who did."

Chapter Fifteen

Every time she remembered what she'd said, she blushed. She blamed the alcohol, of course, thought back to all those times in London she'd had a bit too much to drink, out on the town with her friends, the scrapes they'd got themselves into, the men they would sidle up to, dance close to. It was on one of those occasions she'd met Adam, been taken in by him and his clear blue gaze, agreed to see him again. Alcohol had a lot to answer for.

Alcohol aside, she liked Gregor, she really did. He was turning out to be a solid friend, and she was grateful he'd stayed at the castle with her overnight. But what she'd said and the way she'd said it, impassioned slightly…scrub that, *clearly* impassioned. *Thank you. For being here. For staying. Because you're the only one who did.* She must have been referring to Alexander as well as Adam. Oh, what the heck, she didn't know. It was all a blur. After that first bottle of red, they had opened another, they'd eaten, Gregor helping himself to more, but for her part she'd barely touched the food, hence why she'd become drunker still. The night had passed, and they'd each gone to their respective rooms, and she'd slept fine knowing he was there, deep and dreamlessly. When eventually she'd woken, grabbed her dressing gown and entered the passageway, she could see his bedroom door was open, the bed neatly made and the window ajar, allowing a burst of fresh air in, perfumed subtly with pine and wood smoke, she swore it.

On entering the kitchen via the living room, there'd been a note from him.

Got up early to go home and shower. See you later at work. Thanks for last night. G.

She'd smiled on seeing it, held the paper in her hands and then remembered...what she'd said, and the blushing had started. Later, she indeed saw him in his domain, the gardens, planting more rose bushes as she'd requested, flowers destined to bloom various shades of pink, white and red. God, what he was achieving with the grounds that surrounded the castle! She was knocked out by it. Some species were already in bloom: the narcissi that were also abundant in the forest, the heathers and the tulips too, as well as plenty of ground cover, geraniums that would lend colour month after month after month. The lawns were also lovely, neatly mown in spite of the soggy ground beneath, and, courtesy of the Rotary Club, two sets of tables and benches were arriving soon.

Wondering whether to rush past him – she had the castle to open up – she stopped when he spied her. Lifting his arm, he hailed her over.

"Hey there!" she said, pulling a face as she approached him. "How's your head? Hope it isn't hurting as much as mine."

"Head's fine. Thanks for dinner last night. You sleep okay?"

"Like a baby," she replied. "Hope you did too."

"Babies scream and wail, don't they? So, no, I'd say I slept like a charm instead."

"Fair enough," she said, laughing. "The gardens look

great, by the way."

"Aye, well, there's a lot to do still beside cosmetics – about a million bushes to trim, a thousand trees to prune, the works – but it'll get done."

"A full-time job."

"I'm part-time, remember?"

"Oh yeah, of course. But you know what I mean. Wonder if it'll be a busy day today."

"Who knows? But summer's coming, along with the school holidays. In Scotland the kids break up end of June and go back August. In England, it's different, isn't it? They end slightly later? At least staggering it staggers the holidaymakers too, all eager for a Scottish castle."

"I was thinking we should hold some events here, like a ball or something in the main hall, an evening with the bagpipes, something like that."

"You can, if you think it's necessary."

"That's just it. I don't know if it is. Jean never really did, but then I get the feeling she wanted to keep it as a gem to be discovered, somewhere to chance upon unexpectedly."

Gregor had been tilling the soil whilst chatting to Kenna, but now he stopped and leaned against the hoe instead. "And do you?"

She shrugged. "I want what's best for the castle, really, to keep it afloat."

"Seems to me it's kept afloat for centuries just fine."

"Well, not strictly true. There was a time it was derelict, apparently. Abandoned. Home to mice and rats and nothing more."

"Ah yes, a short period of time, though, relatively speaking."

She paused, thought about this, turned from Gregor to

the castle itself. "A jewel," she mused. "It is, isn't it? Just that."

Gregor's voice was also wistful. "Aye. Aye, it is."

"The roses"—she faced him again—"we need some at the front too."

"That can be arranged."

"So that…so that…"

"So that what?" he prompted.

"So they can be seen from Rohaise's bedroom."

He nodded, not questioning her further, again just accepting what she said, seeming to understand her thoughts even though she didn't fully understand them herself. "I'll see to it. There's an ideal spot, actually. I'll plant a couple there."

"They have to be red."

"I know they do."

"And I'll think about what we've said, have another word with Jean, see what state the finances are in. But you're right, I don't want to spoil the uniqueness of this place."

"And you never know, the summer might be busy enough."

"It might be, especially if you're here." Shit! There she went again, blushing. "I meant doing such a good job, making the gardens as well as the castle somewhere people really want to be, a place to spend more time, to tell their friends about."

Stepping forward, she cupped the bud of a rose in her hand, wondering what colour it would be.

"Red," he said, as though reading her mind. "That particular rose will be deep, deep red."

"If it blooms."

"Oh, it'll bloom, Kenna. It'll come to fruition.

Everything does."

"The cycle of life and death," she murmured.

"You see it as a gardener, played out every day."

Still holding the bud, she couldn't help but look again at Drumlin – or the next thought that flared. As keeper of the castle, could you see *beyond* death sometimes?

* * *

The summer was indeed busy. May melted into June, into July and then August, and with them came visitor after visitor, all of whom dutifully oohed and ahhed over the castle, declaring it such a wonderful find, so different to castles they'd already explored in the region – 'less polished' one described it as before hastily adding, 'but all the better for it!' They were hungry for information about its history from conception to present.

Kenna did her best to accommodate them, and sometimes when it was busy verging on frantic, Gregor came in from the garden to assist, taking those that wanted a tour of the castle, explaining endlessly, it seemed, how the Buchannans were gifted Drumlin, then lost it, then reclaimed it; its links with Robert the Bruce and Mary, Queen of Scots; the monk, of course, who'd been buried in the wall; and the love affair between Alexander and Rohaise, how she'd helped him escape certain doom, only to face her own.

The visitors lapped it up, wanting to know more details, especially about Rohaise. What happened to her? How did she die? What happened to Alexander? Did he escape? If so, did he ever come back to the site of his former home, where his lover had perished?

"We don't know," Gregor had to confess. "We've been trying to find out, at least about Alexander Buchannan, but the history books remain annoyingly vague. As far as I know, there's no record of his existence after leaving the castle, so we have to assume the worst, that he didn't make it. Having said that, there's no record of his execution either."

"He could have died a thousand different ways," someone pointed out.

"Aye, he could. If he made it to the coast, intending to go to France, he could have perished on the sea, as many did in those days."

There was a slight pause before another visitor posed a question, Kenna nearby and eavesdropping. "Was Rohaise a princess?"

"We don't think so," Gregor answered, and then using Kenna's words exactly, he added, "We think she was a child of the forest, the one that surrounds us."

"A peasant?" the visitor said, disappointment evident in her voice.

Gregor countered that claim. "Someone not of royal blood, like you and me, but noble even so. For isn't it the most noble act to put someone else's life before your own?"

On hearing that, Kenna wanted to punch the air. *Sock it to 'em, Gregor!* The story of Rohaise was what really intrigued the visitors, intrigued *her*, the romance of it – and the tragedy. For it *was* a tragic story, and people thrived on that, wanted their stately homes not just drenched in history but a dark history. If Rohaise had been burnt at the stake for being a witch, right here on these grounds, then it was dark indeed but also something thankfully hard to dwell on, not on a bright summer's day with the sun shining.

When the day had passed and the visitors left the castle,

a few stragglers remaining on the grounds usually until five or six o'clock, the team would also call it a day. Because they were so busy, Gregor was helping more and more to take tours, Kenna wishing he could be paid for it, but he waved her concerns aside, insisting it was good experience for him. Connor and Laura were working flat out too, feeding so many guests. They all needed time to unwind, so, as the sun sank behind the castle, bestowing a final burst of amber brightness before disappearing, they'd sit together with a glass of wine or a cold beer.

In her previous life, she would have called this 'team bonding' or some other corporate duty, but here it felt natural and genuine. A community. A unit. The four of them were indeed that. Their company was easy, amusing even, particularly Connor and Laura, who were still skirting around their feelings for each other, enjoying the thrill of the chase instead, perhaps. She and Gregor would look on, amusement in both their gazes as they sat round one of the tables that had been provided by the Rotary Club, the younger pair's antics childish but so endearing.

"You were a lazy sod today, Connor Dalgleish!" Laura had said one such evening. "Too busy in front of the mirror, making sure your hair's perfect before helping to serve the customers."

"What rot!" he'd retorted. "And you're the vain one, not me."

Laura had given him a shove, making him spill his beer. "Preening yourself for the girls that come here, are you? Hoping to catch someone's eye, eh? What would they see in you, I wonder? You're not a laird, just a skivvy."

"Look who's talking! And I saw you today, don't think I didn't, chatting away to a group of lads, giggling and fluttering your eyelashes, waggling your hips, going the whole hog!"

"I was *serving* them, Connor! That was all. No way I was interested in them."

"Who are you interested in, then?"

"Not you, that's for sure!"

Oh, it was painful, because that was a lie Laura had told, a blatant one. Whenever they'd get up to go, Kenna and Gregor would roll their eyes, silently plead for one of them to admit how they felt about each other.

"The tension's too much for me," Gregor would say to Kenna afterwards.

"Aye," Kenna would agree, Gregor laughing at how she'd adopted the native language.

"Kenna's a Scottish name, isn't it?" he asked her on another of those balmy summer evenings, firelight flickering in front of them courtesy of several candles in jam jars.

"Allegedly," she replied, explaining her links to Scottish ancestry.

"And yet this is the first time you've visited the place?"

She nodded. "It is. I came, I saw…"

"You conquered."

Wry laughter escaped her. "I hope I'm doing okay running the castle. Had no complaint from Jean so far."

"You're doing a great job." He reached for his beer and took a sip. "The punters love you, you can tell. No one goes home disappointed from Drumlin."

"Thanks, they love you too. It's kind of you, you know, to help with the tours. It's not as if you're not frantically busy yourself. This garden looks – and smells – amazing."

And it did, the roses still in bloom and resplendent, their sweet fragrance as heady as the wine in her glass. The rose bushes he'd planted in front of Drumlin were doing well too, somewhere she'd often wander towards to admire them, her gaze always, *always* directed back to the castle and upwards to Rohaise's room.

"So you've been here a good few months now," Gregor said.

"Five," she confirmed.

"Technically, you've only another seven to go."

She frowned at that. "Yes, yes, I suppose you're right. But…"

"But what?" he asked when her voice drifted off.

"I'm thinking Jean wants me to stay."

"No doubt about it. So…will you?"

"Um…I don't know yet, to be honest. I arrived in spring, and summer, well…summer's been glorious. I thought it rained constantly in Scotland!"

"Just a myth," Gregor assured her. "As you've found out."

"A cruel rumour," she teased.

"Vicious."

"But winter in Scotland, that's no rumour, is it?"

"Winter can be hard," he admitted.

"Snow?"

"It's more the wind and rain, the freezing temperatures." He gestured towards her flat. "You'll be warm enough. I'll make sure the log supply is never-ending."

"Thank you, and in answer to your question, I'll have to see how the winter goes and whether I can hack it."

"Och, you'll be all right."

"There won't be many visitors in winter, though, will there?"

"You'd have to ask Jean."

Another thought occurred. "And what about the gardening? You won't be able to do that in torrential rain or hard frost!"

"There'll be days when I'm laid off, that's for sure."

"Study days?"

"Aye, I'll be immersing myself in that more and more." There was a slight pause before he added, "I'm sorry, you know, about Rohaise, not being able to find out anything more about her. About Alexander's fate too. It's not for want of trying."

She shook her head. "I know you've done your best."

"I'll keep on at it."

"No need. Really. You've said before that perhaps it's better we don't know. Maybe you're right. That way we can think the best."

"Aye," Gregor said, but his expression had clouded, indicating he didn't think the best, quite the contrary.

Eventually she decided that all that really mattered was the present, the here and the now, and enjoying some time with a friend. With that in mind, on their evenings together, she began to steer conversation away from Rohaise and Alexander, from anything to do with Drumlin. It was just too easy to get bogged down here with other people's lives rather than their own. Gregor took the bait, and they chatted about books and films instead, her former work and life in London and his former life too, once again Kenna admiring his honesty, how he made no excuses for his wrong choices – although she *did* think he had an excuse. Originally from Glasgow, his childhood, it seemed, had been no picnic. She didn't dare say that, though, knowing he wouldn't appreciate it, that it wasn't sympathy he was after.

Noble. He'd said that about Rohaise. When someone had called her a peasant, he'd defended her. And he was noble too, Kenna decided, Gregor Lockart. More and more evenings passed, the candles often burning right down to the wick, the two of them always lingering, getting to know each other further. They'd sometimes meet on Sundays too, and he'd take her to places in the region that he knew of, other castles, where they'd make a joke of checking out the competition, their turrets fanciful, ropes around everything so you couldn't touch, couldn't immerse yourself like you could at Drumlin.

"No competition," Kenna would declare, Gregor nodding his agreement.

He also took her to small fishing villages on the northern Aberdeenshire coast, some so lonely, so deserted even in the height of summer, forgotten by tourists who tended to head to the western Highlands, who forgot about this corner of the country. She found herself pleased that they did, because to have the villages to themselves, just her and Gregor strolling round, imagining what it was like in days gone by, how different it could be, was special. The lack of people made it easier to do that, her brain storing it all up, fodder for the novel that still eluded her but she would one day pen; she was growing more certain of it. Being here was enriching her, her life in London the thing to grow hazy, the memory of Adam too, whom she'd since given up trying to contact. Too much time and space between them now.

Lovely days, these were, like the days from childhood – *her* childhood, at least – filled with endless sunshine, although it did rain occasionally, she had to concede, and when it did, it rained cold and it rained hard, a taste of things to come. More often, though, the weather was kind, helping to cement the relationship she was forging with this country. An ally. She'd entered a brave new world alone, scared and bewildered at first, heartbroken, or so she'd thought, but her heart was feeling more whole now. It was a world she'd quickly owned, learning to rein in her imagination, to sleep in the castle alone again, to stare in the mirror and see only her own reflection, to stand in Rohaise's room and think kind thoughts, not those laced with horror and nervousness. She loved it at Drumlin, in summer, anyway. Winter might test her; she also knew that.

But again, that was hard to think about on clement days, she and Gregor exploring not just fancy castles owned by huge trusts and organisations but those that were abandoned, set right on cliff edges, and more villages lost in time – *all* of it seemed lost, although she was finding herself, as she'd hoped, wanting the summer to last forever, to be endless.

But it did end, and the past refused to relinquish its grip entirely.

With summer almost gone and autumn just around the corner, a visitor came calling.

Chapter Sixteen

"Surprise!"

"Sal! Wow! I didn't... You never said... Sally Jane Hopkins, what the hell?"

It was around noon, early September, and Kenna was standing behind the counter in reception checking stock records. They'd sold out of so much over summer, benefitting both local craftspeople and castle funds, and, although she knew full well that she didn't need as much for winter, she'd need something, at least – definitely more fridge magnets, bookmarks, tins of shortbread, and postcards, all with an image of Drumlin emblazoned upon them. Chocolates and sweets flew off the shelves too, plus mugs, coasters and felt figures of lairds in kilts and ladies in tartan dresses, so there was plenty to occupy her. More stock was also needed for the kitchen, although both Connor and Laura were reducing their hours over autumn and winter. Laura, like Gregor, was catching up on studying, though she was interested in criminology, not history. Connor, on the other hand, had bagged a few shifts in a friend's pub in Tulce – continuing to hone his cheffing skills.

"I'll give Jamie Oliver a run for his money one day, I'm telling you," he'd declared.

At which Laura had rolled her eyes. "If you earn what he does, I might take you seriously."

"Have a little faith, Laura. I'll prove myself, to you and to everyone else. You'll see."

"I was joking, Connor. I do have faith. Only you've never really noticed."

Kenna, who had witnessed this exchange, was surprised to hear that all teasing between them had taken a brief hiatus; rather, like she and Gregor were with each other, they were being candid, opening up, revealing themselves.

She'd been musing about this as well as deciding what to order when Sal had crept through the doors of the castle and plunged her from a state of reverie into one of shock.

Sal was a good friend, someone she'd known since they were at college together. She was pretty, shorter than Kenna, with an hourglass figure and tousled blond hair. Always made up, even now her lips were crimson and her lashes long courtesy of the extensions she favoured. *So out of place*, was the first thought that formed inside Kenna's head on seeing her again. *You don't belong here!* Thoughts which she quickly subdued.

"Oh, Sal!" she said again, this time far more enthusiastically, rounding the desk to not only stand before her but to hug her – hard. "It's so good to see you."

"You too, Kenna. Been a long time."

"It has. It really has."

There was silence whilst the two girls continued to hold each other, and then Kenna took a step back, noticed a trolley bag beside Sal.

"You're staying?"

"Damn right I am. Just for a couple of days. Is that all right?"

"Of course! I'd be glad to have you. But what are you doing here in this part of the world? Why didn't you let me know you were coming? I could have booked time off."

Sal shook her head, tossed her hair over her shoulder. "Sorry. I was in Newcastle on business, and I thought before going home I'd pop here and see you. It was a last-minute decision, kind of. I was just so close, well...*closer*. I couldn't resist."

"Pop here? As if anyone just 'pops' here!"

"They do now! Are you going to offer me a coffee or what? The train trip was a bit of a nightmare, and then the taxi – well, you don't want to know how much the taxi cost! Forty miles from Aberdeen bloody station. I had no idea!"

"Sal, I'll split the cost—"

"You'll do no such thing! It's on account anyway. Just get me some hot, strong coffee and, shit, Kenna, tell me about this place. It's so...old!"

"Yep, it's that, all right," Kenna agreed.

"I want to hear all about it, about everything. How you've been doing, you know, since...since..." Rather than finish her sentence, she changed tack. "Just look at you! You're amazing. Your hair, your skin. I've never seen you this healthy. I'm gonna need sunglasses, you glow so bright! Who'd have thought being Lady of the Castle would suit you so much. He whom I won't bother naming missed a trick dumping you like he did."

Kenna couldn't help but sigh. "His name's Adam, Sal. And it's fine. I'm over it. I've moved on, literally and figuratively. As you say, being here suits me."

"Good, pleased to hear it. I've been worried about you, we all have, how you're coping."

"We've kept in touch. I've told you I'm fine."

"Yeah, but...I wanted to see for myself, you know. Silly, really, but..." She stepped forward and hugged Kenna again, only briefly this time, but it touched Kenna that she'd been genuinely concerned for her, created an ache for the past and the times they'd spent together. Not just that, they'd *grown* together, from teenagers into adults, supported each other through thick and thin. She felt even guiltier now about that first thought she'd had – *you don't belong*. The initial horror on first seeing her, a ghost from the past.

"Kenna? You okay? You've gone all distant."

Kenna blinked. "What? Yeah, great, everything's great. Right," she said, clapping her hands together, the resultant boom loud, "let's get you a coffee and introduce you to Laura and Connor whilst we're at it, and then, I suppose, you'll want a tour of the castle."

"Absolutely!"

"Brilliant. Leave your trolley bag behind reception – it'll be fine there – and follow me."

Sal did as she was told and, with Kenna in the lead, the two of them headed to the archway, Sal's heels clattering on the floor, making a racket.

"And, Kenna," she said as they continued to the kitchen, "don't disappoint me."

Kenna turned to her. "Huh? In what way?"

"On this tour, I want tales of ghosts, okay?" Sal said, and although there was a smile on her face, her eyes were intent. "Plenty of fucking ghosts."

* * *

Kenna was thankful the day had been quiet visitor-wise. Besides her long-lost friend, just a handful had come through the door and had a mooch around, one couple staying for ages, having lunch in the restaurant area, then cake and more tea, but the others had exited quickly enough, going off to see other castles in the region.

"Fyvie's a good one, isn't it?" said one visitor, a man with a face that reminded her of the actor Christopher Eccleston. "We'll head there."

Perhaps it was stupid, but the way he'd said it made her bristle. *Fyvie's a good one, isn't it?* As if Drumlin wasn't, as if it were some kind of poor relation. How protective she was getting of her new home! *Lady of the Castle*, Sal had called her, going on to use that name several times during the day, especially on the tour Kenna had given her.

"You're in clover, aren't you?" she'd said. "Or should I say heather? Far more apt."

After having tea and cake too, they'd climbed the turnpike staircase, Kenna taking her in and out of each room, the main hall a place Sal had described as being 'wicked' for a party, whereas the library was 'eerie' and the bower 'hardly good enough for a queen'.

"Why'd she get that room? It's the smallest! If I was Mary, I'd have complained!"

"She got it because all the other bedrooms were occupied, I suppose, and it was winter when she stayed, after the Battle of Corrichie. This is a small room with a big fireplace. She'd have been warm here, comfortable, and maybe, just maybe, not all queens were divas, you know? Maybe she didn't go around demanding the best everywhere she stayed. Maybe she was more modest than that."

"Whatever." Sal had shrugged. "If I was queen, I'd be the biggest diva ever."

"I don't doubt it," Kenna had retorted.

The pair of them smiling, Kenna had led her upwards to more bedrooms, Sal admiring the four-poster beds and

Kenna assuring her she'd be sleeping in one tonight in her flat. "You can have it all to yourself if you like. I'll take one of the beds in the spare rooms instead."

Sal shook her head. "No way! We'll share, just like we've always shared in the past. Snuggle up together."

Kenna smiled wider. "If you insist."

Nearing the sixth floor, Sal started moaning.

"Bloody hell, I'm knackered! Is there much more to go?"

"No," Kenna assured her, taking each tread easily, her stamina having built up over the months due to tackling them so often.

As they approached the Rohaise Room, butterflies danced in Kenna's stomach. Now here was a tale to tell, one she'd been saving till last, excited about imparting it.

"Oh okay," Sal had breathed on entering. "It's just another bedroom."

Just as she'd bristled at the man who'd seemed to compare Drumlin less favourably to Fyvie earlier, Kenna did so again.

"It's not just a bedroom, Sal, it's…her bedroom, the true Lady of the Castle."

"What did you say her name was? Ro…what?"

"Rohaise."

"Rohaise? Never heard of it."

"It's Gaelic. It means 'rose'."

"Oh okay, yeah, I can see that. It does sound like 'rose' but with a weird twist to it." She ventured further into the room, ran her fingers over the quilt on the four-poster bed.

"Be careful," Kenna whispered, but if Sal heard her, she gave no sign. Instead, she picked up a vase, another ancient thing, and turned it over.

"It's got a few cracks in it."

"Sal"—Kenna's voice was louder this time—"you're allowed to touch, but just be careful." It was incredible, being as no signs warned you to keep your hands to yourself, that so much survived intact. Visitors always seemed to respect the place, with parents making the effort to rein children in. Sal, though, was a law unto herself.

As Kenna told her about Rohaise and her love affair with Alexander, the sacrifice that she had made, Sal went from item to item, continuing to handle them, to peer at them, her expression far from impressed. On the dressing table, she picked up the hand mirror, stared hard at it, then grimaced, actually grimaced.

"So, when the king's men came for Alexander, he and Rohaise fled. There's a tunnel in the grounds, although we don't know where, but that's where they headed. If she went with him initially, she came back. We think to better conceal the entrance to the tunnel, to concoct some sort of story that he'd fled overland. Misdirecting them would buy him time, you see, give him a better chance of escaping. She didn't escape, though. She was killed by the king's men. She was…she was… Sal? Are you even listening to me?"

Sal had replaced the hand mirror and turned back to face Kenna.

"It smells in here," she said at last.

"What?" As taken aback as she'd been when Sal had first appeared, seemingly out of nowhere, she was surprised again. "It doesn't!"

"Who cleans it?"

"Cleans it? Well…I do. That's one of my duties. But it doesn't take long, to be honest. A castle like this doesn't have to gleam. What sort of smell is it?"

Sal stood there – she was something that did gleam,

overrefined – and screwed up her nose further. "It's…what's the word…*acrid*, that's it, and it's getting worse the longer I stay here. It's a horrible room. The worst of the lot. It feels…oppressive in here."

"Oppressive?"

"Yeah, exactly that. You know what, it's a castle. Wow and all that. It looks impressive from the outside, imposing, despite having no turrets, all the things you'd expect from a castle. But inside, I don't know, I just want to escape, especially from this room. Sorry, Kenna," she said, heading for the door, "it's hard to breathe in here. I need fresh air."

As Sal took to the staircase and descended it, Kenna remained where she was, somewhat stunned. After a few moments, she sniffed. Was her friend right? Did it smell? Had she just got used to it over so many months that she didn't notice it anymore? Had she *ever* noticed it?

Roses. That was all she could smell. Perhaps because that's what she *imagined* she could, because of her name, because of Rohaise. During the summer, when the roses had been in full bloom, big, blousy and beautiful, she'd picked several at various times and placed them in the room, in a vase that stood alongside the lamp in the window, the lamp that was on a timer and would come on soon, that would glow through the night.

The vase stood empty now. As each bloom had withered and died, she'd replaced it, but now there were no longer roses outside; they'd withered and died too. She sniffed again. A stench? A smell that was bitter, *acrid*? No, Sal was wrong, quite wrong. The only smell she could detect was that of age and to be expected.

"Kenna! Where are you? I'm downstairs, hurry up!"

Sal's voice reached her from below, making her jump.

ROHAISE

She'd clean this room more thoroughly than she had done so far, just in case Sal was right. She'd check for mouse droppings although pest repellents were in every room, discreetly hidden. Make sure too that Sal had replaced things properly, spying the hand mirror was askew and rushing to correct it. *Rohaise likes everything in its place.* Another rogue thought, but one she agreed with, the sentiment, at least. It was about respect, and Sal, as far as Kenna was concerned, had shown none.

In fact, she thought – as she finally left the room and hurried down the stairs – Sal had treated the whole Rohaise experience with nothing less than contempt.

Chapter Seventeen

"You sure you don't mind taking over for the day?"

"Not at all, go, have a day out with your friend, enjoy it."

"Thanks, Gregor, I really appreciate this. I don't think there'll be many visitors."

"Aye, they're beginning to wane."

"Seems so," Kenna said. "But you know what, the winter will give me time to do other things. I've decided I need to clean the castle thoroughly. Not make it spotless, I don't mean that, just…chip away at the layers of dust. I have to make a list too of repairs that need doing, some light plastering in places. I'll discuss it with Jean, see what we can do. You need a greenhouse, don't you? The one we have is pretty dilapidated."

"A bigger greenhouse would be nice, but I can manage."

"I know, but we've had a good summer, and maybe the Rotary Club could get involved with raising funds for a greenhouse. After all, the upkeep of the gardens is vital. Look how many came to Drumlin in the warmer months and stayed to picnic."

"Aye, then went into Tulce to spend money there in the shops and restaurants."

"Exactly. It's a win-win situation."

On the pathway outside the castle where they stood, Gregor looked around him. "What does your friend think of it?"

"Sal? Oh look, here she is. You can ask her yourself."

Sal rounded the corner and headed towards them, tottering over the gravel due to inappropriate footwear, her hands wide for balance. But then this had been an impromptu visit, Kenna reminded herself; if not, she would have packed more suitably, surely?

"Hey there!" she called, her face lighting up at seeing the man standing beside Kenna. "And who are you? Kenna, come on, introduce us!"

Kenna did as she was asked, Sal adopting her biggest smile, peroxide teeth flashing.

"The estate gardener, eh? Not sure I've ever met an estate gardener before!"

Gregor was clearly bemused. "Hope you're not too disappointed."

"Not at all! You're a nice surprise, actually."

Kenna intercepted. "Gregor's kindly offered to man reception and greet any visitors today." It began to rain as she said it, verifying that perhaps it was the best option for him anyway. "So we can go exploring. There are some gorgeous little towns a few miles away on the north coast, really historic. Banff and Cullen and—"

"Aberdeen," Sal said. "I'd like to go there."

"But…" Kenna looked at Gregor, saw he was as nonplussed as she was at this request. "Aberdeen's just another city, Sal, not quite London but along those lines. Why not try something different? The small coastal towns, they're amazing, so beautiful."

"Any shops there?"

"Shops?" Again, Kenna looked at Gregor, saw the frown on his face. "There are, yes, a few of them, local shops, you know, bespoke."

Just as she'd done in the Rohaise Room, Sal screwed up her nose. "I prefer the sound of Aberdeen. I want some hustle and bustle, a bit of life. Man, I can't believe you spend your nights here alone, Kenna. I was terrified when it was just the two of us!"

"Terrified?" Kenna questioned. "You slept okay."

"I did, yeah, thanks to the wine we drank, but I'm telling you, I needed that wine!" She shook her head. "No, couldn't do it, I'm afraid, no way." Eyeing Gregor in that way she had, flirtatious, suggestive, she then said, "I'd have to have company *every* night, know what I mean?"

Kenna grabbed Sal by the arm and shuffled backwards with her.

"Right, come on, let's go," she said. "Thanks again, Gregor. We won't be too long."

"No worries, take your time," he replied, "and…enjoy Aberdeen. I'll lock up when I leave and post the keys through your door. The Granite City, it's known as," he added, maybe by way of appeasement, Kenna thought, trying to make it sound more interesting than it perhaps was, for her, at least. "There are some buildings of note there."

In the Volvo, Sal briefly complaining about that as well and how old it was – 'a rust bucket', she called it – she then returned to the subject of Gregor, enthusing about his dark eyes and hair, his 'gardener's build'. "Hauling soil is clearly good for your muscles!"

Kenna listened as she drove but only with half an ear, declaring when she was asked that, no, she didn't fancy Gregor; they were friends, just friends, that was all she wanted right now, it did her very nicely indeed, thank you.

Another part of her was drifting, trying to recall if Sal had shown any signs of being terrified the previous night as she'd claimed.

When they'd got into bed, Sal had snuggled close, but then she always did. That was just her way. She'd been giggling, asking if the flat was haunted, insisting it had that same heavy feeling there was in the castle, stating as she'd done in front of Gregor that she didn't know how Kenna coped, asking if she'd give 'this gig' up soon and return to normality, unable to believe it when Kenna said she had yet to decide.

No, she hadn't been terrified, but what she'd been was as disdainful as ever.

"Nope, couldn't live here," she'd told Kenna when she'd given her a second tour, this time of her flat.

"It's very comfortable," Kenna had insisted.

"It is, but…so bloody old-fashioned. And your bedroom, it's impressive, befitting, I suppose, but everything in it feels dusty with age. That's the thing about this place, Kenna. The past suffocates everything. Give me the bright lights of home any day."

And she got her wish, because the only full day she had here – Sal was due to travel back to London the next morning at the crack of dawn – she'd chosen to spend in a place that mimicked where she'd spent most of her life. Thinking this, *realising* this, Kenna was even more grateful she'd made the break from London, that she was experiencing something different, for surely the more experiences you had, the more rounded a person you became? London life, any kind of city life, no longer appealed. So how she'd cope with Aberdeen, the Granite City, as Gregor had called it, she had no idea.

She was right to be wary. She didn't enjoy Aberdeen at all. Parking was stressful, for a start, in one of those multistorey carparks that squeezed you in, leaving no room on the ramps either, Kenna not used to tackling them and praying she wouldn't damage the car, scrape the sides of it – rust bucket or not – as she drove higher and higher to find a space. Having finally parked, and with her nerves shot, they made their way into a covered mall packed with shops they were both familiar with. The sound of so many people, chatting as they walked and laughing out loud, continued to jar.

Sal, however, took it all in her stride. She dragged Kenna into practically every shop, Kenna spending ages waiting for her whilst she tried clothes on, then paraded herself in front of Kenna, wanting an opinion. Sal worked in finance in the City; she was an advisor and earned a substantial amount, more than Kenna had ever earned in publishing. She had cash to burn and always looked great, able to afford quality clothing rather than the more disposable kind. She purchased a dress, two shirts and a pair of shoes higher than the ones she had on, so high they made Kenna's eyes water just to look at them.

Tired, hungry and laden down, Kenna was relieved when Sal suggested lunch. Instead of heading towards somewhere relaxed, however, she led them to a bar where music pumped out onto the street, the interior dark and moody, more laughter from people in booths that conspired with the music to burst your eardrums. They duly sat in one of the booths, a waitress swooping in on them, greeting them as though they were long-lost friends, doing her job but just too overbearing. The whole thing was. With food ordered and drinks too – Sal fancied a porn-star martini, her favourite cocktail, whilst Kenna stuck to sparkling water – Sal then proceeded to shout at Kenna, albeit conversationally, having to raise her voice as it was impossible to be heard otherwise.

By the time they left the bar, Kenna's head was thumping. She was ready to go home, but Sal insisted on visiting just a few more shops, needing some makeup.

Finally, *finally*, they left Aberdeen, Kenna actually unsure how she was going to drive, she felt so drained. As she'd done on the journey there, Sal chattered all the way home, Kenna wishing she had the guts to tell her effervescent friend to pipe down so she could focus on the dark, winding roads.

As they turned into the driveway that led to Drumlin, nothing but trees surrounding them now, monoliths too but more welcoming than granite, Sal did indeed fall silent.

Despite wishing for this, after a few moments Kenna felt obliged to check on her.

"Sal, you okay?"

"Yeah, it's just, I don't know…it's so…spooky here. I'm missing Aberdeen!"

Opposites, that's what they'd become and in so short a space, mere months. Kenna no longer craved city life; she wanted this, and Sal didn't. Sal *hated* this.

"Only one more night to go," Kenna said in an attempt at humour. "A few hours, that's all, and we'll have you in that taxi and out of here, on the train south to your comfort zone."

Sal shuffled in her seat to face her. "Kenna, I don't like to leave you."

"What?" Taking her eyes off the road for a few seconds to gaze at her friend, Kenna saw it, a nervousness in Sal's eyes, in her whole demeanour. "I'm fine! Honestly! Okay, at first I was nervous, and one night, well, one night, Gregor had to stay. In the spare room, before you ask. But since then, I've put my big girl's pants on and been fine."

"Really? Because…something doesn't feel right. I mean it."

"It seems isolated," Kenna continued to reassure her. "But it's not. Jean, who ran Drumlin before me – remember I told you about her? – she isn't so far away. She lives on the edge of the estate, about a ten-to-fifteen-minute drive. Tulce, the local town, is also about ten minutes away and Gregor not much further than that."

"Ten to fifteen minutes?" Sal declared. "Ten to fifteen fucking minutes? And that's by car, not even on foot! Christ, if the wage was a million pounds a month, I still wouldn't take this position. You are *so* isolated, Kenna, and…and…it's not right."

As they continued along the driveway, she tried again to pacify Sal, not least because her agitation was rubbing off. Kenna had found herself in an unusual situation, granted, hard for city dwellers to feel at ease in, but, oddly, in spite of being a former city dweller herself, she really did. Not only easing into it, *falling* for it a little more each day.

She was about to try to explain this when something caught her attention. Drumlin came into view, silhouetted against the night, the moon above it burning brightly. But that's all that was. There was no light on in the Rohaise Room.

A frown on her face, she checked the dashboard. Even though Gregor had said not to worry about time, they'd been longer than she'd intended.

Why was there no light in there? Once the idea had

occurred to Jean, she'd been adamant about it, that it was a good thing to do, leave a light on at least somewhere in the castle, dispel some of the darkness that otherwise shackled the building.

Shackled?

"Kenna?" Now it was Sal checking on her. "What is it?"

"Nothing, it's just…usually we leave a light on in the castle, on a timer. Jean's idea. It's not on, though, not tonight. I wonder if Gregor turned it off."

Sal shrugged. "Does it matter? It's just a light."

"It mattered to Jean."

"Why?"

"It's in Rohaise's room, you remember?"

"The room that stank."

"It didn't stink, Sal! You're being oversensitive."

"It did. It reeked. Anyway, why are you slowing the car down? Let's just get to the flat and lock the door behind us. It doesn't matter about the light."

"Jean thought it did," repeated Kenna. *Too much darkness is never a good thing.* That's what she'd said. *Don't know why I never thought about leaving a light on before. I should have.* And now it was off. The darkness back in its entirety.

"I'd better see to it," said Kenna, more to herself than Sal.

Sal picked up on it, though. "You're going into the castle? At this hour?"

"It's only just past six o'clock!" Kenna tried to force a laugh, but it never fully materialised. She'd gone into the castle early evening before, alone, and she'd fled from it too, something not quite right, as Sal had just said.

"I'm not going in!" Sal declared. "Wild horses and all

that."

"You don't have to. I'll drop you back at the flat and pick up the keys, then just run back, check what's happened."

"You're being serious, aren't you?"

"I'm the keeper of the castle," Kenna told her, a little perturbed. "It's my job."

"Then change it, jack it in. Because you know what? It's not a job that's fit for purpose."

Her nostrils flaring, Kenna refused to bite back, driving the car to the rear of the castle. Hurrying from it, she opened the door to her flat and, sure enough, found the keys to the castle posted there. A note from Gregor too. Turning on the lobby light, she read it: *A few visitors today, and all wanted food. Not a bad day in all. Hope you had a good one! See you tomorrow.* No mention of the light in the Rohaise Room and what had happened to it. Had it only just winked out?

Sal came huffing and puffing up behind her. "Shit," she said, "my bag is stuffed to the gills as it is. Didn't think of that when I was buying all this stuff."

"It's not so much. It'll pack down," Kenna told her. "But if it doesn't fit, I've a bigger trolley bag you can borrow. Right, go on up. I'll be back in a minute."

Sal came to a halt. "You're going to leave me here? Alone."

"Um...yeah. Just whilst I check on the lamp."

"It's a bloody lamp! Seriously, what's the big deal?"

"It's not a big deal, it's just... Go upstairs. I won't be long, honestly."

Sal continued to look furious as she stepped inside and dumped her bags down in the lobby. "You're determined about this, aren't you?"

Kenna nodded. "Yeah. Yeah, I am."

"Stubborn. You always have been."

"What? No, I haven't!"

"That's why you stayed here, even after…after…"

"Adam," Kenna said, slightly exasperated. "I've told you, you can say his name."

"When you knew he wasn't coming – *Adam* – why didn't you come back to London and confront him? There might have been a dozen other reasons besides the one he gave you – that he needed time and space. I thought you'd want to grill him, that you loved him."

"I did love him," Kenna protested. "Why are you so concerned suddenly? You should be glad we split up. You never liked him, not from the moment you set eyes on him."

"No, I didn't, because…there's something about him too."

"What? Come on, spill. What did you see that I didn't? And this place"—she gestured around her—"what can you sense that I can't?"

"Really? You sense nothing?"

"What are you, Sal, a fucking medium? Because if you are, you kept that quiet!"

There was silence. The two women glaring at each other but also wondering, for Kenna's part, at any rate, why she'd got so irate and so quickly. She was infuriated with Sal and her attitude, but she also had to calm down. Arguing would get them nowhere.

"I'm sorry." She tried so hard not to say it through gritted teeth.

"Yeah, me too," Sal replied, sounding far more genuine.

"Let's not talk about Adam, waste what little time we have together on that loser."

"I know, but I can't help being curious, that's all."

"Listen, I felt out of place when I first arrived here too, felt it was frightening, but, Sal, being here changes you, and it does it so fast. The world I came from, your world, it doesn't suit me anymore. Being in Aberdeen today, it just gave me a headache, to be honest. There's so much noise. I…I've moved on, in more ways than one. I don't think of Adam much, not really, hardly at all. You were right about him, that feeling you had. But this castle, this place, there you're mistaken. This is home now. For better or for worse."

Sal frowned. "For better or for worse? You're not married to it!"

"I know, but—"

"It's how you feel right now, Kenna, but that may change and just as fast as it did in the first place. You said yourself when we were talking last night that you're worried about the weather, about no one coming to visit during the winter. It'll be deserted."

"Not quite. Gregor will be here, and Laura and Connor, part-time."

"And you full-time. *Just* you."

"That's right. And I'm fine with that. I'll manage."

"I hope so, I really do."

"What is it you're so worried about? Come on, spill."

"Okay, if you really want me to."

"I do," Kenna insisted. "Please."

Sal's expression grew darker than the night. "That you'll get buried out here. That this place, it'll just…consume you."

Chapter Eighteen

Sal refused outright to stay alone in the flat.

"Safety in numbers," she'd said just a few moments after she'd admitted what was worrying her. Tired of arguing, Kenna agreed.

"Come on, then, let's get this over and done with, and then we can have some wine." A large glass was exactly what she needed.

They left the flat, closing the door behind them, Sal clutching at Kenna's arm, talons painted bright red sinking in a little too deep. Despite this, Kenna didn't reprimand her, her own words ringing in her head: *Get this over and done with.* Halfway to the castle, rounding the corner by the ruined chapel and dovecote, Sal dug her heels into the gravel.

"Kenna! What's that? There's someone there!"

"Where?" Kenna said, looking at where Sal was pointing, towards one of the outhouses.

"A figure! By that barn or whatever it is. I'm sure I saw a figure."

"There's nothing."

"There is!"

"Sal, it's just the dark, that's all. It'll play tricks on you if you let it. There's no one there. Why would there be? Now come on."

"This place," Sal breathed, moving again. "This bloody place!"

"There's no one there," Kenna reiterated, gently, though, remembering her own fear when she'd been on her own and had done this, how her imagination had galloped.

They were at the castle door, Kenna inserting the key into the lock, still having to force it in spite of it having had a good squirt of WD-40 recently. Finally, it opened, and there was the darkness – the *usual* darkness – both at their backs and to the front of them.

"I'll get the lights," said Kenna, entering.

When they came on, Sal sighed. "Is that it? Is that how bright they get?"

"You're not supposed to have neon lights in a bloody castle, Sal!"

"I realise that, but this is taking it from one extreme to the other, surely?"

"There's enough light to see by. You staying here or coming upstairs with me?"

"What do you think?"

There it was, that edge to Sal's voice, anger that had erupted, then simmered down, back on the boil again.

She had to be quick. Get this situation under control. *Both* situations.

Sal followed her as she crossed over to the archway, turning on more lights before setting foot on the turnpike staircase.

"It's so quiet," Sal said, her voice shaking likely as much as she was.

"It is." In contrast, Kenna was grateful for that.

"And that bloody stag's head, the way it glares at you, that'd be the first thing to go if I was in charge."

They climbed upwards, past the first few floors, rooms leading off into more darkness.

"Which floor's the library on again?" Sal asked.

"The fourth floor."

"And you're sure that monk, what was his name, Joseph something?"

"Joseph Buchannan."

"You sure he's gone, that his ghost really doesn't haunt here?"

"Not so keen on ghosts come nightfall, then?" Kenna teased.

Sal sounded far from amused. "Who the fuck would be?"

No one sane. That's what she meant, Kenna again irritated by the intimation.

"Almost there," Kenna said, wanting to distract both Sal and herself.

"Her room would be at the bloody top, wouldn't it? Couldn't have left a light on in a room on the ground floor, could you?"

Kenna rolled her eyes. "What would be the point of that? It needs to be seen."

"By whom, though, Kenna? By whom?"

Alexander.

The answer came to her, a lightbulb moment. *That's* why Jean had wanted it on, because maybe, just maybe, if he ever made it home, in spirit rather than body, the light would guide him. A strange concept, but…it made sense. Added to the romance.

The door to the Rohaise Room was slightly ajar.

"I'll go first," said Kenna, glad Sal was with her now, even if she was being annoying.

The light switch. Where was it? The door opened to the

left, and it was on the right, on the wall there, so why couldn't she find it? It was so dark despite light from the sconces in the stairwell, light that – unlike the last time – didn't seem to reach this room at all. As if it had been eschewed, evicted, *all* light. Not wanted here, by her, Rohaise.

Rather than struggling to locate the panel, she walked further into the room, drawn in there. She could smell it now, something unpleasant, a stench, as Sal had described it, that crept into her mouth and lingered there.

She spun round. "Is this what you smelled, Sal? You're right, it's—"

Any further words stuck in her throat. Sal was closer behind her than she'd realised. She was standing there, *silently* standing if not for her breathing, which was laboured.

"Sal, what's wrong? Look, don't worry, sweetie, I'll get the lights. Sorry, I should have done that, but that smell. I didn't know what you were talking about earlier, but I do now. You're right, it's awful. Where the hell's it coming from? Sal? Sal, speak to me, come on. It's all right, I'll get the lights, okay? Hang on. Just hang on."

"Witch."

Had Kenna heard right? Had Sal just uttered something. *Witch?*

"Evil. She was evil."

"Sal, what are you talking about? *Who?*"

"Evil witch!"

Still Kenna was confused. "Sal, come on, you're not making sense. I told you about Rohaise yesterday, but I didn't think you were listening, that you were interested." Both true, but at no point had Kenna mentioned her suspicions that once the king's men had hold of her, Rohaise might have been burnt as a witch. *This child of the forest.* So what did Sal mean? Why was she saying this stuff? *Terrible* stuff.

"Deserved it. Had it coming. The lynching. The burning. Trickster! Changeling. The fey. Doesn't belong amongst civilised men. Heathen! Unnatural. Vile."

Forgetting about the light, Kenna took Sal by the arms and shook her.

"Snap out of this, Sal. I don't need this. You're being fucking weird."

This close and another smell assailed her, like that of charred meat.

"Sal," she cried again. "For God's sake, what's got into you?"

Sal opened her mouth again, emitting a blast so rank it forced Kenna to screw her eyes shut. Sal smelled of Jo Malone's Lime, Basil and Mandarin normally, not this.

Her eyes open again, Kenna began to beg. "Sal, stop what you're doing. This isn't funny, this isn't…right." She was now using the very words Sal had. So quickly panic rose up. "Sal? Sal! Sal!" She was reduced to screaming her name. "For fuck's sake, Sal!"

The light came on, not the chandelier overhead but the lamp in the window. Dragging her gaze from Sal, Kenna stared at it aghast.

"Kenna? What are you doing? Why are you digging your nails into me? Ouch, my arms, let go! The lamp's on, look. There's nothing wrong with it. Can we go now, please?"

Turning her head from the lamp to Sal, then back again, Kenna's shoulders – so rigid before – slumped. A physical sign of relief, perhaps, but her mind refused to play catchup.

"What was wrong with you?" she breathed. "All the things you were saying!"

"Saying?" Sal repeated. "I didn't say a word. Too bloody scared."

"You did! About Rohaise, you called her a witch, other names too, said she deserved what she got."

"Kenna! I said nothing of the sort! She was just another person who lived at the castle, wasn't she? I can't remember what you said, exactly, a princess or something?"

"No, no, the mistress of Alexander Buchannan. You said awful things about her."

Sal shook herself free, still denying it. "And I thought I was the one letting my imagination get the better of me. Talk about the pot calling the kettle black! I didn't say a thing, and you know it. Stop trying to scare me, because it's bloody well working. I followed you in. It was dark, and then you must have flicked the lamp back on, because there it is, glowing merrily away. Now can we go? I really can't stand it in here a minute longer. It's a funny old place this, strange, I'm telling you," she continued as she turned and stomped out of the room. "Something's not right, it's not right at all, and it looks like you realise that too, deep down, that it's getting to you. Be careful, Kenna, okay? You don't have to stay here, not for the winter. Bugger the contract, you can just pack your bags and leave, come back to London. With your experience you'll pick up a job anywhere, a *decent* job."

Kenna gazed in astonishment at the retreating figure of Sal until she disappeared out of sight, heading down the stairs to the exit.

Her mouth still open in shock, she glanced around her – at the lamp in the window that hadn't been working but now was, at the panel on the wall, which was exactly where it should be, hadn't disappeared somehow, and at the darkness that wasn't as intense as before. Had she imagined it, the words that had fallen from Sal's mouth, that had been *spat* out? Laced with hatred, with fear and with loathing. A depth of terrible emotion that Sal wasn't capable of, not even in jest. No. No way was she responsible.

As Kenna at last left the room, one question plagued her. If Sal wasn't guilty, who was?

Chapter Nineteen

Trickster! Changeling! Heathen! Witch! Witch! Witch!

Before they touched me, there'd been words, words as cruel as their hands. Their terror, their hatred, was genuine — they truly saw me as something despicable. A woman who had helped their quarry escape, denying them the pleasure of tearing him apart. Who refused to talk, no matter what they threatened. Therefore, I could not be a woman but something other, evil. A certain irony in saying so, when it was love that held my tongue!

The light...the orb... Is it that which keeps me from sleeping? This light that continues to burn so stubbornly. If I am a witch, then it follows I am powerful, doesn't it? Within me is the ability to extinguish the orb. I want the dark, only the dark, for in it there is nothing, just as there was nothing in the eyes of the king's men, the soldiers, certainly no mercy.

"Where is Alexander? Where has he gone? Tell us, witch, if you want to live!"

No mercy, no light, and only lies spewing from their mouths.

They would not let me live. But what they could do was make my death harder. If I would not tell, I would suffer, and suffer dreadfully.

It was Alexander's eyes that kept me strong, the way he looked at me, always.

'You have entered my life, and suddenly the world is somewhere I want to be. Not full of fear and treason but the

sweetest place. Because of you, Rohaise, it is heaven.'

Drumlin was heaven, with him and me in it, then it was hell, then it was…nothing. Limbo. But that limbo is no more because of the echoes, because of the orb, a light I focus on, willing it to disappear, to snuff itself out. Success! Once again there is darkness, me at the centre of it, not a witch or a heathen or a trickster, just nothing. Oh, if only I could sleep!

Red hair was another sign I was in league with the devil. An incubus, an acolyte, a scourge upon humanity.

"No natural woman could suffer this," said one, tall and thin, his cheeks pockmarked.

He took a poker from the fire, one wrought in iron, and prodded me with it, sticking it in my side whilst demanding I speak. When I refused, he raised it high, then brought it down again, hard. I heard the crunch of bone in my arm as I tried to defend myself. He heard it too. Tossing the poker aside, he grabbed that same arm and twisted it, causing me to wail, to scream, to pass out. Darkness again, such a comfort but so fleeting!

My hair was ripped out, great clumps of it, my head held in an iron vice as it was parted, a blade taken to it as well. Blood that flowed just as red, staining white skin crimson.

"There she is!" declared another. "That's more like it. Rohaise in her natural state, that consorts with the devil, that covets him. A filthy creature, she is an abomination!"

I struggled to get away from them, not far but to crawl, as a beetle might crawl, into the corner of the room they held me in. If only I could escape them and, like the beetle, scurry further into the cracks, into the very fabric of the building, where no man could follow.

"If I were a witch, I'd do it," I screamed. "I'd disappear. I can't because I am innocent!"

Only laughter greeted my protests. More kicks, more blows, the easy snapping of bones.

Why do such memories refuse to fade?

Oh, Alexander, I endured this for you. And I would endure it again to keep you safe. I hated what they did to me, how quickly I was reduced to something feral when you had raised me so high, how they spat on me, how they talked amongst themselves of what else they could do to make me pay for my sins, but, Alexander, I would still rather I suffered than you. I was right to come back, to protect you, to conceal the entrance to the tunnel, because they couldn't find it! Try as they might, it confounded them.

Whilst they conspired, I was left alone, there in my corner, fingertips scrabbling at the wall, no dresses now adorning my body, the gowns that you'd given me, the red velvet and the green, colours to match the jewels you had placed upon my fingers. All that was gone, the dress ripped off; only an undergarment remained, a soiled thing as wretched as I was.

But I was alone, and that was something to be grateful for, that there was some respite. And rather than descend into madness, for the pain in my body threatened to drag me there, into the depths, and my mind kept slipping, I held on, remembered the reason for this.

So you could live, Alexander, so you could breathe.

I could barely breathe, my chest was wracked with sobs, but your memory drew at least the ghost of a smile.

You used to stroke my hair, remember? As we sat by the hearth or lay together in my bedchamber. You would stroke my hair and gaze down upon me. You don't forget torture, but neither do you forget gentleness such as that. You were older than me by several summers. I was a child when first we met, but with you, I became a woman.

'Will you take a wife one day?' I'd asked. I hadn't meant me but someone of your own rank.

'Never!' you declared.

'But isn't that the way of men? They must take a wife and produce an heir?' A child of the forest, maybe, but I wasn't naïve about these things.

You took my face in your hands and kissed my lips.

'Rohaise, we may not marry, but as I have told you, over and over, we will live here, you and I, all the days of our lives. Just you and me, I promise. To hell with everyone.'

I had pushed you away, shaken my head. 'I would not let you live as a recluse. Besides, you would grow tired of me, resent me.'

'I would not!' Your voice was so full of passion I could no longer doubt you. You would make it happen, our future as you saw it, because you loved me as much as I loved you.

"Witch!"

The men returned, all wearing expressions that were gleeful. They had conspired, and they had indeed found another way to torment me, to break me. Fools that they were! They could not break the bonds of love!

Even when they dragged me from the corner into the centre of the room, when they pushed the rag I wore aside, when they forced my legs apart and took turns at me, one after the other, grunting or snarling or both, their sweat dripping onto my face, they could not break me, break us.

The vows we made were too strong.

Even for that.

"Trickster! Changeling! Heathen! Witch! Witch! Witch!"

Despite their disgust, they used me still.

"You deserve it, all that's coming to you. Evil! Evil! Evil!"

Their voices are all I can hear. Then another voice joins

them, that of a woman's, repeating those terrible words, another female voice crying out in protest, begging her to stop. No use. Her pleas are in vain. For there was no stopping any of it.

Chapter Twenty

Sal left as planned, the taxi waiting patiently on the gravel path outside Kenna's flat just after seven the next morning. Not another word had been said about what had happened in the Rohaise Room and the words Sal had spouted, apparently unconsciously. Rather, the two of them had sat together in Kenna's living room the rest of the night, eating and drinking and touching on just about every topic under the sun other than Adam or the castle.

Kenna stood on the doorstep, waving until the taxi disappeared. She had, of course, offered to take Sal to the train station, but Sal had refused.

"I've told you, the cab's on expenses."

And Kenna had felt relief at that, that their time together wouldn't be prolonged. Sad too as she headed back inside. There was a gulf between them now, she and her best friend. Time, space and distance had had an effect – being *here*, at Drumlin, had. *You don't belong.* That's what she'd thought on first seeing Sal, and, as she climbed the curved staircase, she *still* thought it. Sal didn't belong, Kenna did, yet it was Sal who'd been…what? Possessed in the Rohaise Room? Who'd felt all along something wasn't right with the castle and then, conversely, had no recollection of any strange happenings.

Possessed. As Kenna headed to the kitchen for breakfast,

that word kept repeating, that notion. It couldn't be true, but how to explain it otherwise? Had Sal instead engineered what had happened? Deliberately denying it afterwards because…because…she wanted to force Kenna's hand? She'd made no secret that she wanted her to leave this position at the castle and come back to London, but what a way to go about it! It was…nasty, conniving, when Sal had never been nasty or conniving before. A first time for everything, Kenna supposed. Maybe talking to Gregor would help. Then again, would she appear mad in the telling of it? What she couldn't deny was that Sal's words were similar to the thoughts that kept popping into her own head. Could it be, was it possible, that Rohaise had been branded a witch and burnt at the stake for it?

Forgetting breakfast, she headed to the kitchen table and her laptop. Clicking on Google, she typed in the search bar – *did they burn witches in Scotland?* They did, she knew that. Gregor had said so too, but she needed to know more. *Just what did the king's men do to you, Rohaise? How badly were you treated?*

Information regarding the Great Scottish Witch Hunt of 1597 immediately popped up on-screen. Selecting a page, Kenna read. During March to October of that year, at least four hundred people had been put on trial for witchcraft. How many of those had been executed remained unknown, but it was thought to be at least two hundred. There'd also been an earlier witch hunt in Scotland between 1590 and 1591, then three more in the seventeenth century. Rohaise had lived at the right time to be subject to such treatment. It was James VI who'd reigned in Scotland from 1567 and who'd become King of England and Ireland too in 1603 until his death in 1625. The only son of Mary, Queen of

Scots – and the great-great-grandson of Henry VII – he'd penned *Daemonologie*, a tract that passionately defended the punishment and persecution of witches. Indeed, Kenna read, he had personally supervised the torture of so many individuals, identifying several signs of witchcraft, including the presence of a devil's mark 'upon some secreit place of their bodie' as proof, subjecting his victims to further humiliation. Although it was claimed he'd grown less fanatical about the existence of witches in later years, the damage had been done, with Scotland having executed five times as many people as elsewhere in Europe per capita, the king's men – the true acolytes – given carte blanche to treat them abominably, not just by James VI but by the Bible too: 'Thou shalt not suffer a witch to live,' an extract from Exodus 22:18.

Kenna took a deep breath, imagining the true horror of this terrible history. The persecution of witches in Scotland was part of a craze that had swept Europe, more than eighty per cent of them women, both young and old, who'd been dragged from the sanctuary of their homes and brutally murdered. Terrified women, women who'd named others, pointing the finger at someone, anyone, in a bid to save themselves, and could Kenna blame them? Not everyone would put themselves in harm's way for another, especially when it involved such pain and torture.

Red hair. There was something about red hair too, some snippet of information she'd heard or read or been told about. She ran her hand over her own hair, an almost protective gesture, before typing in the search bar again: *red hair the sign of a witch?*

Sure enough, despite the fact that two queens had red hair, two *warring* queens – Elizabeth I and, of course, her cousin, Scotland's very own Mary – red hair was associated with witches, a colour that represented fire, blood, hell and all things bad. Add to that the fact you'd bewitched a laird, a simple forest girl, and you never stood a chance.

She read further. The belief that redheads possessed supernatural powers permeated culture after culture around the world. Even today where voodoo and magic were still central to belief systems, redheads were thought to be witches. Though having red hair was generally not common, here in Scotland it was less of a rarity. Whether you were a forest dweller or from a village, town or city, red hair could have branded you during such hysteria and sealed your fate. History. It was as fascinating as Gregor claimed, but it could make you angry too, the ignorance and stupidity of humankind.

There was prejudice after prejudice. *The Proverbs of Alfred* in medieval times warned against choosing a red-haired person as a friend, and the *Secretum Secretorum* issued another warning against using redheads as advisors. And Judas, Christ's betrayer, was commonly portrayed as a redhead! Why? Of all the European countries, it seemed the French had the lowest opinion of red hair, actually dubbing it '*poil de Judas*' – hair of Judas – as far as into the nineteenth century. In amongst so much prejudice, she could only find one positive quote about red hair, ironically from a Frenchman, Cyrano de Bergerac. He wrote, *A brave head covered with red hair is nothing else but the sun in the midst of his rays, yet many speak ill of it, because few have the honour to be so.*

She stood up, the chair scraping against the flagstones. She needed coffee. After the kettle had boiled, she filled her mug with instant and took it over to the window at the far end of the kitchen to stare at the grounds, the garden being created – *lovingly* created – by Gregor, which would bloom year after year, with roses especially.

She was evil. The words that had left Sal's mouth came to her, etched upon her mind, it seemed. A suggestion that she deserved it, all that was coming to her – Rohaise? For whom else could she have meant? *Trickster! Changeling. The fey. Doesn't belong here.*

Perhaps the latter was true; Rohaise didn't belong at Drumlin but to the forest. Even so, here she had found herself, in the arms of a lover before lies had forced them apart.

Kenna clutched her mug tighter.

Despite not belonging, despite it being so long since her death, did she still remain?

* * *

Surprisingly, it was a busy day at the castle, with car after car winding its way up the driveway, their tyres crunching over gravel, then parking at the front before their occupants headed inside. Kenna greeted them all, was glad of them, the life they injected.

As usual, some opted to explore the castle under their own steam, some preferred a tour. Almost all of them wanted sandwiches, tea, coffee and cakes, Connor also preparing an autumnal vegetable-and-lentil broth with tattie scones that was proving very popular. On one of the tours, there was a family with a son whose hair was the brightest of auburns. Aged around ten, he commented on Kenna's hair, pointing to it and saying, "We're the same."

"We are," Kenna agreed, although her hair was a darker

shade of red than the boy's, hair she'd brushed in the mirror in her bedroom this morning, making sure it gleamed.

Accompanying the family around the castle at their request, Kenna delivered the set spiel, and in one of the bedrooms, the boy returned to her side, his parents busy admiring the fabrics and furnishings and reading Captain John's laminate cards.

"I get teased about my hair sometimes," he said. "I get called Carrot Top and Gingersnap. Do you get teased as well?"

She used to, as a child. As an adult, though, that had stopped, although people did comment all the time, complimenting her, insisting they wanted hair like hers. Adam had loved her hair, or so he'd said. Then again, Adam had loved *her*, then dumped her, via email, disposed of her. As far as Adam was concerned, she couldn't trust a single word he'd said. This child, though, and the way he was looking at her, there was such innocence in his blue-green eyes, and sadness too.

People can be so damned cruel! Again, she thought it.

With his parents still occupied, she bent slightly so her face was close to his, securing the connection the boy was struggling to make.

"I did get teased," she said. "I got called names too, but you know why I think they did it?"

"Why?" the boy – Rory – asked.

"Because they were jealous. Red hair is rare, and because it is, it's special. When you get home, look in the mirror and study your hair. Truly study it. There's a richness to it, a dozen different tones that perfectly combine. Your hair shines, Rory, it dazzles. It doesn't matter what anyone says; be proud of it and who you are. Never let others make you think otherwise or try to force their opinions on you. Own your hair, wear it like a badge of honour, as a reflection of how unique you are. If you do that, magic will happen."

"Magic?"

"That's right. If you believe in yourself, others will feel it and believe in you too."

The boy eventually returned to his parents, neither of whom were redheads, and as he did, Kenna straightened, reaching out a hand to steady herself. She'd become quite emotional during that little speech, tears forming in her eyes that she had to wipe away, the parents turning to her, done with reading and expecting the tour to continue.

In the Rohaise Room, tears pricked at her eyes again, prompting the boy's mother to ask if she was okay.

"It's the dust," Kenna replied. "A bit of an allergy."

"Oh," the husband said, "inconvenient, given your job."

"Very," Kenna said, forcing a burst of nervous laughter.

"So, who's Rohaise?" the woman asked.

Who's Rohaise? Kenna didn't know, not really, but it didn't stop her from launching into another passionate speech. She told them who she *thought* Rohaise was, what could have happened to her, and each word she spoke compounded the belief she was right.

"Christ," the woman exclaimed when Kenna had finished. "Poor woman." She looked around, then went over to the four-poster bed. "These are roses on here?"

"That's right. Rohaise is Scottish for 'rose'."

"Wow," she said again. "I think…I think that's the best story I've heard at any castle I've visited. Like, really romantic."

Romantic? Maybe, Kenna thought, at least initially. How it had ended, not so much.

The man wanted to know if Rohaise was buried on the grounds.

Kenna shrugged. "We're not sure. If she died here, then it's possible, but not in any marked grave, that's for sure."

"I wonder where, then," the woman mused.

"In the forest?" Rory piped up, who'd been as fascinated by the story as his parents.

"That would have been the ideal resting place, but somehow I don't think so."

"She had red hair," he said. "Like you and me."

Kenna nodded. "A kindred spirit."

The boy squinted, looked at her oddly, as did his parents, Kenna wincing slightly. Why had she said that? It was going too far. And yet, as they filed out of the Rohaise Room, she couldn't help but glance back over her shoulder. If she stared hard enough, would she see her again? If, of course, it had been her when she'd looked in the mirror – both here and in Kenna's own room. Did she want to see her again? This woman she was so curious about? There'd been a hardness about her, nothing gentle or soft. A rose, a red, red rose, and yet roses had thorns.

Kenna accompanied the family back down to the ground floor, where they exchanged goodbyes. As they left, Connor and Laura appeared, Connor shaking his head and declaring what a day it had been, Laura wondering if the winter would be as busy as the summer, worrying that if it were, what Kenna would do, as part-time staff wouldn't cut it.

Laura needn't have fretted. The next day and the day after were back to hosting a handful of visitors, and some of those merely glanced around before leaving, back on the castle trail and wanting something perhaps a little grander than Drumlin. That was the thing, Kenna thought, watching them as they left. You either got this place or you didn't. But those who did, really did. As Jean had said once, it got under your skin, Rohaise, at least.

As autumn deepened and the weather closed in, a handful of visitors became one or two, and on some days, there were none at all. The castle must remain open, though – Jean had stipulated that during the interview – closing only for a few days over Christmas, just as other castles in the area did. If they were ever going to compete, they had to adopt the same policy. Kenna agreed and was pleased when, on windy days and rainy days and days where the temperatures plummeted, some still turned up, these visitors determined and, because of their determination, enthusiastic and a joy to host.

On quiet days, when Laura and Connor were busy elsewhere, and Gregor too, she busied herself cleaning, as she'd promised herself, although the stench that had been in the Rohaise Room had all but disappeared. She no longer felt too uneasy despite being alone so much of the time there, but she dwelt, she had to admit, on the tragedy more than the romance of the castle, finally searching – feeling a compulsion to do so – to find something that remained elusive, that even Jean didn't know the location of, the severed artery in the body of the castle grounds that had leeched the lifeblood from Drumlin.

The tunnel.

Chapter Twenty-One

In the kitchen area of the castle, Gregor scratched his head as he looked around.

"You'd think it'd be here somewhere, wouldn't you? The business end."

"That's what I thought, and I've looked and looked for any sign of a possible opening, but if it was sealed up, someone did a good job of it. There are no cellars as such or an undercroft. There's nothing else below this except…maybe a tunnel."

"To be honest, the tunnel could be anywhere on the estate. We won't know unless the site is excavated, a dedicated archaeological team brought in to comb the grounds over, and I can't see that happening. You know, magnetometry, like they use on *Time Team*. It would cost a bomb. I've kept an eye out in the gardens whilst digging, wondering if I might find something, but no luck so far. I've even looked on satellite view on Google to see if there's a shadow of it on the ground, but again nothing."

"Damn," Kenna said. "It's a vital piece of the jigsaw, and it's missing."

"Kenna, a whole lot is. As we know, not everything's recorded."

"No, history fails quite spectacularly on that score, doesn't it? The lives of people, *real* people who suffered because of stupid beliefs and rules and superstitions, people who weren't even granted a final resting place, who were just…fucking disposed of."

"I know, I feel angry and frustrated about it too, and…I'm sorry I've not been able to find out more about Rohaise or Alexander."

Immediately, Kenna felt embarrassed about her outburst. "Ignore me, please. I know how hard you've tried despite how busy you are with work and studies. I'm just… It's being here, immersed in it. The history of the castle is on my mind all the time." *She is.*

And it was true that last thing at night, lying in bed, she'd think of Rohaise. In the morning, on waking, Rohaise was there, on her mind. She'd stare in the mirror, thinking she still saw something of her, that they were similar to look at with their pale skin, green eyes and red hair. She'd dream of Rohaise. Only last night she had, which she now told Gregor about, trying to recall every detail as she leant against the counter.

"It was like she…floated around this castle, not as a ghost, I don't mean that, but as a living, breathing person dressed in…green. That was it, green velvet."

"Go on," Gregor said when she paused, his interest as deep as hers.

"She floated around the castle, and she was touching things, the walls, the hearths, furniture, and there was wonder in her eyes all the while. She loved it here, couldn't believe she was here because…it was a place she'd never imagined living."

Adjusting her gaze, she stared beyond him.

"It was like *I* was Rohaise in the dream, and…I was so happy. What's the saying? My cup runneth over. That's what it was like, as though my heart was brimming with happiness and love. I'd been blessed, and I had no idea why I should be." A thought occurred to her. "Gregor, perhaps happiness like that can be hard to bear – for others, I mean. Because it is hard sometimes, isn't it? If life isn't going so well for you, to witness it going brilliantly for others? I think we're all guilty of envy on occasion."

Gregor nodded his dark head. "Aye, yeah, true enough."

"I say that because Alexander was betrayed by someone, so why not a member of his own household, a servant, perhaps? Someone who questioned his loyalty and let it be known it was in question, let it also be known that a woman had bewitched him, a peasant girl from the forest, a girl whose wide smile and sparkling eyes were just too hard to bear."

"It's a theory we've discussed," Gregor reminded her.

"A theory that's making more and more sense," Kenna insisted. "I know I'm filling in the gaps here, but I'm carefully filling them in, at least. My theory's not so outlandish, I hope."

"Not at all. The dream, though…"

"Ah yeah, the dream. So, there I am, floating around. As Rohaise, I love this castle, Gregor, I really do. It's my home now. And yet…I'm missing something."

"Missing what?"

"The forest. It's so close, but I hardly go there. Alexander doesn't want me to, you see; he wants me here, in his home, in his bed, and I'm happy about that, but…the forest, it was my first home. The animals, the birds, the herbs and the trees – I was a part of them, and they were a part of me. But I'm also a part of this now, Drumlin. And it's fine, it really is, because despite how my heart aches sometimes,

Alexander is worth it. Worth everything. Even so, in the dream I start crying, really sobbing, because suddenly I'm so terribly homesick, and…and…I just want to go home, Gregor. I have to. I must go home!"

"Kenna! Hey, come on, snap out of it."

"What?"

Gregor reached out and touched Kenna's cheek, wiped away something, a tear? "The dream, you're getting a bit too into it."

She touched her cheek too, found it was indeed damp. "Was I? Oh wow, sorry." She closed her eyes, took a deep breath. "The dream was intense. To be honest, everything's a bit intense sometimes, this whole Rohaise thing."

His smile was as gentle as his voice. "It's understandable."

"Being here," she continued, "I love it like Rohaise, but maybe…"

"You need a break, a proper day off. When was the last one?"

"With Sal a few weeks back, when we went to Aberdeen." And she had hated it; all she'd wanted was to go back to the castle. "Do you think I'm obsessed?" she asked, adopting a wry smile. "For God's sake, I'm dreaming about her now!"

"How busy is it today?"

"In the castle? It's not."

"Shall we close it?"

"And go where?"

"To the forest, to clear our heads."

"I think it's supposed to rain."

"You've a raincoat, haven't you?"

"You bet. Heavy duty!"

"Then get it, and let's go."

"What if Jean—"

"You're the boss, not Jean."

"The forest?" she said and again smiled. "Okay. How can I resist?"

* * *

Being closer to nature was like being closer to something bigger than both of them.

"Not God, I don't mean God, per se," Kenna was saying as, alongside Gregor, she crunched over twigs, leaves and copious amounts of pine needles that littered the forest floor. "I'm not religious or anything. I can just understand Rohaise, the dream Rohaise, I mean, and her love of this, the open air, the freedom it gave her, the fact that she answered to no one. I wish I had the time to come out here more, but, like her, I seem to be stuck. During the day, at least, by the time I knock off, it's too late and night's come."

"What have you been doing on Sundays lately?" Gregor enquired.

"More often than not I work still, fill out stock sheets, that kind of thing. I want to expand the shop, make it bigger, provide a real showcase for local crafts. So, if not doing paperwork, I'm heading out, striking deals with people. That's mainly it. Oh, and sleeping. On Sundays, sometimes a lot of what I do is watch films and sleep."

"No need to feel bad about that. It is a day of rest, after all. What about writing? During the summer you said you were gathering ideas."

"That's right. They're coming along."

"Anything to do with Rohaise?"

"Gregor! Not everything's to do with her."

"But is it?"

She closed her eyes briefly, screwed up her nose. "Yeah. All right, okay. Some of it is. They're just notes at the moment, but, ya know, there's quite a pile of them!"

"Good for you," he said.

"Good for me, why?"

"Because you're dragging her out of the darkness and into the light."

"*If* I write about her," she reminded him.

"I think you will. One day."

She glanced at him. "Really?"

"Yeah." He had turned towards her too, and there it was in his eyes: belief. "But enough talk of Rohaise. We're trying to get away from her, and here she is following us."

Kenna looked over her shoulder. "God, I hope not."

"Come on, this way," Gregor said, taking her arm and leading her off the path.

"Where are we going? Deep into the forest again?"

"You were scared that time, weren't you? When I stumbled across you."

"Yeah. Yeah, I was. At one point it got so dark."

"Let me show you there's nothing to be frightened of. It's beautiful there."

With his hand still on her arm, and Kenna glad that it was, she followed him. He increased his pace, and so did she. He was full of eagerness to show her yet more of nature's treasures, and she was just as eager to be shown.

Latin names fell from his lips as they continued onwards, names of plants and flowers that she'd never remember. There were larch trees as well as pines – giants, all of them – the moss-covered floor beneath them a veritable carpet and as vivid a green as the dress Rohaise had been wearing in the dream. Most plants were hibernating, he told her. Even so, the air was a mix of such heady perfumes, not just pine, clearing her mind just as Gregor had intended, making her feel more and more alive.

"Imagine this in the snow," she breathed.

"What? You didn't come here when it snowed in the spring?"

"I meant to, but I was just too occupied with the castle."

"Och, you'll see it soon. There'll be snow aplenty this winter."

"It'll be a wonderland."

"It will. When I..." He hesitated before continuing. "When I was inside, surrounded by nothing but grey walls, it was here that I'd escape to – in my mind, I mean, the forest surrounding Drumlin. It kept me sane, made me *want* to change my ways. I couldn't stand being in a prison cell. If I kept repeating the same mistakes, kept going in, I'd be lost. Thoughts of the forest wouldn't save me then. They'd torment me instead. There really is no place like it. You're right, you feel so free here. Do you, Kenna, do you feel the same?"

"Yes!" she replied, bolting forward. "Yes! Yes! Yes!"

The path ahead was narrow, the forest beginning to darken again. She was so unused to this, winding pathways that stretched on forever, climbing the rise of a hill one minute to then descend into a valley, with a stream that would be a torrent when the snows from the surrounding slopes thawed in the spring. On first discovering all this, she had been enchanted, then become afraid of it. Now, with Gregor alongside her, she was euphoric. Higher than a kite. Learning all the while about her new environment, to understand it.

ROHAISE

Laughter escaped her, and she could hear Gregor laughing too, striving to catch up with her. He'd have a job, though; the wind really was at her heels. With the trees vying for space, some branches hung precariously low, but she avoided each one, feeling not as though she were running but flying, actually flying.

At last, the trees thinned, and she realised again with wonder that she was in a clearing, the same one she'd been in before, perhaps, and the rain that had been threatening was now falling in earnest. Panting heavily, Gregor reached her.

"You set quite the pace when you want to!"

Although she heard him, she continued to look around her.

"This place," she whispered. "It is, it's incredible."

Reaching out, she grabbed his hands, then tipped her head back, enjoying the feel of the rain on her face, her red hair no doubt turning so much darker, almost black.

"What are you doing?" he said, but she could tell he was caught in the moment too.

She began to move round and round, forcing him to do the same. Willingly, he obeyed, took over from her lead, the pair of them spinning in a clearing in the woods, more laughter punctuating the air, no whispering, only the birds singing louder as if trying to compete. Eventually, with her body slowing but her mind still spinning, Kenna let go of his hands and slumped to the ground, lying back against it, eyes skywards. Gregor lay beside her, not flat on his back as she was but propped on one elbow, gazing down at her.

Still the rain fell, cold but refreshing.

"What do you see?" he asked.

"I see…I see intricate cobwebs that decorate the trees like

fine silk, woven through branches. I see fresh morning dew and an icy cold frost that's glistening white. I see the night sky. There are so many stars you could never hope to count them, even if you spent an entire lifetime trying. I smell wood smoke, pine, of course, and the smell of the earth is pungent too, Mother Earth, my mother and yours, who gives so much. I hear clear sweet notes, some high, some low, from early morning until dusk, the birds serenading you."

From lying down, she sat up and hugged her knees to her chest, eyes now probing the darkness of the trees. "How can a place like this ever be frightening? It's *bursting* with life, that which we see and that which we can't, which remains hidden from sight. At every hour of every day, year after year, century after century, there's life here, the humming of bees, the rustle of leaves as ants move over them, the eyes of the deer that track you. And there's food all around. You'd never be hungry here, or thirsty; there's enough for all."

When she had finished, when Gregor finally spoke, he whispered only a few words as she turned towards him, words that made her skin tingle further.

"Bewitching," he said. "Kenna, you are quite bewitching."

Chapter Twenty-Two

It felt like rats deserting a sinking ship.

Connor was unwell, and now Laura, both of them suffering stinking colds. Although only part-time, they couldn't work at all now, not for a few days at least.

"And mind," Laura said, who'd phoned after Connor, "the fact that we're both ill with a cold at the same time is mere coincidence."

"If you say so," Kenna replied, tongue in cheek.

"It really is!" Laura continued to protest, perhaps a little too much, as Jean had said. "It's not me he's been kissing, I can tell you that."

"Not because he doesn't want to." There, she'd said it. The truth.

"Kenna!" Over the phone, the name burst from Laura, causing Kenna to hold the phone at a bit of a distance whilst wincing.

"I'm just saying, that's all," Kenna replied.

"There's nothing between us!"

"I know."

"So what do you mean?"

"That maybe there should be?"

"Kenna," Laura said again, a short coughing fit preventing her briefly from carrying on. "The ball's in his court. I'm waiting, ya know, for him to stop being such a dolt and grow up."

Being as the pair had known each other since childhood, Kenna disagreed. "Maybe it's you who should take the reins and force the issue. You know what, Laura, you're a strong woman, clever and funny and beautiful, and he thinks all those things too, I'm certain of it. I've caught the way he looks at you when he thinks you're busy. I've seen it in his eyes that that's *exactly* what he thinks. But men, they can be a bit…"

"Backwards?" Laura said scathingly when Kenna faltered.

"Hesitant," Kenna corrected. "Shy, even. Sensitive. Remember who you are, *what* you are, and if you want something, go for it."

Laura was quiet for a moment before replying. "Yeah, yeah, okay. Food for thought, I suppose, whilst I'm lying here in my deathbed."

"You're not dying just yet." Kenna laughed. "Take it easy, though, and feel better soon."

"Sorry, Kenna, about this. I feel really guilty."

"No need, you can't help being ill."

"And thanks, you know, for the advice."

"Anytime."

The phone call ending, Kenna stood behind the desk in reception, the surrounding shelves bulging with unsold goods. *That'll change*, she reminded herself. Come spring, come summer, she'd have a job to replace it fast enough.

Although she looked longingly at the door, willing someone to walk in, it remained closed. The day wasn't too bad weather-wise, the sky more grey than blue, admittedly, but not as cold as it could be. She was alone in the castle again, with not even Gregor for company, as it was his day off.

ROHAISE

Gregor. That day in the forest. How long ago was it? Just two or three weeks, but it seemed longer than that, an age.

Bewitching, that's what he'd said. He had stared at her, dark eyes not just alight but blazing, and said, *You are quite bewitching.*

And then…then he'd shaken his head, as if he'd been in a trance of some sort.

"Sorry," he'd continued, that word indeed breaking the spell, not just the one he'd been under but her too. As for the words she herself had spoken, where had they come from? So eloquent, so…nostalgic, somehow.

They'd climbed to their feet, and Kenna could tell he was as embarrassed as she was. Brushing themselves down from the wet leaves and twigs, shivering too, the more unpleasant effects of being drenched to the skin beginning to make themselves known, they'd left the clearing, retraced their footsteps out of the forest and back to Kenna's flat, where she had fetched towels so they could dry off. After a hot mug of tea and some leftover shortbread from the kitchen, Gregor had left, and that was that. The day was over. Whether there'd been any visitors to the castle in her absence, as she'd worried about, she would never know. Certainly there'd been no fresh tyre tracks on the gravel.

He'd left, and she could kick herself about that. Because she hadn't wanted him to go, and she didn't think he'd wanted to go either, but she'd just let it happen. And yet here she was, despite that faux pas, dishing out romantic advice to Laura.

"Best get on with cleaning," she muttered as she came out from behind the desk and headed to the kitchen.

It was so lonely in the castle with no one there but her. She kept listening out for more noises, kept thinking she'd caught movement out of the corner of her eye only to turn and see nothing but empty space. Being alone could make you imagine things. Being alone in a castle, well, that took it to a whole new level. Keeping herself busy helped, though. She'd give another of the bedrooms a really good clean. She'd done several rooms now, including the Rohaise Room, polished and scrubbed and cleaned, making it look as pristine as possible, glad the strange smell hadn't returned.

With a bucket of cleaning products in hand, she climbed the turnpike staircase.

She hadn't wanted Gregor to leave that day, so what had she wanted? For him to stay, for something to have developed between them? A kiss? More than that, even? A blush suffused her cheeks. She could feel the heat of it. He was a friend, just that. Why ruin it? When it became more it got complicated – exciting at first, absolutely, but it could lead to disappointment. *Once burned, twice shy.* Perhaps. But Adam *had* burned her, severely.

She shook her head. Best not to think of Adam, which was a coping mechanism, actually, something that being so far from him at least made easier. What if he'd dumped her when she was still in London and regularly bumping into him? How excruciating!

Focus on the task ahead, that's what she'd do, clean the rooms, scrub the floors. Pass the hours until she could return to her flat. Christmas was coming, and the school holidays, so she could think of something to attract the visitors. Festive lunches, perhaps. Why not? Just simple, tasty fare that she could help Connor and Laura prepare. She'd float that idea with them, hoped they'd be enthusiastic about it, devise a menu. She'd decorate the castle too, order a

Christmas tree, a huge one, to stand in the entrance hall, adorn it with baubles, red, green and gold, put lots of tinsel up too, and bunting, and deliver leaflets to Tulce and other nearby towns. *Enjoy Christmas at the Castle!* A great idea, one that could work, that would give her something to do other than cleaning and staring at a doorway. People. It was all about the people. *Imagine Christmas alone!* She couldn't.

A sound at last, something other than the thoughts that rattled inside her head.

A creak.

She was heading to the fifth floor. Had it come from above, the sixth floor?

Still on the stairway, the wall sconces flickered too. Although daytime, very little light encroached due to the grey skies, and so it had been necessary to turn on all lights as she'd climbed. But now they were flickering, on-off, on-off.

A rustle?

Had there also been a rustle? *The swishing of skirts.*

Being here at night was one thing; of course you'd get scared after dark. That was normal, only to be expected. But in daylight, should she be scared then?

Her skin tingling and her blood freezing, her breath also caught in her throat.

Murmuring. As before. Such a low sound. One voice or two?

There was no one at the castle but her. No one could have entered without her knowledge. Could they? When she'd gone to the kitchen for cleaning supplies, she supposed she'd rummaged around for quite a while to get the things she needed. Had lingered after that too, still wondering where that confounded tunnel was, stamping her foot on the ground to see if it sounded hollower in places, something she'd done several times already, declaring beneath her breath it was just another myth. There was no proof of a tunnel, no castle plans, just a snippet of a tale handed down through the ages that would have become embellished at every telling. Sighing with frustration, she'd eventually swapped the kitchen for the staircase. Had someone come in in-between times, whilst she'd been preoccupied? Let themselves in and headed upstairs?

Possible. Entirely possible. A logical reason when before there'd been none.

"Hello," she shouted. "Is anyone there?"

She'd have to check, couldn't just turn tail and run, although she felt like doing exactly that, especially when there was no reply. If people were here, innocent visitors, they'd respond, surely? Say something like 'Oh sorry, we called out when we entered, thought it strange there was no one on reception, but we thought we'd explore anyway, come downstairs afterwards and pay then. Hope you don't mind.' And Kenna would say of course she didn't mind, tell them to carry on, that she hoped they enjoyed the experience.

But no. No such exchange took place.

From her position on the staircase, she gazed out one of the deeply recessed but narrow windows. No sign of a car having been parked, not at the front, anyway, but they could have gone around the back of the castle. Some did, just naturally gravitated there.

Strange how there was no reply. Perhaps they weren't so innocent after all.

She swallowed hard. Considered going downstairs and surreptitiously calling Gregor. He'd come round if she asked him. *In a heartbeat.* They could check the castle together.

Vulnerable. That's what she felt. Not just alone in the castle but on this vast expanse of land, all immediate neighbours a car drive away.

Isolated and once again frightened.

What if someone knew she was alone and was deliberately trying to frighten her, meant to harm her, even? With no one to hear her screams, she was an easy target.

She dropped the bucket, heard it clatter as it hit the stairs.

If someone was there, that sound would have startled them too, provoked a reaction.

Her hand delving into her pocket to retrieve her mobile, she held it aloft as though it were some kind of weapon, heading upwards rather than down, to the sixth floor, forcing her legs to move whilst shouting she had her phone on her, had called the police.

"Sorry if you think I'm overreacting," she continued, "but you should answer me. I've given you enough chances. Come on, show yourself. Don't play games, don't hide."

The door to the Rohaise Room was closed. Usually it was ajar.

So there *was* someone in there, doing just that and hiding.

"Bloody hell," she swore under her breath. Why did people have to act so stupidly? "I told you I've phoned the police, and they're on their way. I'm sorry I wasn't at reception when you entered, but effectively you're trespassing. You need to pay to come into the castle; this is private property. Look, if you just come out, we can sort this. If it's a misunderstanding, then fine. Please, come on, come out of there."

The lights had stopped flickering, one thing she was

grateful for, but she was still shaking. This job – keeper of the castle, as she'd dubbed it – as interesting as it was, had a darker side. She *was* vulnerable. Here on her own. Anyone could come by, a psychopath, for that matter. Really, there should be someone with her at all times. And she supposed there was, in effect, Laura and Connor when Gregor wasn't and Gregor when Laura and Connor weren't. But illness had scuppered that. In the future, other plans would have to be made; Jean herself could step in. Because this…this was not on. Sal was right about that.

Her hand on the door, her heart hammering, another thought occurred. *Always her room.* Whenever anything strange happened at the castle, it involved the Rohaise Room. Elsewhere was fine, safe, even the library where a body had been bricked up in the wall! But here… *Unstable.* That was the word that sprang to mind. *The atmosphere is unstable.* Because Rohaise was? The *ghost* of Rohaise?

Ghosts don't exist!

On that further thought, she threw the door open to stand there in the doorway, defiantly, her green eyes blazing, she knew it, her hands thrown wide and her shoulders straight, making herself as tall as possible, wider, more formidable.

About to demand yet again that whoever was in the room, *whatever*, show themselves, any words shrivelled in her throat.

No person, no ghost, but the room itself was a mess, like a tornado had hit it, a whirlwind. Cushions were scattered, the ancient, delicate patchwork quilt pulled back to lie in a crumpled heap on the floor. A table was overturned, books torn from the shelves, and the lamp in the window had been smashed, shards of glass glinting on the floor.

Again, she froze. Who'd done this? Who could *possibly* have done this? Such…vandalism. A couple of days ago, she'd been in here and it'd been fine, just fine. But now it wasn't. Someone *must* have got in and headed upstairs without her knowledge. Either today whilst she'd been in the kitchen or yesterday when she'd been elsewhere cleaning. What about the other bedrooms? Had havoc occurred in those, too?

She turned on her heel, ran down the steps to the fifth level. All was as it should be. The same for the fourth floor and the third. She continued checking other levels but knew she'd find everything in order. It was just the Rohaise Room affected.

Always her room, she thought again, feeling more vulnerable and alone than ever.

Chapter Twenty-Three

Alone at the castle. Even the king's men left eventually. There is only so much you can do to a body, only so many ways in which to violate it. At the end, not one man would willingly touch me, a broken, bruised and hideous thing, truly a hellish creature. And what should be done with such a fiend? It should perish in the fire. For only fire can purify.

And so I was dragged from the castle and into the grounds, hoisted high above a pyre, roped to a stake driven into the middle of it.

Though my eyes were blood encrusted, I sought to open them, prizing my lids apart because I wanted to see one last time our home, the castle, holding firm. I wanted to remember the love that had blossomed within it, the depth of it, the purity. His eyes. I must not forget his eyes and the words he whispered to me, his passion which mine was a match for, the feel of skin against skin, the cries that sprang from our throats as love reached its peak. It felt like we'd been together for an age, and yet truly it was no time at all.

Smoke...I can smell smoke. Not a smell that's welcome anymore, the promise of a gentle warmth. Now the heat of the flames will ravage me, become something lascivious. So sharp, it fills my nostrils, wrings tears from my eyes that mingle with blood, threatening to blind me again. No! I am not yet done with seeing! The crowd shout and scream, call me witch still, an imp, evil, and there, in amongst them, is a familiar face – not the face of so many strangers, so many men, but Eilidh, a servant. Is it true? Can it really be her? Standing there and also shouting. It is! It's her! A woman who had come to accept me, whom I would treat with simple salves and potions whenever she fell ill, who would thank me for doing so, bow deep. Who was always there, I realise, in the shadows of the corners, not waiting to tend me as I had thought but spying on me, watching, waiting, biding her time until like a snake she could strike. It is her, and the truth dawns: it isn't just men that hunt witches. She is the one who betrayed us, Alexander and I, told untruths. And yet…if I examine her further, if I try to, there is something other than glee in her eyes, there is…horror. But horror of what? Of the way the men have treated me or what their treatment has reduced me to? Like them, does she think that what she sees now is the true Rohaise? This wreck? Does she think also that she is safe, that when they are done with me, they will not turn to her, enquire more how she knew of my wickedness?

"Run," *I want to tell her, my mouth indeed opening to say so, although no sound emerges, none that is recognisable, that is human, something guttural instead, horrific, even to my own ears. Still, I try to warn her.* "Run! Run! Run!"

For what they have done to me is exactly what they will do to her. Some are looking at her even now, their eyes narrowing. These men hunger every bit as much as the flames.

Oh, Mother, Mother! Your words haunt me!

'I want you to be happy, my rose, but you must be careful. Your hair, your beauty, will attract men. They will want you, but they will also seek to use you.'

'Are there no good men?' I'd asked. After all, I had a brother. I didn't want to think of him as someone women had to be wary

of. Oh, what did I care about men? I was young when she told me this, too young, and yet still she warned me until the day she died.

The day she died…

She lay on a bed of straw I'd made comfortable with animal pelts. Her body was ravaged by disease rather than men yet just as savage. Despite being so weak, she lifted her hand and beckoned me closer. I immediately obeyed, although I had to swallow, take a deep breath and hold it.

'Live,' she whispered. 'For me.'

'I will, Mother, I will.'

'Your hair…your glory.'

'Mother, rest now.'

'Unlike mine.'

True, she had dark hair.

'Like his.'

My father.

'There are men…'

'I know, you have told me so many times.'

'Don't leave the forest.'

'I won't.'

'Stay.'

I nodded avidly, still trying to hold my breath but failing, hating the smell because it was the smell of death, creeping closer.

'Safe here.'

'Yes, Mother.'

'Stay safe.'

Those were her last words, pleading with me. My mother, once brave and strong – who'd fled to the forest for reasons she never told me and cultivated a life there, who'd lived well and lived humbly, who'd taught me to do the same – was gone. The howl that left me as her spirit rose was enough to rival any the king's men could drag from me. I searched for some trace of her, an essence, eyes wide and frantic, but there was nothing. She'd gone.

I obeyed her, the dutiful daughter, until him, until Alexander. If my mother had lost faith in men, in turn eroding mine, he restored it.

I was not wrong about Alexander!

But it was because of Alexander I encountered men like these, a breed apart.

Ah, the flames! The breeze has risen, colluding with them, fanning them. God, if you exist, then take me now! End this suffering!

But the suffering continues, on and on.

Eilidh, you fool! Be wary! Do not believe they respect you, that they are grateful. Look around, can't you see what you have birthed here? You have given them power, and once they have tasted it, they will want so much more. I am their victim, just as you will be, as so many will. And to end this way, it is wrong, their verdict a nonsense.

I am not a witch; I am not an acolyte, the devil's mistress. I was his mistress, Alexander's, and proud to be. A good man, the best, he betrayed no one but was betrayed instead by you, Eilidh. And so if you burn too, then I hope you burn forever, in flames as hot as those that now lick at me, your flesh melting just as mine will melt, your eyes bulging from their sockets, mouth wide open and emitting sounds no human should make and no one should ever hear. And yet, as it is music to your ears, it will be music to mine. I will dance as you burn, do you hear me, Eilidh? As blackened a thing as you, shrieking but with laughter, relishing your torment, praying to whomever – the devil if I have to – that it is eternal, that pain will be heaped upon pain,

pain beyond all imagining, beyond even this.

Ah, no, no, have they broken me? Have they succeeded? I'm struggling to remember the reason I suffer. My mind is a cauldron, boiling too.

I open my eyes, perhaps for the last time, expecting a host of faces again, each one hideous, as contorted as mine. We are a mirror of each other, the darkest kind. But it is not them I see, only what lies beyond, not even the castle – not this time, no matter how high it looms – but the forest. A forest that is older than the castle, that is truly eternal, that will endure the storms that seek to thwart it, and be there, always. A place where I would have been safe, that always sought, as Mother did, to protect me, one of its own. I miss the forest! The gentleness of each day there, the harmony that existed between all living things. The hazy sunshine of summer mornings and the cold snap of winter evenings, the blue of the sky, the glow of the stars, a springy green carpet beneath my feet, and the birds that sang so joyously when the sun rose, so triumphantly.

My final breath is near. It has to be! But my longing remains.

Oh, Alexander, Alexander, how long must I wait here? Alone and suffering still.

So, so alone.

Chapter Twenty-Four

"Oh, Jean, I'm so sorry to hear that. No, really, don't concern yourself with me. I'm perfectly fine here. Honestly, I am. Of course you have to be with your sister at this time. I'll hold the fort…well, the castle. I'll hold the castle until you return."

On the other end of the phone, Jean was clearly flustered and with good reason. Her sister, younger than her by several years – in her early sixties – had suffered a heart attack, a severe one, by the sound of it. Although she was married, her husband had health issues of his own, and so Jean was helping whilst she convalesced. In Berwick-upon-Tweed. A couple of hundred miles away.

Kenna again forced breeziness into her voice, assured her over and over that it was no problem, that she could work a Sunday or two, whatever it took.

"It's not exactly busy, although I'm hoping it'll pick up during half-term holidays."

"You're cleaning, are you?"

"Yes, basic cleaning, of course, not touching drapes or linen, just sprucing the rooms up a bit, making them look their best, plus I've been working on Christmas plans. I want to get a tree in, decorate the entrance hall, the entire castle, in fact, offer a festive menu from the kitchen too and try to promote it all on a Facebook page, then keep it updated for events."

"Good ideas, all of them."

Kenna was curious. "Did you…um…ever put a tree up at Christmas?"

"Aye, a small one, just on the desk in reception."

"Oh right, like I said, I was thinking of going the whole hog. Is there enough in the budget to support these ideas?"

"Aye, of course, just. It's been a good summer. Busy."

"Unlike now."

"It has its peaks and troughs during the autumn and winter months, that's for sure. Kenna, are you sure you're coping?"

She thought of what she'd discovered earlier that day, the mess in the Rohaise Room, stuff thrown to the floor as if…as if in a whirlwind of fury. A guest or guests responsible, it had to be, mysterious guests, those that had come – and gone – without her knowing. And she'd meant to bring it up with Jean, phone her and tell her about it, but had delayed. Instead, she'd tried to rectify it, putting everything back where it should be, sweeping up the glass, fetching a new lightbulb from the office for the lamp, all the while wondering how she could have missed someone in the castle and hoping, *praying*, they'd got their senseless kicks and left.

Was she coping? That was the current question. If the situation with Jean's sister were different, Kenna would have said that whilst she *was* coping, she could do with an assistant, that she didn't want to be here on her own, day in, day out, that Laura and Connor were both ill, and so during their absence, perhaps Jean could help. She couldn't say that now, though. Jean had phoned her, not the other way around, and was in distress. No way she'd add to the load.

"I'm coping fine," she said eventually. "It's not hard

work, it's just…"

"Lonely?" Jean suggested.

"Yes," Kenna replied although, actually, right now, not lonely enough.

"Sorry," was the word that left Jean's mouth, such gravity attached to it.

"Don't be! Ordinarily Laura and Connor would be here, and there'd be guests, Gregor too, and you. It's just…unusual. A blip. It'll all be back to normal soon, as you say with peaks and troughs over autumn and winter, but if I can do it up for Christmas, offer well-priced meals from the kitchen, get the word out, I really think it'll do the trick, draw the crowds in again."

"Yes, yes, it will. I'm afraid I never really had time to plan events and suchlike. There was always so much else to keep me busy, including the kitchen. Laura and Connor have only been at the castle for a couple of years, so teas, coffees and cake, well, providing those fell to me too. Ach, my time there, the days, went so swiftly, like no time at all. Kenna," she continued, her voice still solemn, "you're not…frightened, are you?"

"Frightened?"

"Yes. Do you…sense anything?"

Kenna frowned. Sal had asked her this, and now Jean. "Sense what?"

"Well, that's what I'm asking. You tell me."

Should she do it, tell her about the Rohaise Room? She was tempted, especially because it was only that room that had been targeted, and if she'd sensed anything, it was upset so tangible you could almost reach out and grab it. Why would any would-be vandal be furious? *Always her room.* There'd been other things that had occurred in there, of course – when Sal had gone into some kind of trance, for instance, said all that stuff, and then afterwards denied it, had just…brushed it off, looked at Kenna as if she were bonkers when she'd kept insisting it had happened. Also, when she'd looked in the mirror in Rohaise's room, when she'd first come to Drumlin and possibly seen the face of another. Mad, all of it. Even so, she *would* tell Jean. Just not now.

"Jean, if I sense anything, it's just events that I've imagined have gone before. Sometimes my mind goes into overdrive, and because of that, yes, I'll be honest with you, I can get a bit spooked. But it's not because I'm sensing things. Gregor is trying to dig deep into the history of the castle, fill in some of the missing gaps."

"Yes, yes, I know he is."

Kenna was surprised. "You do?"

"Oh yes, the boy's a budding historian!"

"He is, and working at a place like this, well, it's perfect for him – and me because…I've come to appreciate history too. It's Alexander and Rohaise we're primarily concerned with. They're such an important part of Drumlin, and yet so little is known about them."

"Yes, and it's not for want of trying on my part either."

"Really? You've done some research of your own?"

Jean hesitated briefly. "You could say that."

"And?"

"And nothing, I'm afraid."

Kenna's sigh matched Jean's. "It's such a shame. She deserves to be known about."

"Oh, she does!" Jean's tone was ardent. "Most certainly. But whilst you're there alone, be…careful. By that I mean don't let your imagination take over. I've been there alone too, countless times, and I know how easily it can do that. I'll try to be as quick as I can at my sister's, a few days, a week or so, maybe. And then…then we can talk more about it."

"Yeah, yeah, sure." Kenna's frown only deepened. Despite what she'd claimed, was Jean withholding something from her? Just a few moments ago, she'd wondered if she would sound like an idiot confiding in her, if Jean would scoff in derision. Perhaps not.

Whatever the case, she'd take her advice, adhere to it, her spine tingling despite this.

"Focus on your sister for now, Jean. That's the priority."

"You're right, dear. I know you are…" Again, there was a moment of silence. "But keep in touch, okay? I'm on the end of the phone. If you need me, I'll be there."

"Thanks, Jean," Kenna said before ending the call. Maybe her imagination was once again the culprit, but there'd been agitation in Jean's voice at the end, *increased* agitation, as if she was torn between her duty to her sister and Kenna too, her successor.

A successor. That's exactly what she was, thought Kenna, her eyes on the door again – keeping guard, as it were. *Jean's* successor. And like her, like Rohaise too, she had a job to do, lonely or not, spooked or not. She was paid to protect the castle and, come hell or high water, she'd do exactly that.

* * *

Rats deserting a sinking ship. It wasn't so long ago she'd thought that, a couple of days, in fact, when Laura and Connor had called in sick and then Jean had been asked to help tend to her ill sister. Abandoning Kenna.

Not that she'd been abandoned yesterday, as Gregor had

been in, chopping wood and bagging it up, the excess due to be sold to local people, adding to the castle coffers.

"October's a chilly month," he'd said.

"And there's worse to come."

"Aye, but you'll not want for anything, I'll make sure of it."

She glanced over to where logs were neatly stacked in one of the outbuildings to season for future years. There was enough to heat the entire castle, she thought, not just her flat, but he denied it.

"You'd be surprised. The log burner eats those things like Smarties."

"There's central heating in the flat," she'd pointed out.

"Aye, there is, but there's nothing like a log fire, is there? Watching the flames leap and dance, the colours of them, such bright shades, orange and yellow."

"No, that's right, there isn't," she said, thinking how romantic he made it sound, also about the nights she'd spend alone in front of the fire, unless…

"You know you're welcome for dinner anytime."

"Aye, thank you."

"We can eat in front of the fire."

"That'd be lovely. I'm happy to come over whenever you want."

Not lonely, not at all. No need to feel that way. He'd come over whenever she wanted. And she did want him to, she *really* did. An intelligent, caring, *interesting* man, he'd also called her 'bewitching' in the forest. The first man ever to do that. She'd take it over 'fit' any day, as Adam tended to describe her, much preferring the old-fashioned charm of it. Despite what had happened between them – and the term of endearment he'd used, the way he had said it – they remained friends, just that, Kenna liking the simplicity of it, and perhaps he did too.

"Gregor…" she said, wondering how to put into words what had happened in the Rohaise Room, when, lo and behold, visitors arrived. And not just one but an entire carful! "Tomorrow evening," she said instead before hurrying over to them. "If you're free, come by then, and I'll do us a chilli or something." That's when she'd tell him; they could discuss it at length, also what to do about security, how to broach the subject with Jean, who had never even hinted there'd been any problems in the past – until their last conversation, that is. *Whilst you're there alone, be…careful.*

She heard his agreement just before greeting the visitors, who stayed for well over an hour and then wanted tea and coffee after, which she gladly prepared, offering them cake too. As she served them, they were keen to continue chatting with her, and so she duly told them about her plans for Christmas, which they said they'd spread the word about.

When they left, she felt happy, buoyed by their visit and the prospect of Gregor's the following evening. After work that day, she'd head into Tulce, to the supermarket there, do some shopping, get some red wine in, a really decent bottle. She'd also chat to the cashiers, whom she'd got to know more over the summer – Jenny, Lewis and Sonny, their banter something she always looked forward to.

Whilst locking the castle that day, she thought she could tell the cashiers about her Christmas plans too. No doubt they'd also spread the word, allow her to advertise in the store window. All the shops and restaurants in Tulce would. It could be a success, a raging success, loneliness a mere memory.

Gregor had already gone, busy now delivering wood. It felt like a gaping hole at the castle when he was absent, but no matter because he'd be back soon, everyone would, and there'd be more visitors, she'd ensure it. And any strange goings on, well…she'd put them to one side, maybe stay out of the Rohaise Room, try to stop thinking about her. Do a jigsaw in the evening or watch TV or read, a quiet time for quiet pursuits.

She hummed to herself that evening whilst preparing dinner, happy, she realised, quite content. Her contract ended in April, and she could choose to stay or go. A few times she'd contemplated what to do for the best, but now she knew – she couldn't face going back to London, and not just because of Adam. This felt like home now, Scotland. She'd stay, get two years under her belt, perhaps, before moving on, try to see – budget allowing – what differences she could make. A second year would also give her more time to contemplate her book. Every day she was getting closer to taking the plunge.

Around eleven, she went to bed and slept well, then woke up not with Rohaise on her mind, just the day ahead and the tasks she needed to carry out.

Gregor was due in today, and tonight they'd be eating together in front of a log fire. She'd invite him to stay the night too, if he wanted, like he'd done before in the spare room. He could have more than one glass of wine, then, truly relax.

She was in the bathroom, towelling off after a shower and shivering slightly – the heated towel rail in there not quite enough to fend off the chill that had pervaded the atmosphere – when she heard her phone ringing. After wrapping the towel around herself, she hurried out of the bathroom and along to her bedroom, her mobile on the bedside table there.

Before picking it up, she noticed the name of the caller: Gregor.

If she'd shivered before, she did so again, also noting the time. It was early, just past 7.30 a.m. What did he want at this hour?

"Gregor?" she said. "Are you okay?"

"Kenna"—there was pain in his voice, she was certain of it—"I…um…had a bit of an accident yesterday."

"Oh God, really? Are you okay?"

"Aye, yeah, don't worry, I will be."

"What is it, then? What's wrong?"

"I delivered all the logs, got home and then, would you believe it, slipped right outside my front door, twisted my ankle."

"Oh no, you poor thing! How can I help?"

"There's nothing you can do. I just need to rest it."

"I'll come round later, cook for you at yours."

Before she could answer, he broke into a hacking cough.

"I'd love you to, really, but I think it's best you stay away. I was delivering logs till late, in the rain." The rain? That was right; it had rained heavily. She was getting so used to it she'd barely noticed. "The thing is," he continued, "I've caught a chill, a bad one, probably due to getting drenched, then falling and hurting myself and not being able to warm up properly, you know, in the shower. You'd best stay away, Kenna. I can hobble to the kettle well enough, and the fridge, so I'll be fine. I just need a few days, then I'll be back."

"Sure, okay, but if you change your mind, if you need me, call."

"I will, I promise. You'll be all right?"

"Me?"

"Yeah, at the castle, what with Connor, Laura, Jean…"

And now you, she thought but didn't say it.

She looked outside at a day that was still drizzly and heard something – thunder? Surely not. There was going to be a storm? No visitors today, then.

"Kenna?"

"I'll be all right," she assured him, just as she'd assured the others, her voice breezy again. "Get well soon, Gregor."

"I will. I'll do my best."

At a loss for what else to say, she ended the call, trying not just to quash her disappointment – none of her colleagues could help what had happened to them – but put it into perspective. Aside from any visitors, she'd only be alone for two or three days. No big deal. She hadn't been abandoned. No need to keep thinking that.

Another rumble of thunder, but it was low, distant. With a bit of luck, if there was a storm, it might just head the other way or blow itself out.

Sinking down onto her bed with the phone still in her hand, she found she was trying to quash something else too – fear, on the rise again. Being alone really didn't appeal. Alone…but not alone. *Always her room. Always…her.*

The storm wouldn't pass, she was suddenly certain of that.

It hadn't even begun.

Chapter Twenty-Five

She didn't have to go to the castle today; it could remain locked. No one would be turning up in such grim weather at the end of October. Halloween was looming, All Hallows Eve – or Samhain, as it was known in the Pagan calendar – and, at this rate, unless one of her colleagues made a miraculous recovery, she'd be alone for it at Drumlin Castle.

Kenna shook her head. You couldn't make it up, even a novelist couldn't; it was just too contrived. Because wasn't Halloween a time when the veil between life and death, the past and the present, thinned? Not that she'd taken much notice of the beliefs and superstitions surrounding the festival. Maybe as a kid she'd enjoyed a scary movie during the evening with her family, but as an adult, it was precisely that: kids' stuff. In London, some dressed up and roamed the streets come sundown, trick-or-treating, but not so much in her neighbourhood. It was just another night, not something of relevance.

It was relevant now, though.

Just a couple of days away, that's all. Surely one of her colleagues would be back by then? Although…

A thought occurred. Leaving the bedroom and heading to the kitchen, she checked the work calendar. Even if Connor or Laura did recover in time, they weren't due in until next week. The weekend was coming, and the thirty-first was a Sunday, Kenna's day off. Not this Sunday, though, not without Jean here.

If only she'd thought ahead and planned an event, then she could have been assured of people at the castle, during the day, at least. They would lift the energy, lighten it, that lightness always carrying into the night. Without others, this place was just too heavy.

Shit! What should she do? Call it quits? Stay holed up in her flat? Wait for it to pass?

For what to pass, exactly? What did she think would happen? *The best thing you can do, Kenna, is to go about your normal business. Not worry so much, not fantasise.*

Fantasising…she was guilty of that.

And yet, could she be blamed? Being here, not just at the castle but *right* here in Scotland, surrounded by pine forest, such a natural setting, so removed, closer to something else, as she'd said to Gregor, something…*super*natural?

"Stop it! For God's sake!" No way she'd give in to such nonsense. She'd open the castle but close the kitchen. One person could only do so much. And she'd stay in reception, no real need to wander around elsewhere and certainly not up to the sixth floor. Gregor was hardy, so he was bound to be back sooner rather than later. As for Jean, who knew, but with the other three still nearby locally, she'd be fine. She'd just sit at reception and wait. She might even get lucky. Hordes of visitors might turn up, a stray coach party.

With that decision made, she returned to the bedroom, dressed, then went back to the kitchen to drink coffee whilst scouring the internet, catching up on national and international news. Trying to *stay connected.* As terrible as the news often was, it helped her to do just that. She could take her laptop to reception, but the signal within the castle itself, because of how thick the walls were, could be temperamental. She was only grateful it was stable enough in her flat, although again it dipped in and out sometimes.

And with that storm coming...

One hand reaching out, she closed the computer lid, deciding to take a book to reception instead, something light and fluffy. A little before ten, she went down to her front door and opened it, gasping as a gust of wind hit her so hard it stole her breath.

She was going to need a hat, gloves *and* scarf just to go a few yards. Retreating inside, she donned those items as if they were armour, which she supposed they were against the elements and a ferocity she would soon become well acquainted with. Suitably attired, she tried again. It wasn't hard rain, not yet, but the wind was foe enough, making you battle against it in order to remain upright, the sky above dark and brooding, clouds clashing as if conspiring about the mayhem they could bestow on mere mortals below. Twice Kenna thought to turn back, longing for home comforts, but she continued onwards to the castle to take up position, fulfil the role she'd been appointed for.

Jean would have had to contend with this sort of weather, and empty hours too, and she'd done it for years and years – the keeper of the castle, the *real* keeper, unlike the Buchannans in LA, Duncan et al, who owned it on paper but shunned it for sunshine. Could they be blamed, though? Would Kenna do the same if she had half the chance?

Not so much reaching the castle door as falling against it, Kenna inserted the key, willing it, just for once, to open easily. *Come on! Hurry up, just hurry up, will you!*

Eventually it was defeated, and she hurried inside,

quickly closing it again whilst panting heavily. Her breath returning to normal, she listened. No sounds, nothing but silence. *Get on with your day!* She would, she'd head to the kitchen, switching on all lights en route, grab another coffee and then, back in reception, liberate her book from her bag and turn the radio on too so there *was* noise, the acceptable kind. Hopefully, by the time she left at four o'clock, her duty done, the wind would have subsided.

One thing she'd do before going to the kitchen, however, was lock the door, just during her absence. This was Scotland, *rural* Scotland. Stuff wasn't supposed to happen here. You could leave your door open; Gregor had told her that. And people often did – certainly Gregor never bothered to lock the door to his cottage. But something *had* happened, although she realised no one but her was aware of it. She hadn't yet told anyone.

Tired of thinking, of reasoning, she put her plan into action, settling afterwards in reception, the radio presenter chatting merrily away in between playing a selection of pop songs from before she was born. Sipping from her mug, she glanced at her watch. Half an hour of blissful tedium gone; only five and a half hours of official duty left. It was cold in the castle this morning, though, more so than normal, prompting her to drag the Calor Gas heater from where it was stored in the office and fire it up.

Rather than immediately retake her seat, she reorganised the giftshop shelves. Once items had been shuffled around enough, each and every one perfectly aligned, she checked her watch again. Good! Another hour had passed, and quickly too. She'd forego lunch, as she often did, and just eat this evening when she got home. At the flat, she'd call Sal or maybe her mother, just for a chat – for the sound of a familiar voice – longing for that. Whatever the weather was like outside, the silence in here was always so complete, except, of course, when it wasn't. *Don't start...not again!*

She picked up her book, then finally returned to her seat, the warmth from the gas heater beating back the cold. Not her usual reading material – it had been on the bookshelf in the living room, something she'd just selected: *Mischief in Cornish Cove*. A chick lit, she supposed, wondering who it had belonged to. Not Jean, surely? Although, like Kenna, maybe she'd needed something lighter too on occasion. Whether her usual type of book or not, it'd do. It looked pleasant enough. *Inoffensive.*

She kept glancing at the entrance as she read but less and less, the glow of the heater really quite fierce, deciding she'd get up and turn it down now that the room had warmed up so nicely. She'd do that in a minute or two, after another paragraph and then another, feeling really quite cosy, really very, very warm, the book becoming heavier as her eyelids closed, as she sank back further into the chair, not nervous at all now but relaxed, completely. Hardly noticing when it fell from her hands, barely hearing the thud as it hit the flagstones below.

* * *

It was as if she was walking through...mist. Layer upon layer of mist, thicker than the clouds above. She wasn't frightened; she was comforted. The mist enveloped her; it *cloaked* her. Offered a haven of sorts, a respite, the nothingness she craved.

How fleeting it was, though, the mist clearing suddenly, mysteriously, when she didn't want it to, when she begged for it to remain, crying out, "No! Please! Stay." But clear it did to reveal the faces of men before her, so many men, their eyes as mad as hers.

In her sleep, Kenna jerked as she looked down at her dream self. Was it really her body she was looking at, with barely a cloth to cover it? *Her* skin? Instead of soft and pale, it was red with blood that had become thick and crusted, but more than that, *worse than that*, was what had been carved into her flesh. Crosses? They were! So crudely done and all over her. Crosses that were upside down. Each and every one.

She was a woman marked. Branded.

If only she could shrink from herself, avert her gaze, but all she could do was stare, the pain returning, the memory of those crosses being carved, the blade driven deep.

How many tears could one person cry? In amongst sheer horror was amazement that, whatever source grief sprang from, it was endless.

Every inch of her was ruined, her hair yanked from her head to leave only tufts and bloodied scabs. She was a pitiful creature that clung to corners, whimpering and babbling.

They'd taken everything from her, smashed her mind against the rocks, over and over, damned her. What more could they do? And at the end, was there truly nothing? Is that what she hoped for? For if nothing existed, then neither did Alexander. She wouldn't find him again. Such agony! If there was one thing she clung to, one thing she prayed for, it was to see him, in life or in death, what did it matter? They would meet, and he would hold her, cleave to her as she cleaved to him, and in his arms the healing would begin. A love such as theirs could transcend this horror, surely? Erase the memory of it. She'd be whole once more, her skin unblemished, her red hair abundant, bewitching.

"Witch!"

No peace. Gone, all gone. Shattered.

She was in a room that had become a cell, the door opening, the light creeping in and blinding her, hurting her more. Why did it do that? Wasn't the light something infinite, something good? Had it turned on her too? Had it done so because she truly was a witch, a child of the forest, a mistress, bewitching? All the things a woman shouldn't be. Not in a man's world. And yet a man had loved her despite this. 'My heart is not my own anymore. It is yours, Rohaise. You have captured it.'

Could hearts be destroyed?

Could hope?

The cloth she wore fell to the floor, her body wearing a cloak of bloodied crosses instead, every broken limb horribly distorted as she was hauled from the filth she sat in.

His face – Alexander's – she would see only him as she was dragged outside. He would give her courage and strength, curb the terror that was building and building. Because there it was, what she dreaded most, what she knew was coming. The stake.

So many men, cheering and jostling, the king's men but, despite this, lower than worms that crawled in the soil. How could any king sanction this? Believe it to be right?

She tried to scream, break free of their hold. She had borne so much, but this…

"Oh God, no, please no."

This was for him, for Alexander. She had *chosen* this, to protect him, to allow him to escape. She *must* endure. And yet fear was a force as well as love. So was anger.

How had it come to this? How?

And so quickly.

The mist…there it is again, rising all around me. Hands bound to the stake, I wish I could reach out and drag it closer. The mist is where all pain will ease. If there is nothing in the mist, no Rohaise, no Alexander, so be it, for I cannot bear this!

The mist…why does it choke me? Why does it fill my lungs so readily?

Smoke, not mist.
Of course it is smoke.
Belching and billowing.
Murderous.
Why must I relive this? Why?
Burn, then burn again.
Witch! Witch! Witch!
Burn! Burn! Burn!
Endlessly I burn!

Chapter Twenty-Six

When dawn arrived, she was awake still.

After the dream – the nightmare – Kenna had left the castle and hurried back to her flat. Having climbed the steps, she'd made it as far as the living room before slumping down on the sofa there, her body trembling and her eyes downcast. Just as time had passed so quickly whilst in the castle, it passed again, it slipped, because when finally she lifted her head and looked over at the window, daylight had faded, and it was dark.

When she'd left reception, the storm, such as it was, remained only a threat. A mist had arisen instead to surround the castle, engulfing both it and her. A mist that Rohaise had liked to hide in, that was so like the smoke, a precursor to the flames that would soon burst into life.

A sob broke rank. This dream, like the other she'd had about Rohaise, had been all too real. Every detail savage, every second vivid. She had *lived* the dream, been Rohaise, this time a tortured, disfigured thing. How could anyone do that to another human being? And with such unbridled joy? People did, though, even today, treated each other inhumanely. What had happened then – the persecution of innocents – happened still, just in other guises.

The shock wearing off, to be replaced with overwhelming despair instead, more sobs escaped her, her chest heaving painfully, her eyes red and sore.

At last she'd risen and padded through to the bedroom, not to lie down on the bed, as exhausted as she was, but to stare into the mirror there as she'd done so many times before, again time slipping. No matter. Drumlin was a place where the past and present melded, became as one. And if time didn't matter, then it mattered not how long she stared, her face not changing although she willed it to. Rohaise had been beautiful with pale skin, red hair and green eyes, just as Kenna had pale skin, red hair and green eyes. Her beauty had captured a laird, bewitched him. He had brought her out of the forest and into his home, called it theirs. She had loved him, and he had loved her. They'd been happy. And then they'd been betrayed. *Rohaise* had. A rose torn apart.

If her face in any way resembled Rohaise's, it was only fleetingly. For they had destroyed the woman's beauty too, her innocence gone as she'd been driven mad with pain and fear.

Were you insane, Rohaise? At the end?

The woman in the dream was something diabolical. Oh, they had made her look the part, that was for certain. Even Kenna, despite her sorrow for Rohaise, her compassion, flinched at the memory of what she'd become. And those crosses! Inverted crosses, so many of them on her arms, her legs, her face.

Immediately, she reprimanded herself. *It was just a dream, a terrible, terrible dream. You don't know it really happened.* But somewhere deep inside she *did* know – a woman had been tortured at Drumlin, burnt to death there in defence of her lover and the home she had shared with him, and that woman was Rohaise.

The night deepening, Kenna had torn herself from the

mirror to lay on the bed. It was cold, silent, and yet she didn't slip beneath the covers, because…because… *I want to suffer too*. She wasn't averse to sleep, it might be dreamless this time, but her eyes never closed, just stared at the far wall, unwavering.

And then night begrudgingly withdrew, dawn rays entering the room through open curtains. When full light eventually arrived, it was weak, her body stiff as she forced movement into it, pushing herself off the bed and onto her feet. Rather than go to the window to peer out at the new day, her usual habit, she ventured down the passageway to the living room, descended the stairs to the lobby and opened the door there.

The mist hadn't receded. If anything, it was thicker than before. A *wall* of mist, one she walked into, that allowed her passage, knitting back together again behind her.

She could barely see anything, not the grounds that Gregor so lovingly tended, only the tops of the pines trees that encircled them. More alone, more isolated than ever. Just her and a castle that had witnessed so much. The best of life and the very worst.

She carried on walking, measuring each tread, past the dovecote and the ruined chapel wall. If the chapel had stood when Rohaise was alive, had the men that tortured her prayed in there before, during and after her death? Had they sought guidance, divine support for their actions? Had the God of their own minds answered them, confirmed *they* were indeed the righteous ones, carrying out His will and banishing evil? If so, she was glad the chapel was a ruin, for it deserved to be. Here on this ground, it served only to aid delusion.

The only sound to reach her ears was the crunch of her

own feet against gravel, all birdsong silenced, her own breathing silent too. Soon, though, she came to a halt and turned back to the castle.

Halloween was tomorrow, when the past could come closer. When she slept again, as sleep she must, would Rohaise return? If so, could she bear it? Could she help her, perhaps? Reach out and whisper, *I'm so sorry for what happened to you. It was wrong, and I'm just so sorry.* She looked up at Rohaise's window, the mist patchy all around it, and knew what she saw was imaginary – a woman, staring down at her, her dress as green as the forest she'd come from, and hair so red.

Imagination. That's all it was. Nonetheless, Kenna lifted her hand, held it outwards, and the shadow figure did the same. A beautiful figure. Not scarred, shorn or blood soaked, only beautiful.

"I'm sorry," Kenna whispered before blinking away fresh tears. In a second, the figure was gone, as she knew it would be. Pure imagination. Once, though, Rohaise had been a whole lot more, as substantial as Kenna was now, as filled with emotion.

She wouldn't open the castle today. She'd decided that when leaving yesterday. Not until someone was here with her. It was a place no one should be alone, no living person.

"Sorry," she said again, turning from the window, heading back to her flat, where she would stay, where she would pray, like Rohaise had, for respite from all that haunted her.

* * *

The music was blaring; the TV was on too, Kenna encouraging as much noise as possible as the day wore on, trying not to glance out the windows but cherishing what little daylight there was until, finally, it was gone. Light and darkness. Always rotating. But tonight the darkness was grey in tint, at least, the mist still hovering, Kenna eventually succumbing and peering out of the living room window as a newscaster spoke in the background, wondering if the mist could solidify somehow, form shapes, one shape in particular…

"Kenna! For Christ's sake!"

She returned to the TV and changed channels, seeking something blander, a cooking programme, maybe; that would do. She was tired, her eyes kept drooping, but unlike last night when she couldn't sleep, she now fought it, just too afraid of what it might bring. The presenters of the programme were laughing, two of them, their Geordie accents thick. For a moment she smiled too, glad of some normality, but the smile wouldn't hold. She lifted her hand and started chewing at her nails, something her mother used to reprimand her for and a habit she'd long since broken. Now, though, the urge was irresistible.

She would have phoned Gregor, phoned Sal, her mother or father if she could, but the phone signal – likely because of the weather – was weaker than usual, barely even two bars showing. She *had* phoned Gregor, knowing his voice would soothe her, but the phone just kept on ringing, refusing to connect. A temporary issue, that was all. The weather would clear and the signal grow strong again. Plus, there was always the landline in the office at the castle. If she grew desperate enough.

Kenna stood and began pacing whilst giving herself a pep talk.

"You're fine, you're safe. What happened was just a

dream. Rein it in, see sense. The past can't hurt you, as Gregor said. It's done and dusted. You are utterly, utterly safe."

She was, she knew it. Strange, though, how Jean had been called away, how Laura and Connor had gone sick, and now Gregor, the last bastion, who'd come at the drop of a hat if she wanted, was out of reach too.

Gregor. She'd go to him, and to hell with the chill he'd caught. On the main road, out of the mist, she was bound to get a signal, could call and tell him she was on her way. The idea took shape. She couldn't stay at Drumlin. Not alone. For Halloween, Samhain, the Feast of the Dead.

On feet that were practically flying now, she ran to her bedroom, grabbed a rucksack from the wardrobe and threw some clothes and a few toiletries into it. Oh, Gregor! She couldn't wait to see him. She'd tend to him, help him get well. The sooner the better.

Her rucksack packed, she returned just as swiftly to the living room, looking around only once before descending the curved staircase. In the lobby, she grabbed her coat from the stand and shrugged it on, then headed to a shallow dish kept on the windowsill. There it was, the means to an escape – the key to the Volvo, that beautiful ancient rusty Volvo that would steer her out of here. What a relief! For a moment, she thought the keys wouldn't be there, had been spirited away, the Fates conspiring against her again. Not an outlandish theory, not really, because right now anything seemed possible, this land so different to London, so much more ethereal. *The land of the fey.* Never had she believed it more.

Her hands closing around the keys, the coldness of the metal like a gift, she again hurried, wondering why she hadn't thought of this plan earlier in the day, why she'd stayed, allowed herself to become so fretful. *Tortured yourself.* That's exactly what she'd done. She shook her head, almost laughed. *Too empathetic for your own good!*

She yanked the door open and then slammed it behind her, walking into the mist, to the dormant car, her hand shaking as she tried to insert the key into the Volvo's lock.

"Almost there. Almost there," she told herself.

Behind her the castle was in darkness, the only light left on at night being the single lamp in Rohaise's room. At the back where Kenna was, the mist obscured the windows anyway.

"Come on!" she shouted, working harder to steady her hand.

At last, the lock complied, and she opened the rear passenger door to throw her rucksack in. It landed with a satisfying thud. Soon she'd be out of here and by another man's fireside. Together they'd be laughing about this, her mad dash.

Turning the key in the ignition, nothing happened.

"What the fuck?" she breathed.

Telling herself to slow down, she repeated the procedure, the engine turning lazily this time and catching but only slightly before dying out.

"No," she whispered. "No, no, no. You cannot be serious! You're an old car, fine, I get it, but you're supposed to be reliable. You're a fucking Volvo – you go on forever!"

It *had* been reliable so far, always starting straightaway. Not now, though.

She tried again and again, gunning the key over and over until finally she had to accept it. The Volvo was going nowhere tonight. This mist perhaps too much for it, damp in the electrics, an old thing that had just…given up.

The only option left was to walk down the driveway and onto the main road, wait until she got a signal, call Gregor and tell him, sprained ankle or not, to come and get her.

She'd do that, give it a go. Getting out of the car, she retrieved her rucksack from the back, slammed both car doors and started walking.

Earlier in the day, she'd likened the mist to a wall, but it had parted readily enough for her. This time, as she ventured further round the path to the front of the castle, it did no such thing. It was a *shield* wall, preventing her from seeing anything. At least this part of the way she knew by heart, how many steps almost exactly. The light in Rohaise's room would also help, act like a beacon, something to keep in the corner of her eye. Except – and she was sure she had reached the front of the castle, her eyes searching for the familiar glow – there was none.

The light that Jean insisted stay on, was it off again? The lamp dashed to the ground as before? If so, who was responsible this time? The castle was locked. It couldn't be breached, not by burglars or pranksters or anyone. It had kept an army out once; it could keep them out too. *If* they'd come calling. Because, really, who would? In this weather.

Jean's words when they'd first met came flooding back. *Why are you here? Why are you* really *here?*

"I don't know!" She screamed the words as if somehow, someway, across the great divide, Jean could hear them. "I have no idea why I'm here!" And then, in a much smaller voice: "I wasn't supposed to come alone. I wasn't…I never bargained for that."

Why did the lamp keep going off? Who had vandalised the room? Not kids. That certainty grew within her too. No living, breathing person was responsible.

She knew she couldn't make it to the road, not on foot. The mist ensured she had to stay, as there was no way she was entering the main body of the castle again, not on her own, not after dark, to try the landline there. The flat was the only sanctuary on offer.

With a sob in her throat, she retraced her footsteps, counting each one, determined not to veer off track. She'd return to her flat and…she'd hide. Get into bed, perhaps – for she was tired, so very tired, every bone heavy, every limb like lead – succumb to sleep but not before asking a God she'd only recently railed against to protect her, a true God, a God for everyone, not just men, an entity that shone its light on all.

"Keep me safe, please keep me safe."

She was still muttering those words as she opened her front door, as she climbed upwards, as she headed to the vastness of her room – darkness pooling in the corners, her mind going against her again, seeing more shadows, demons…

"Please, please, please."

She climbed into bed, so small in the room but not small enough, curled her body into the foetal position, wanting to make herself smaller still. Soon she began to drift, a plea still on her lips. *Keep me safe, even in dreams, keep me safe.*

There *was* comfort, nothing but darkness in which no shadows dwelt, a void that welcomed her, closed in around her as the mist had. Sweet comfort in which she was suspended, hoping to remain there for as long as she could.

A sound woke her, a fierce banging.

Kenna sat bolt upright and glanced at her watch. It was late. She'd slept for hours. What was making such a sound?

Who?

Swinging her legs over the side of the bed, she stood. No way she could ignore it, not something that loud. But who could it be?

She crept towards the light switch, arms outstretched, but then thought better of it. Perhaps she shouldn't alert anyone to the fact she was in residence. They might get bored, then, and go away. Because the banging was coming from further along in the flat, not inside but outside, someone at her door. At midnight. *Frantically* at her door.

Trembling again, terrified again, she continued along the hallway in darkness. Tomorrow, as soon as dawn broke, she'd leave this place one way or the other and never come back. She was angry too with those that had abandoned her – Jean, Connor, Laura and Gregor. Gregor in particular, as if it was his fault what had happened to him, as if he'd engineered it.

The mantra of before was replaced with another: *Go away. Go away. Just go away!*

Who'd come calling in the mist? What had managed to reach her?

"Kenna, for God's sake, are you in there? Open up! It's bloody horrible out here!"

A voice! A recognisable voice! She could hear it now, over and above the banging.

"Kenna, you have to let me in!"

Warmth flooded previously frozen limbs, and she started running, almost tripping over herself in her haste, into the living room and down the stairs to the lobby.

"Kenna!" she heard again, and his voice was like manna from heaven.

Unlocking the door, she yanked it open and threw herself

into his arms.

"Adam!" she breathed. "You're here at last!"

Chapter Twenty-Seven

Adam was uttering so many words, but Kenna didn't hear them, didn't want to know. One minute the past was all that mattered, the next, it was of no consequence whatsoever. All she cared about was that he was here, that someone was. She was no longer alone.

Releasing him briefly, she tugged at his hands instead, pulled him over the threshold, the mist at his heels, but she shut it out. Standing together, she saw the wonder in his eyes, surprise too, but also such familiarity. This was Adam, *her* Adam, the man she was supposed to love, that she'd wanted to start a new life with, and finally, *finally*, he'd come.

She kissed him, her lips hard against his. Immediately, he responded. Again and again they kissed, until at last they had to part, had to draw air, the pair of them, Adam starting to laugh, Kenna also laughing, not wanting this moment, this joy, to evaporate, for it had done what she'd thought was impossible and obliterated all else.

He spoke again, trying to explain his absence, it seemed.

"I'm so sorry. I was stupid, a coward. I know I bailed but—"

"Not now, Adam, later. Right now, just…be with me, stay."

"I want to, but I didn't know—"

ROHAISE

Again, she interrupted him. "Adam, please. We can talk later. I just want to hold you and be held by you. Come upstairs, come on."

With astonishment still on his face, he allowed himself to be led into the flat. When they reached the landing that opened onto the living room, Kenna turned left, still with her hand in his, leading him down the passageway all the way to her bedroom.

When they reached it, he gasped, as she knew he would. "Bloody hell, Kenna, this is…vast. And it's all yours?"

She almost snapped at him. *It was supposed to be ours, Adam!* She didn't, though; she held her tongue, releasing his hand as he wandered round, taking in the grandeur.

"Impressive, the whole place is, what I could see of it in the mist, at any rate." A frown developed. "The weather, though, I hope it's not always like this! It's treacherous out there, Kenna. I've crawled here, literally crawled. Almost left the road a couple of times too. So fucking scary. I would have been here much earlier otherwise."

She closed the gap between them. "It isn't always like this. This weather's…unusual. Adam, do as I ask and hold me, please."

As soon as his arms came out, she started kissing him again, her hands also busy trying to rid him of his coat, something he all too eagerly helped her with. Steering him backwards, they fell onto the bed, Adam lifting his head briefly to laugh again.

"Never had sex in a four-poster," he said, but she quieted him with more kisses, needing to feel skin against skin, the pulse of life rather than so much death.

An image tried to force its way into her mind, that of Rohaise in the dream, how she had squatted so pitifully in a corner of one of the rooms here, but she banished it and clung harder to Adam, her fingers digging into the small of his back, Kenna not just closing her eyes but squeezing them shut, desperate to focus only on the moment, on them.

All too soon it was over, and Adam tried to push himself off her. She wouldn't have it, wasn't ready to release him. There were still many hours until daylight and, as far as she was concerned, only one way to spend them.

Only when the gloom of night receded did she settle in his arms. She'd sleep, she had to, but with Adam wrapped around her.

It was late morning when he stirred, stretching wide and declaring how hungry he was. Grudgingly, Kenna opened her eyes, her exhaustion somehow more intense.

"Got any food in?" he said. "I need to refuel if you're going to use me like that again!"

Use him? He was joking. She knew it, but, actually, was that what she'd done? Because she was just so desperate? Another uncomfortable thought that she dismissed. He was right; they'd worked up an appetite, the pair of them, Kenna ravenous too.

She sat up, wrapping the duvet around her.

He frowned. "Why so shy all of a sudden?"

"What? No, I'm not, I just…" She tried to laugh. "I need a shower and then, yep, I'll cook some breakfast. Unless you want to, that is?"

"Yeah, sure." Adam stretched languidly, pushing a hand through his blond hair. She used to like how he did that, thought it sexy. Did she think that now? She loved him. It wasn't possible to love someone, then just turn that feeling off, no matter what they'd done. He'd made a mistake, one he clearly wanted to rectify or he wouldn't be here, surely, but the look on his face as he rose from the bed and pulled on his clothes, just tossed on the floor there from last night, wasn't endearing. There was something about him as he left the room, humming some tune to himself, that irritated her. A certain smugness, was that it? He'd come here expecting Kenna to turn him away, deservedly so, but instead, she'd dragged him to the bedroom, torn off his clothes and had sex with him, over and over. And now he was smug, thought he was off the hook.

Only as she emerged from bed, heading to the bathroom, did she remember what day it was. Halloween. Instead of horror washing over her, she felt relief that she wouldn't be alone for it. Stuck here, at Drumlin. If some forces were conspiring against her, clearly others were on her side, bringing Adam to her door. Reminding herself of that, all irritation vanished. She was just so grateful. Why he'd changed his mind, had effectively – and ironically – ghosted her, plus how long he intended to stay were all questions that needed to be asked, but right now, the smell of bacon permeated the air. She'd get in the shower before eating, but, oh, how her stomach growled.

Breakfast was leisurely, Adam dishing up with his usual theatrical flair, keeping them topped up with fresh coffee too and chatting more about the weather and how cold it was here compared to London, where it was still mild. He also talked about his work, how stressful it had been but how pleased his clients were with him. It just kept on flooding in, apparently, even though he'd hiked up his prices, no one batting an eyelid about that.

She listened as he talked – there was little opportunity to do much else – and couldn't help but make a comparison between him and Gregor. She'd not noticed before, but

Adam was all harsh lines and angles, from the sculpt of his chin to his cheekbones and slightly pointed nose. Gregor was much softer to look at, a product of nature rather than the city. Would Adam have done what Gregor had that day in the forest, when they'd spun round and round and laughed like children? Would he ever call her bewitching?

"So…shall we?"

Kenna shook her head, unaware her attention had drifted. "Shall we what?"

"Explore the castle, of course! I want to see what all the fuss is about."

"Fuss?" she questioned. "What fuss?"

"Oh, you know, what's cool about it, if it's worth…"

His voice trailed off.

"If it's worth what, Adam?"

He hesitated. "Nothing, nothing."

"If it's worth giving up everything for?"

A moment of silence again, his blue eyes not warm at all, really quite cold. "Well, is it?"

"I love it," she declared, her chin jutting with defiance. "It's…unique."

Adam stood up, all schoolboy eagerness. "Let's see it, then! I'll grab a shower, then you can give me a private tour."

She did love it, she'd just said so, but going in there today? No way.

"We'll…um…tour the castle tomorrow. Today I want to…I want to…" What the hell did she want? "To get away from work, that's it! Go to Aberdeen or something. It's not far, and it's a great city, interesting. We can grab a late lunch or early dinner there."

Adam screwed up his nose, looking more like a petulant child instead of a man.

"Really? I've just come from the city, but, hey-ho, if that's what you want. I thought you'd be busy today, that's all."

"Why?"

"Because it's Halloween! It's a castle. No ghost tours, then?"

"No, Adam, no ghost tours." How wry she sounded. She stood up too, seeking to urge him on. "Go on, get ready. I'll clean up here."

"Okay," he said, still despondent, she had to admit.

Before he left the kitchen entirely, she had to know. "Adam, how long are you staying?"

He turned to face her, his nose shiny under the kitchen spotlights. "Just a couple of days, and then I'll have to go home, sort out some things."

A few days? More relief. The others would be back by then.

"But after that, when everything's sorted," he added, smiling at her again, smug again, "I'll be back." Taking his eyes off her, he looked around him. "I like it here. It's nice, better than I expected. Yep, when I return, it'll be for good."

As she watched him eventually head off, that relief, strangely, evaporated.

* * *

Bright lights, chatter all around her, people rushing back and forth, children in costumes, and shops decorated with pumpkins, spider webs and witches.

Witches…soft toys and puppets dressed in black, hag-like creatures with long, gnarled noses, stringy hair and warty skin. Either sitting on broomsticks or hunched around a cauldron, stirring, stirring, stirring, creating mischief and mayhem with the spells they cast.

Staring at one such tabletop display, green smoke puffing intermittently from the cauldron into the witch's face, all else around Kenna blurred into the background as she focused on what was being represented. A witch. A woman. A lie. One that was worldwide, fed to people from young in storybooks, in films and at Halloween. And Kenna, like most others, had readily accepted this portrayal, didn't tend to question it. Until now. She not only questioned it, she *reviled* it.

"Wrong," she whispered. "It's all so wrong."

So many women in Scotland, in England and Wales, the world over, through the ages, wronged. Accused of witchcraft, the trials they faced were the true abomination. *Dunk her*, they would say, *into the river. If she floats, she's a witch. If she drowns, she's innocent.* Kenna shook her head at the barbarity of it. No way out. Not once you'd been accused. You'd be murdered in a number of different ways, but in Scotland they tied you to the stake and burnt you. Not because you were a witch but because they could. Because *they* – the king's men, the judges, the self-appointed marshals – had the licence to do so.

"Kenna, hey, what are you doing? Come on, I need to go into Next. They've got some great shirts, really funky. Why are you just standing there? Staring? Fancy dressing up for me later, do you? I like the idea of a sexy witch. You'd look good in a laced bodice."

Kenna whipped her head around, her eyes blazing, she knew it.

"What? What did you say?"

Adam flinched. "I just said… Look, forget it. Stand there if you want. I'm going in here."

She was glad how quickly he removed himself from her sight, didn't bother to follow him. Instead, she made her way over to a nearby bench to sit there and wait, her head down now, her eyes no longer on the display, unable to bear it, for it was an injustice too.

Of course, that latest dream was why she felt so raw about it all. She just couldn't shake it, the images returning despite efforts to dispel them. Once seen, never forgotten, she supposed. And she had seen. She'd *become*.

Her breathing a little uneven, she lifted her head and caught the eyes of a little girl who was holding her mother's hand. A girl in fancy dress, a witch's costume, of course.

The little girl smiled at Kenna, and Kenna did her utmost to smile back. After she'd passed, Kenna continued to stare after the girl until she disappeared from sight amongst the melee of people, some embracing the season, others not. *The season of the witch.* Samhain. The veil thinning, when at Drumlin it was thin enough already.

"Sorry I kept you waiting. I popped into another couple of shops whilst I was at it."

Adam was back, a couple of carrier bags in his hand.

She shook her head. "That's okay, no worries." In truth, she hadn't noticed the time. Just as it had done in the past couple of days, it had slipped again.

"Fancy that late lunch we talked about?" he continued.

She agreed, despite not feeling hungry at all.

Like Adam, Kenna had no real idea where to eat in Aberdeen, what was considered good and what wasn't, but there was certainly no shortage of places to choose from. In the end, weary of trying to decide, they opted for an Italian restaurant close to the town centre and itself housed in one of the city's famous granite buildings. It was bright and cheerful inside, a contrast to the place she'd visited with Sal, which had been dark and moody and loud. They were shown to a table towards the rear of the restaurant, somewhere quiet. Once seated, Adam reached across to hold her hands, his cheeks still pink from the cold. So different to yesterday, her first instinct was to retract her hands. It took effort not to do so.

"This is great, isn't it?" he enthused.

"What?" she said, despite knowing full well what he meant.

"Us. Being here. Together again. Kenna, I've really missed you."

"When?"

"Huh? What do you mean?"

"When did you start to miss me?"

The colour in his cheeks deepened. "Oh…um…"

"You just cut me off, Adam. Discarded me."

He shook his head, blond hair flopping. "No, I didn't. I tried to explain."

"You explained nothing!"

His grip on her hands tightened. "Kenna, I thought we were okay. Last night…you were glad to see me." He released her. "Look, if I've read this wrong, then sorry."

"You didn't even warn me you were coming."

"I did! Check your phone! I called a few times."

Not believing him, she freed her hands, reached into her bag and rummaged for it. Eventually, she stopped. "I don't seem to have my phone with me."

"Check when we're home, then." The way he said it made her bristle. It was her home, not his. He adopted a gesture of surrender. "I'm trying to make amends," he continued. "That's why I'm here, why I hired a car and drove all this way, through shocking weather too, not least on the approach to the castle. I know I've got a lot of explaining to do, but the simple truth is this: I bottled it, okay? I was scared to leave everything behind."

"But, Adam, I did!"

"I know, I know. What can I say? You're braver than me, clearly." He shrugged. "I'm a coward. I was also very stressed. Work really was getting to me. It was like…like I was *drowning* with work." He hung his head low, Kenna certain that just before he did, his eyes had begun to glisten. "You know what I really think?"

"What?" Her voice was softer than she'd intended.

"I think I had a mini breakdown."

Kenna frowned. Seriously? Was he telling the truth?

Adam lifted his head, held her gaze. She was right. There were tears in his eyes. "There was never anybody else, Kenna, if that's what you're thinking."

She inhaled. That was *exactly* what she'd thought.

Adam reached across again. "Kenna, I love you, *only* you. I've been lost without you. I don't know if I can do it, move up here, leave London entirely despite what I've said, how I encouraged the idea, but if you'll let me, I'll give it my best shot."

He looked so genuine. Everything about him did, his eyes, his expression, the weight of feeling behind his words. He wanted to come back to her, come to Scotland, try living with her, a dream they'd held, or she had *thought* they'd held. And yet he had shut her out, apparently had a breakdown. Hadn't confided in her.

Her hesitation prompted him to release her hands again and gather his bags.

"Adam," she said, alarm bells ringing, "what are you

doing?"

"It's okay. I get it, Kenna, I do. Despite last night, I have read this wrong. I thought we were okay, that you'd missed me as much as I missed you. That somehow, everything that's gone before, the *mistake*, didn't matter anymore. Of course I have to explain, I know that, and I will, I want to, even if I'm having trouble getting my own head around it, but sometimes I suppose there's no turning back. Not if both parties aren't willing to at least try and understand." With Kenna still staring at him, he stood. "I'll take you back to Drumlin, and then I'll leave. You're the one who needs time and space now, not me. And I respect that, I do. I'll drop you back and find a hotel nearby, then head to London in the morning. Hey, I might just drive through the night, not bother stopping at all."

So many words and all being thrown at her, hard to process, except those last few.

She stood up too. "You can't go, Adam! Not tonight."

"Kenna, I said I'll drive you home first. It'll just be easier—"

"No!" she said again, she *shouted*, not caring if she attracted the attention of nearby diners. "You have to stay with me." God, her voice! There was such a whine in it. But no way could he leave her alone at the castle, not again. Not tonight of all nights.

"Adam, I'm sorry. Drive me back to Drumlin, sure, but stay. I can't... Please, Adam!"

Clearly baffled, he sat down again, a hovering waiter heading elsewhere.

"Kenna, what is it? Are you scared or something?"

Should she do it, confide in him when he hadn't confided in her? When she had told no one else, not even

Gregor?

He had to stay, that was all she knew, and so she sat back down too, and the words flew from her mouth about Rohaise and Alexander, the love story, the tragedy, what she thought had happened – to Rohaise, at least – and what had happened to Kenna herself. So many strange things.

"And you think it's her? Rohaise? A ghost?"

When he said it, she wished she'd said nothing. How sceptical he looked!

"No…I don't know. Of course not, but—"

"So if it is Rohaise – odd name, by the way – what's she doing there still?"

"Rose," Kenna said. "That's what Rohaise means. As for what she's doing there…I don't know. Waiting, maybe?"

"For Alexander? For the love of her life to return?"

"Well…yeah, she could be." There was amusement in Adam's eyes, definite amusement. "Oh, Adam, like I said, I don't know. I just imagine stuff sometimes, get—"

"A bit dramatic?" He was going to do it, burst out laughing, but she mustn't get angry.

"Yeah," she admitted at last, "being alone at the castle, I suppose I tend to."

"Kenna," he said, reaching for her again, "of course I'll stay tonight, and tomorrow if you'll let me. I want this to work between us. Little hiccups, we'll get over them."

Little hiccups? The waiter appeared at last, not the one she'd seen hovering but a different one, a tall woman, hair dyed as black as the night, eyes rimmed with kohl and wearing a pointed hat, fitted top, and long black skirt over laced-up boots.

Kenna inhaled again. Witches, witches everywhere. There was no escaping them.

Chapter Twenty-Eight

When they'd reached a distance of five miles from the castle going to Aberdeen, the mist had cleared, revealing a normal day, grey-skied certainly and cold but what was expected for Scotland in autumn. On the journey back, they'd encountered the wall of mist in exactly the same location, building and building the closer they got to Drumlin, the day fading too.

"Can't see a bloody thing," Adam muttered at the wheel. "This weather's ridiculous!"

"You know, London used to get really bad fog too," Kenna told him. "I read about this one time back in the early 1950s when the fog was so bad literally no one could see their hand in front of them. Smog, they called it. Industrial pollution and freak weather conditions caused it, and it hung around for days. Thousands of people died, not just in car and bus accidents but because they *choked* on it."

"Really?" Adam sounded far from convinced. "You sure you're not exaggerating again?"

"I'm not," Kenna declared. "It's all there on the net should you want to educate yourself."

"Maybe." His tone was dismissive, but, as she reminded herself, he was concentrating on the roads. She shouldn't talk to him anymore. Having mentioned car accidents, she was suddenly fearful they might have one too.

The last leg of the journey seemed to take forever.

"Here," Kenna said eventually, her voice hollow in the confines of the car, "turn left."

"How the bloody hell can you tell?" Adam said, obeying her despite his misgivings.

"Because I live here, Adam! I know these roads."

"Just as well," he said, sighing heavily. "You're right, this place is spooky at night."

She should have felt triumphant on hearing that, being validated, but it was just too true to be comforting. Wasn't it? She leant forward and peered through the mist as he was doing, the castle a silhouette, something hazy in the darkness, definitely otherworldly.

"Beautiful," she breathed, surprising herself as well as Adam.

"Beautiful? Really? I don't know, Kenna, perhaps I'll change my mind again, but right now, I'm not feeling it."

She turned to him. "Change your mind again? What do you mean?"

Another sigh. "I just meant it's fine in the day to look at. At night it's different."

"Different how?"

"I don't know. It just is. And it isn't beautiful. It's practically a ruin."

A second time she had to clamp down on a response. What the hell did he expect?

Deciding to change tack, dispel some of the atmosphere between them that hadn't quite abated since dinner, she adopted a smile and snuggled a little closer. "You'll be all right," she said. "I'll protect you."

He laughed, but he also pulled away from her slightly, continued to focus.

She straightened up. "Not far now," she said, wishing she could maintain the joviality in her voice. "Just a few more yards. Park in the front if it's easier. We can walk from there."

"I'll park as close to the flat as possible."

At last, the car came to a halt, their journey at an end and Kenna relieved every bit as much as Adam, although one thing concerned her. At the front of the castle as they'd passed, the light was on in the Rohaise Room – which it hadn't been the previous night, and it was flickering. The lights tended to flicker elsewhere on occasion too, including the wall sconces on the stairway, leading her to conclude it must be dodgy electrics responsible, not just a faulty timer. She'd get it checked out as soon as possible, give Jean a quick call in the morning and ask for details of a preferred electrician.

Now, though, all that mattered was being inside and getting tonight over with.

Out of the car, they started trudging towards the front door when Kenna had an idea.

"Adam, can I have the keys to your car?"

"What? Why?"

"I was sure my mobile was in my bag. I just want to check it didn't fall out whilst I was in the car, been kicked under the seat or something. Sorry, I should have done that already."

"Fair enough," he said as they exchanged keys. "Want me to come with you?"

"I'll be fine. It's just a quick check. Keep the door on the latch. I won't be a moment."

Wrestling the mist again, she returned to the car, feeling down the side of the passenger seat and checking beneath the seats. Eventually, she conceded defeat. The phone wasn't there; it must be in the flat. Apparently, she had several missed calls from Adam, something she mused about as she hurried back. Who else had she missed calls from? The signal really was bad right now. Maybe Jean had checked up on her. Gregor too… Hopefully, he was on the mend. With Gregor here, she felt fine at the castle, safe.

As she closed the door behind her, she pondered further. Didn't she feel safe here tonight with Adam? She felt better than she would have done if alone, granted, but safe? She had to admit she was still nervous. The light, why was it flickering like that? *Always her room. Always her.* She mustn't think about Rohaise, just get drunk instead, her and Adam, put that plan into motion, and the sooner the better. It was already nearing seven, time passing so bloody quickly. *The witching season. The witching hour.* God, these thoughts had to stop! Besides, Rohaise was *not* a witch, just a woman, young and beautiful, who'd laid down her life for someone she'd loved.

Where was her phone? She'd find it, check it, then head to the kitchen and get that first bottle of red open. At the top of the staircase in the living room, she saw Adam had dumped his bags on the sofa and was already in the kitchen.

"You okay?" she called out.

"Yeah, just wondering what we can have for dinner."

She was stunned. He hadn't long tucked away a huge dollop of lasagne followed by tiramisu, and yet here he was, on the prowl again.

"I'll look and see when I come back."

"You've got onions and veg. Shall I start chopping? I can make a soup or something."

"If you want. I'm just going to the bedroom. My phone

must be in there."

"The bedroom?" His voice had a tease in it this time. "Want any company?"

She couldn't help but laugh. Tonight was going to be okay, better than okay; it might even be fun. Because Adam could be fun when he wanted to. He certainly had been when they'd first met, fun and as eager as he was being now. It had waned, though, that eagerness, as it would, she supposed, reminding herself how work pressures had forced them apart. Exactly the reason they – or rather she – had come to Drumlin, for a more relaxed life. A drastic move, no point in pretending otherwise. Could he be blamed for getting cold feet? If she could forgive him, put it all behind her, would they be able to move forward, do as they'd intended? He hadn't been unfaithful, she believed him regarding that, and nor had she. There wasn't that to contend with.

"Kenna? I said do you want some company?"

"Just keep chopping onions," she said, "and pour me a glass of Merlot too, a large one. I'll want some company in the bedroom, just not right now, okay?"

A few moments later and she'd reached her bedroom. She'd walked happily down the long, narrow passageway into the older part of the building, but now she hesitated. In the doorway, staring into the darkness, was that more thunder she could hear outside those floor-to-ceiling windows? The storm that had threatened yesterday had moved on. Had another come to take its place?

One hand reached out to flick on the light switch. Darkness remained. Frowning, she tried again, turning it off, then on, but no joy. There were several lights in the chandelier. Had one of them blown and fused the others?

ROHAISE

She ventured further into the room, leaving the door open so that light from the passageway could filter in, at least. She made her way over to the bed, its sheets still rumpled from earlier. She could have left the phone on the bedside table. It wasn't there, though, forcing her to go deeper still. Such a big room, vast, as Adam had called it, fit for a queen. All the rooms at the castle were, intended for nobility, and yet here she was, an ordinary person living there. Rohaise too, a commoner, a peasant, a child of the forest.

You don't know that! Again, she chided herself for joining the dots. That was the trouble, she supposed, with a figure as smoky as the mist; there was that temptation.

Where the hell was her phone? She might have to get Adam to ring it if it remained lost. Whether it would ring, though, was another matter, the signal being weak.

Thunder. Definitely. A burst of it making her jump. Thunder *and* the darkness. She really wanted to sort out the lighting. Fresh bulbs, and the fuse box, were in the castle, in the office. Abandoning her search for the phone, she retraced her footsteps back to a lamp beside her bed and flicked the switch on that. Nothing. Leaving her bedroom, she went into one of the spare bedrooms, the one Gregor had slept in. There was a lamp in there that worked when she tried it. She unplugged it and brought it back to her bedroom. It worked again, indicating that circuit at least was okay, but the light was disappointingly low.

Her sigh was heavy. Could she make do with just this lamp tonight, fetch the bulbs for the chandelier in the morning? She could, but…it was different now. If she went to the castle, she wouldn't be going alone or with someone as nervous as her, as Sal had been. She had Adam, no-

nonsense Adam, the least fanciful person she knew, in his rightful place at last, by her side. Whilst there, she could check the light in the Rohaise Room, unplugging it for safety's sake. *It's your job, Kenna, to take care of the castle.*

Her mind made up, she tried one last thing regarding her phone. The dressing table, it must be there. She crossed back into the heart of the room, then to the far end, where the curtains were open, more darkness bleeding in.

It was so dark, and yet she could make out just the outline of her reflection as she approached the mirror that hung over the dressing table, a mirror she'd stared into on so many occasions. Just an outline, a mere hint of herself but compelling even so, her eyes drawn to it, the shape of her hair as it cascaded to her shoulders, one side of her body more defined than the other, the slimness of her waist – very slim, actually, as if she'd lost weight. A slight figure, although she never really thought of herself like that. She was tall; she had curves, but now she looked…delicate. She stopped and squinted. Something else about her reflection was off. She was wearing jeans, but it was as though her figure flared from the waist downwards, like she was wearing a dress.

A trick of the light. Or rather, a trick of the dark. But as she continued to eye the image in the mirror, two words came to mind, words she hadn't summoned: *half awake.* Strange words, words that held no meaning, no context. What was half awake, exactly?

She lifted a hand, an almost involuntary reaction, and reached out. The reflection did the same, nothing odd about that, at least.

"Who are you? Could it be… Is it…?"

"Kenna? What are you doing?"

Adam's voice startled her.

"What the hell?" she said, spinning round. "Why are you creeping up on me like that?"

Immediately, he protested. "I wasn't! I just wanted to see what was taking you so long, that's all. Have you found your phone? Why are you in darkness?"

He walked over to the light switches and, as she'd done, kept flicking them on and off.

"Shit, have they blown or something? And is that thunder I can hear? Are we going to have ourselves a Halloween storm?"

"Yep, the lights have blown, and, yep, I heard thunder too, but it sounds distant."

"Did you find your phone?"

She turned back to the dressing table. "It's got to be here somewhere."

She was right – it was.

Relieved about that, at least, she immediately checked the screen for missed calls and texts. Blank. It was still offline.

Adam was talking again. "What are we going to do about the lights? Leave them?"

We.

Glancing back at the mirror, seeing an outline still, *just* an outline, no flared skirt, no strange words forming in her mind to unsettle her further, she found herself grinning.

"Nope," she said, approaching Adam, "*we* are not going to leave them. You wanted a tour of the castle, didn't you? I think now may be the perfect time."

Chapter Twenty-Nine

"Can you help me?" Kenna said, having to shove her shoulder against the door to the castle, which, courtesy of rain and mist, had swollen, resisting her more than ever.

"Sure," Adam replied, giving it a hefty push. "Hope the lights work in here, at least."

"Believe me, so do I," Kenna answered as they entered.

Having switched on the lights, Adam frowned.

"Hmm…" he said. "They work after a fashion."

She nodded, as dismayed as him at how the darkness soaked up the light, denied it.

"Reception and the office are just over here," Kenna continued.

"I thought we were going to have a tour of the castle first?" Adam protested.

"Well…um…" It had seemed like a good idea back at the flat, a *benign* idea, an opportunity to test the waters, to prove to herself that with Adam by her side she'd be far braver, not so prone to imaginings. But now that she was actually inside the castle, she was changing her mind. She wanted to check the fuse box, grab the bulbs and then go. "Oh, hang on, wait," she said, wincing slightly. "The Rohaise Room, we have to go there, at least."

"Where's the Rohaise Room?"

"On the sixth floor."

"How many floors are there in total?"

"Eight including the attic rooms."

"Okay, so if we have to go all the way up there, give me the tour."

Although she felt hesitant still, courage remaining on the wane, she'd do as he asked and deliver the quick version. They had dinner to make and wine to drink, activities far more preferable than trying to prove some stupid point to herself.

"Follow me," she said, moving towards the archway. Briefly stopping, she pointed to the left, tried to slow her words down, appear more confident. "Over there is the kitchen, the café and the toilets, the nuts and bolts of the castle, if you like. Connor and Laura work there. They're local, from Tulce. They're full-time in spring and summer but otherwise part-time. It's a rota that suits them, as they've other things to occupy them."

"Right, okay," Adam said genially enough. "Loving the swords on the wall, and the stag's head. Wonder who brought him down?"

"Francis Buchannan, allegedly, in the sixteenth century, just before he was exiled."

"Nice work."

As she climbed the stairs, a feeling that was all too familiar bloomed in her chest. Agitation. *No need to be nervous.* The words repeated like a mantra in her head but had very little impact. Adam, at least, seemed completely unfazed, reassuringly blasé.

They covered the main hall, the anterooms, Queen Mary's Bower, the sitting room, the dining room and the library, where Adam started messing about, lifting his hands as though he were a spook and declaring he was the monk returned.

"So, tell me again, who was it who insisted a body was buried in the wall?"

"A local girl, apparently. She was a teenager at the time."

"And they took her seriously?"

"Well, yeah, and just as well because she was right. Some strange things had happened in this room before his body was discovered, items being moved or going missing, phantom footsteps, that kind of thing. Once they liberated him and had him buried properly on consecrated ground, it all stopped."

"So is the castle haunted or not?" When she failed to answer, he prompted her. "Kenna, do you think Drumlin's haunted by this, what's her name, Rohaise?"

How could she answer? *Truthfully* answer? Despite what she'd said in the restaurant, she didn't know what to think.

Adam burst out laughing. "For God's sake, Kenna, you don't really think ghosts are real, do you? That stuff with the monk was probably all made up."

"I don't think it was."

"Well, even if it was true and they found a body—"

"Adam, I've told you, they did!"

"Okay, but all that stuff about spooky happenings beforehand, it's just nonsense."

She was intrigued. "How can you be so sure?"

"Because ghosts don't exist, Kenna, that's how. You've talked about Rohaise, but have you ever seen her? Seen any type of bloody ghost?"

"I—"

"No, you haven't, and nor have I, and nor has anyone else I've ever known. The kind of people that insist they exist are usually bonkers, those bizarre New Age types."

"Right, okay," she breathed, part angry with him but hanging on to his words too.

"If they plonked a monk's body in the wall—"

"His name was Joseph Buchannan," she said, wanting to respect his memory, at least, especially as they were standing in what was tantamount to his former burial site.

"Okay, well, if they interred him here during the Reformation to hide him, to keep him safe as a family member, then that makes sense." He reached out and lightly thumped the wall. "A body has to be put somewhere, so why not in these walls? It's macabre, but...you know, they're thick enough. There's plenty of room if you hollow them out. But all that stuff about his spirit being restless and Rohaise's too, don't buy into it, Kenna. Amuse the punters with it, sure, dress it up for them, but otherwise recognise it for the bollocks it is."

"Fine, I do, okay? Look, can we get on, get this over and done with?"

"Because you're scared?"

He was teasing, she knew it, but she was becoming less and less soothed by his attitude. "Because I want to get back to the flat and have a glass of wine! That's why."

"All right, keep your hair on."

The tour of the remaining floors was not only brief, it was curt, Kenna unable to keep any further irritation from her voice but Adam, as far as she could tell, oblivious. By the time they'd reached the sixth floor, his attention was clearly dwindling.

"I'll just unplug the lamp," she said, "then we'll go back down to the office."

"Sure," he said, following her into the room and doing as Sal had done, wandering around and touching stuff. "So this Rohaise, she was top totty, then?"

Kenna swung round to face him. She'd turned the lamp off, but on her way in had switched the main lights on, saw that they were flickering too. Just what was going on?

"Um…yeah, I've told you this. She was the mistress of Alexander Buchannan, a man who, according to what little we know of him, was betrayed. We don't know who by, but someone suggested his loyalty lay with someone other than the reigning king."

"Alexander Buchannan, who fled to France?"

"Um…I don't know where he went," she said, frowning as the main lights flickered again.

"And her name means 'rose'."

"Yep."

"Hence the roses on the bedposts and the quilt?"

"That's right."

"All in her honour."

"Uh-huh."

"And this is the original bed?"

Kenna nodded.

"Must have seen some action!"

Her eyes on him rather than the lights, her mouth fell open. Adam could be a bit of a lad. Now, though, he was being downright crass. "Adam, can we just get out—"

Her phone, which she'd pocketed before leaving the flat, began to ping, the sound of several messages coming through at last.

"Hang on," she continued. "I think I've got a signal."

Sure enough, when she looked at her phone, Adam turning from her whilst she did so, continuing to run his hands over items of furniture and, similar to Sal, with no reverence at all, no damned respect, she could see that he had indeed tried to call her – not several times, though, as he'd claimed, just the once. More of interest were the missed calls from Gregor, so many of them but also texts, which she hurried to open.

I tried calling, but u not picking up. I've something to tell u. Something I think you'll find very interesting. As had time on hands, I've done more research. I'd like to tell u face-to-face what I've found. Actually, scrub that, I NEED to tell u face-to-face. Hope u ok.

The second text was etched with more worry.

Kenna, u ok? Call me as soon as poss. We have to talk.

The third and fourth more urgent still.

Is your signal dipping in and out? Why u not responding? Look, I'm coming round, my ankle's not as bad, am sure will be ok to drive. See u this afternoon.

Checking the time Gregor had sent the text, it was late this morning. Likely, he *had* called round, but she'd been in Aberdeen with Adam. He'd have seen the Volvo, though, in its usual parking space and might have been puzzled further by that.

There was yet another text, and so, with Adam now staring at himself in the mirror, pulling a variety of stupid faces, she continued to read.

Not sure where u gone in this mist. It's so thick around the castle! Searched the grounds and edges of forest, just in case u gone there, but somehow don't think so. Christ! Hope u okay, that there's a good explanation for all this, that'll put my mind at rest. Because it isn't at rest. Not at all. Call me!

The text continued, her heart thumping louder and louder in her chest, a sound to rival any clap of thunder. Just what had got him so riled?

I found mention of Alexander Buchannan at last. Not him,

exactly, someone related. I printed the page and brought it over to u. A piece of the puzzle solved! I posted it through your door, then wished I hadn't.

The text ended, but another followed it.

Since I got home, I've had the strangest feeling. I should have waited till we could talk about this not just face-to-face but away from castle. Call me stupid, but I really am uneasy about this revelation. Just stuff the envelope in your bag and come here. If u haven't opened it yet, DON'T. If u have, keep it to yourself. If ghosts exist, and I'm not saying they do, Rohaise doesn't need to know. Come over asap. Please.

No more texts, and what did he mean he'd posted something through her door? He hadn't. Not to her knowledge.

She lifted her head and called over to Adam, remembering he'd gone into the flat first. If there was something waiting for her, he'd have seen it.

"Adam, did you find an envelope for me when we got home?"

He faced her. "An envelope? Yeah, there was one."

"Why didn't you let me know?"

"I was going to. I took it into the kitchen with me and then...forgot about it."

She sighed with relief. That was good. Intrigued by what Gregor had said, she would indeed go to him first thing in the morning to hear the full story, Adam could give her a lift. Strange, though, that he'd mentioned ghosts. *Her* ghost. Rohaise's.

She had closed the gap between herself and Adam when it sank in, what Adam had said. She'd told him about Rohaise, blurted so much stuff out, fact as well as the fiction she'd created, but never had she mentioned France as being the place Alexander might have sought refuge. Was he assuming too? Or…

"Adam, that envelope you found…"

"Uh-huh," he said, heading for the door.

"It was addressed to me, right?"

He turned. "Um…yeah."

"It was addressed to me, but you opened it?"

Twin spots of pink flared on his cheeks.

"It wasn't stuck down properly," he defended. "Barely at all, in fact."

"So you read it?"

"I did, yeah. Look, Kenna—"

"That's how you know about Alexander and France?"

"Well…yeah."

"Right. Okay." So he *had* escaped, something Rohaise had wanted. Good news. So why was Gregor so worried? Whatever the reason, she'd find out soon. The very next day.

Her hand reaching for the light switch, she faltered when Adam continued talking.

"So this man Rohaise was screwing—"

"Adam!"

"Sorry, this man, this *lover* she had"—he stressed the word 'lover', again making a mockery of it—"she was besotted with him, right?"

"Well, yeah, I'd say so, you know, if she died for him!"

"Yeah, yeah, she sacrificed herself, all for the love of Alexander."

"Look, we need to go, okay? Get back to the flat in case the storm gets closer."

"Sure, it's just a shame, that's all."

She frowned. What was he talking about now? "What is?"

"That he didn't feel the same," Adam blithely continued. "That if she really does haunt this castle, you know, hanging around for him, so to speak, the love of her life – and her death—" here he chuckled, pleased with the joke he'd made "—it's all in vain."

"Adam…" She stopped, lowered her hand by her side, leaving the lights on. There it was again, a strange smell rising up, the smell of something charred, something…rotten. Her heart hammering again, becoming a wild thing, she swallowed hard. "Adam, don't—"

Adam, though, carried on grinning, carried on talking. "What was in that envelope—"

"Adam, please—"

"Was a snippet, photocopied from a book, it looked like. About Alexander, Mr Lover Lover Man. He made it out alive, to France, married there and had children, six daughters! One of them was famous, Grace Buchannan. That's it, yeah, her name was Grace. She wrote chamber music, was some kind of prodigy, apparently. So, yep, Alexander escaped, lived to a ripe old age off his child's earnings, then was buried in France right alongside his wife, his *beloved* wife, it said. Never returned to Scotland, to Rohaise. Forgot all about her." As Kenna stared at him, unable to respond at all now, he continued. "Poor Rohaise. She should have run, shouldn't she? When she had the chance. Perhaps she can rest in peace now, though, eh? Because if Alexander didn't return when he was alive to honour the sacrifice she'd made, he sure as hell ain't gonna now, five hundred years later!"

Silence at last. A heavy, heavy silence.

And then it was broken by a roar, an almighty roar, one that made the windows rattle as well as all the teeth in

Kenna's head. Not thunder, but certainly thunderous. Words filling her mind, just as they'd done before.

Wide awake.

Chapter Thirty

"What the hell? What's going on?"

If Kenna was wide-eyed, so was Adam. Again he shouted, trying to make himself heard, demanding to know what was happening just as the lights failed in the Rohaise Room, as they burst, every single one of them in the chandelier, raining down glass.

Kenna grabbed Adam's hand. "Come on! Move! Now!"

She hauled him towards the door and through it, just as it slammed shut behind them. Not just a roar, there was a scream, so high-pitched it caused them both to skid to a grinding halt, to lift their hands to their ears and try to block it out. Crashing. Banging. Coming from back in there. Something was flung to the floor to no doubt lie in a broken heap. The room being torn apart as it had been torn apart before, by a ghost, by a force, an energy that *had* survived, long after its earthly body had been destroyed.

Rohaise. She'd been asleep, then had half woken. Because of Kenna, perhaps? Another redhead from another time, who'd become immediately fascinated with her, that fascination becoming obsession and that obsession disturbing her slumber. And now this. She was wide awake, Adam's words dragging her into full consciousness. A revelation that should never have come about, not at Drumlin and certainly not in the Rohaise Room.

ROHAISE

"We need to keep moving," Kenna continued, though her legs felt rooted to the spot.

"I don't understand." Adam's voice was tremulous. "Tell me what's going on."

"Not here. Not now. Too much has already been said."

One hand on the rope, the other still holding Adam, she forced them both down the staircase. They had to get out of the castle, to his car, and – despite the mist – get far, far away. Drumlin was no longer safe, if it ever had been.

A few steps down and she heard a creak, the door to the Rohaise Room opening.

"She's coming," she whispered. "Oh shit, she's coming."

What could she do? What should she say? Shout out loud that Adam had embellished the truth? Reference might have been found regarding Alexander, but surely never that he'd forgotten Rohaise. That he'd *forsaken* her. His actions, though, suggested otherwise.

"Come on," she urged.

They continued to flee, past various floors with various rooms, all of which seemed alive to Kenna now, as if not just Rohaise had woken but other things that had slumbered too, following her example and all so dark in nature.

Had Alexander made a promise to Rohaise that he'd return, he'd come back, one way or the other? It made sense if he had, their last moments together so intense. She could picture the scene, despite striving to focus only on escape: *Promise me you'll return, one day, somehow. Don't leave me waiting here alone.* And promise he had. *I promise, ma cridhe, ma cridhe fiadhaich.* Those last words, what did they even mean? She'd never heard them before. And yet the answer came: *I promise my heart, my wild heart.*

He *had* promised, but he hadn't acted on it. And she had

died for him, in agony, in one of the worst ways possible but also in good faith, because she never doubted him, not once. That belief alone had been her reasoning for the agony, assuaging her anger at how vilely she'd been treated. Now, though, there was nothing to subdue or justify it.

Having reached the bottom of the stairs, Kenna tripped and nearly fell. Only her tight hold on the rope was enough to keep her on her feet.

"The door, head for the door," she said, Adam taking the lead now, obeying her.

There was light downstairs, but the minute they took a step forward and left the staircase, those bulbs shattered too.

"Keep going," Kenna insisted. No matter about the light; they didn't need it. She knew well enough the distance that remained. Movement. A shadow. Something standing by the entrance. Could she trust her eyes? Was it truly there? The darkness played tricks. It had done so several times before. Not this time, though. It *was* a shadow. Waiting.

"Stop!"

The command in her voice was enough to halt Adam.

"What now?"

"There." Lifting her hand, she pointed. "Don't you see it?"

He looked back towards the entrance, their means of escape.

"A shadow, a woman." Kenna swallowed. "It's…it's her. Rohaise."

"Rohaise?" Adam repeated. "She's dead, Kenna, fucking dead! Died hundreds of years ago. I told you, I don't believe in ghosts!"

She took her eyes off the shadow, just for a moment. "And yet you ran just as hard and as quickly as I did. Ghosts exist, and this castle is haunted. By her."

Adam looked back towards the entrance, struggling to see, craning his neck.

"Rohaise," she whispered. "I'm sorry."

Apologies from her were meaningless, failed to quell the anger that burned.

"We can't get out that way," she told Adam. "She's blocking the doorway."

"She's not there!" he insisted. "No one is!"

As if he were the one desperate to prove himself, he darted forwards but soon stopped, then backtracked. He did so because the shadow had broken loose from the umbra to become something quite separate. Petite, feminine, but oh so dangerous, a blackened thing, drifting towards them leisurely, as if it had all the time in the world to torment them, and it would, it knew how to, had *imbibed* the lesson.

Kenna about-turned. "This way," she said, heading back towards the archway.

At first, he resisted. "No! Not further into the castle. We have to get out!"

"Adam"—how bleak her voice sounded—"we've got no choice."

To pass beneath the archway took all her courage, all her strength. Rohaise was by the entrance, she'd seen her, but something was also descending the staircase, again with a slowness that ached, that terrified Kenna further, the certainty of that movement. For this was her territory, Rohaise's. She knew every inch. And, as a witch might do, those of old, she'd conjured the mist that engulfed the castle to hamper them further.

Kenna mustn't look at the thing on the stairs, tried not to, but it caught her eye, something that jerked and writhed and twisted.

"Oh, come on, come on," she was muttering, an instruction to herself as well as Adam to keep going through the darkness, towards the rear of the castle, to the café and kitchen. A tradesman's door to the outside yard was there, the key to it in a drawer somewhere. How she wished she knew exactly where! She'd find it, though. She had to. Or what? In an illogical situation, logic still tried to succeed. *A ghost can't harm you.* Something incorporeal, of no substance. The shadow at the entrance, the movement on the stair, that was all too real, though, what lay outside Drumlin – normality – the fantasy.

Adam yowled as he collided with a chair in the café, then went tumbling over the top of it. The flagstones would not make for a soft landing. Having to force herself to stop, Kenna returned to help him, not so much lifting as yanking him to his feet.

"My ankle," he said. "I've twisted it or something."

"I don't care," Kenna hissed back. "You move. Now. We have to get out of here."

"This fucking place! What's wrong with it? If it's haunted, why did you bring me here, at night on fucking Halloween? What's wrong with you?"

The lightbulbs. It seemed such a poor reason now. A sorrowful excuse. She'd been putting herself to the test, but more than that, *worse* than that, she'd been testing Rohaise.

She lifted her head and looked beyond Adam. No way was it her imagination this time, the shadow following them, feeding off their fear, gorging itself.

Rohaise, what has love done to you?

Something so bright, so beautiful, so full of joy, once so glorious, now the very opposite.

A shadow, that's all she was, but Kenna recalled too well the woman she'd seen in her dream and all that had been done to her, that she'd withstood. All for the love of Alexander. A man who had been both betrayed and the betrayer.

"Follow me, Adam, to the kitchen. It's a key we're looking for, okay? To the back door."

Howling again, Adam scrambled after her, his movements awkward too.

In the kitchen, she pulled open a drawer, instructing him to do likewise.

"It's where Connor keeps the key, in one of the drawers." She cursed again that she couldn't remember which one. The devil was always in the detail.

The Devil's Mistress.

If Adam had yelped before, now she did as more words formed in her head.

That's what they called me.

She swung around to the doorframe, knew what she'd see there – her. Were those Rohaise's words? They had to be, more and more of them tumbling in, witchcraft indeed.

The Devil's Whore! And I railed against them, said it wasn't so. I was his mistress, Alexander Buchannan's, and I was proud to be. But they were right. And I was wrong. I was the Devil's Mistress after all. I'm everything they said I was.

Kenna couldn't speak, her voice as terrified a thing as she was and trying to hide.

Where was the key? As frantically as she searched, she couldn't locate it. And Rohaise, done with talking, was moving closer, something else behind her, another version of her, another aspect, what she was and what she had become.

"Where the fuck is it?" Finding her voice at last, Kenna flung the words out.

Adam also yelled. "Got it! I think I've got it."

Kenna raced over to him and took the key from his hands, hers shaking every bit as much as his. Fearful she'd drop it, she tried to steady her hand as she jabbed it at the lock. The first attempt failed. Spectacularly. The key did indeed clatter to the floor.

"Kenna! What the hell?"

"Hang on, wait."

She daren't turn around, see if the shadows were nearer still. Maybe, though, all this was in vain. Maybe there was nothing they could do but succumb. As frantic as she was, as hard as she jabbed the key at the lock again and again, part of her was beginning to admit defeat, to look at the horror unfolding with something akin to blessed detachment. She and Adam, in the castle, trying to escape, shadows at their backs, full of anger and vengeance, a vengeance sparked with careless words, words that meant nothing to them but so much to Rohaise, that had not just parted the veil but ripped it, right down the middle. Could they fight this? Her wrath?

"Kenna, there's something behind us! Oh shit! What is it? Come on, hurry up! It's coming closer. Oh my God, what is it?"

Adam's voice was at fever pitch and yet so far away. All she could truly hear was the sound of her own heaving chest, the breaths being wrung from her as she tried, maybe for the last time, to find purchase with the key, for it to do its job.

Open, will you? Just fucking open!

Something clicked, Adam's hand shooting out almost simultaneously.

He was out the door before her, calling for her to follow, to hurry.

She had to hurry. The shadows *were* closer. She could feel the heat of them. If they touched, she'd be branded too, physically *and* mentally, dragged back into the darkness, to linger for how long? Time truly was of no consequence here.

Hurry, Kenna, get out!

She told herself this, tried to return to full consciousness, not keep hiding somewhere deep inside, but her legs still wouldn't obey. The mist, the *unnatural* mist, did it offer another hiding place, or was it nothing but a trap? Rohaise waiting at every turn.

"Kenna!"

Adam's voice reached her just as something else did, something scorching.

"I'm coming! Wait for me. I'm coming," Kenna shouted, galvanised at last.

Chapter Thirty-One

"Adam? Adam, where are you?"

She was in the grounds of Drumlin, logic told her that, common sense, but all she could see was grey mist, so thick it obscured all else. No sign of anyone, living or dead.

Her chest sore with the effort it took to breathe, she forced herself to calm. Rohaise knew these grounds well, but so did Kenna. She'd walked them every day for months, seen them go from something wild to naturally ordered, flowers blooming, roses too.

Roses have thorns. Something she'd thought before.

Scanning her surroundings, trying to orientate herself, she felt dizzy when she stopped and no more enlightened as to which direction she faced. A leap of faith was called for; she had to pick a direction and just walk, keep going, her hands held out for balance, and hope and pray she ended up at her flat, her only sanctuary at Drumlin. *Her* space, not Rohaise's, and yet was it really a refuge? She'd seen Rohaise even there.

Not her flat, then, Adam's car. That's what she needed to reach, still in the same direction, parked close by on the gravel there. That's where he'd be heading too, surely? The keys were in the lobby. She'd thrown them in the dish after she'd returned from searching the car for her phone, had kept the door on the latch too.

ROHAISE

Gravel. She looked down. She'd have to rely on it, the feel of the ground beneath her feet and the sound of each step. She could sense the familiarity of the path as it stretched onwards, relished the crunch her boots made against it. It grew softer and deeper at the borders, so she'd stick close to the middle, relieved she'd formed a plan of sorts.

"Adam." She whispered rather than shouted his name, fearful of what she'd attract. "Where are you?"

As she walked, she couldn't help but reach up to the part of her shoulder that the entity had touched, immediately extracting her hand because it *was* burnt, Rohaise's touch the touch of fire.

A sob escaped her. This was crazy. Was she truly awake or dreaming again? Fingers pinched at the skin on the back of her hand now. That pain was real enough too. How could this happen? How was any of it possible? *Ghosts don't exist!* That's what Adam had said. Even Gregor was hesitant in his belief of them. *I'm not saying ghosts exist.* He'd written that in his text, or something like it. Yet he'd been worried about what he'd found, about it being revealed on Rohaise's turf, the consequences of it.

"Rohaise is dead!"

The words burst from her. She *was* dead, and yet she was here, the castle not just haunted but *savagely* haunted, a building that had stood for ten centuries, that housed more than history. It housed *her*. It was a bridge between the past and the present, both of which had collided on this, the darkest of autumnal nights.

Have a taste of my despair, drink deep!

Violently she shook her head, tried to dispel what infiltrated it.

"Your despair is not mine! It's nothing to do with me!"

Words that were in vain, for Rohaise would not listen. She was beyond listening. Kenna definitely had to reach the car. Find Adam and leave here for good.

On and on she walked, straining to make out the castle at least, rising above the mist, towering over it, as steadfast as ever no matter what had occurred there. Rohaise wasn't the only one to have died at Drumlin over the course of so many years; plenty would have taken their last breath there. When Kenna had flown down the stairs earlier, trying to escape, she'd thought the castle was alive with those others, that they had woken too. Was it true? Or was it her imagination, not numbed but enhanced by this terrible situation. Yes, plenty of people would have died at Drumlin, but had anyone died the way Rohaise had, so cruelly? Had they felt the keen sting of betrayal as much?

She shook her head. Only Rohaise. Rohaise, who had been sleeping until Kenna's arrival, Kenna's *obsession*, had started to wake her, only to discover something that would torture her more, tearing not just Rohaise apart but all of them here tonight.

For that's what she intended, to extend her suffering.

Kenna walked faster, the crunch of the gravel still in her ears. She'd left the castle by a side door; her flat was at the back. Pray God she was walking the right way.

Nothing lay ahead, it seemed. No log store, no ruined chapel, no dovecote. There was a low wall at the front of the castle, but that had vanished too. Suspended. That's what she was. In the mist. The world having shrunken to a pinpoint.

Keep going. It was all she could do. She couldn't wander forever, though, alone like this. Something was bound to happen sooner or later.

Tears streamed down her face. In this moment, she *hated* Rohaise for what she was putting them through, but she also hated herself for hating her, because could Rohaise be blamed? The dream she'd had, it wasn't merely that; it was an *insight*, a glimpse of the truth, a snapshot, and that had been bad enough, had left her shaken to the core. But for Rohaise, it had been days and days of suffering, enough to break anyone but not her, not quite. Only the truth had done that, only Alexander.

"You shit!" she swore under her breath, for wasn't her hate, her blame, misdirected? "She died for you, waited for you, right here at Drumlin. You promised you'd come back, whatever happened. One way or the other, you'd find a way, but you didn't. You left, and you left for good. She died for you. She loved you. Did you truly love her?"

A scream! One so wracked with grief and so near.

Kenna shut her mouth, clamped it tight. She mustn't say such things and bait her further. She might not be able to see her, but Rohaise was all around her. She was also *in* her somehow, privy to her thoughts and feelings, just as Kenna had been privy to hers. The castle was a bridge between past and present, but also two redheads.

Kenna broke into a jog. She had to reach Adam and find the car. How long had she been in the mist? An age. Too long. Time slipping away again…or in reverse? Other sounds emerged, those she dreaded as much as Rohaise's screams, for they were the sounds of men, an army, laughing and heckling and grunting. Something else too, crackling and hissing, the flames that would eventually consume the woman they'd called a witch, the mist more like smoke now, much thicker, entering her lungs and making her cough, their laughter only increasing. More than a snapshot, she was living it, Rohaise's past, not only choking, her skin felt like it was blistering. Kenna reached out to look at her hands. The skin was bubbling and cracking. Soon it would split open, blood frothing over.

At the sight of it, she screamed, as loud and as piercing as Rohaise.

"No! No! No!"

She was no witch. She would not burn.

It makes no difference.

She heard Rohaise's scathing reply, ignored it, ran faster, trying to put distance between herself and this other world that had manifested, no longer hearing the gravel crunch but only Rohaise as she repeated, *No difference at all.*

Not Adam's face, it was Gregor's she kept in mind, his gentleness, his earnestness, wishing he were here, that he had come to save her – knowing, though, if there was to be salvation tonight, it would be at no one else's hands but her own. *If…*

"Kenna!"

She started. Someone was calling her name! A male voice. Adam.

"Kenna, where are you? I'm at the car."

Was it true what she was hearing? Not just wishful thinking? Adam was near, had reached the car. They might just pull this off and escape!

"Oh God," she breathed as more sobs left her. "Oh God! Oh God! Oh God!"

Just when she'd thought it was hopeless, hope had arrived.

"Adam! I'm here!" Her voice was a weak thing, nowhere near as loud as it should be, the result of the smoke she'd inhaled. *Not smoke, mist, it's just mist*, she told herself. She had to call again, louder this time. "Adam! Adam! I'm here."

"Kenna?" Miraculously, he *had* heard her. "Is that you? Come on! I'm at the car."

"I am, I'm coming!" Damn her voice for still being so weak, but he'd heard her; that was all that mattered. He knew she was still alive, still out there. "Wait for me. I'm close. Really close. Keep calling, and I'll follow your voice."

"Kenna! Kenna! Ken—"

Silence again, all other sounds dying too.

"Adam? Adam, what's the matter? Where are you?"

The irony if they were within a hair's breadth of each other! If only she could see him. If only he'd keep calling. What had happened to make him stop?

Another sound burst into life, one that struck both hope and dread in her, that of the car engine turning over.

Adam had not only found the car, he was *in* the car. That was good, that was hopeful. So why the dread? Why was it increasing?

If the engine was running, there'd be headlights. Twin beams that would slice through the mist. She'd be able to spot them.

"Adam!" Another croak but growing stronger. "Adam! Adam!"

No answer, not anymore. But a low rumbling, not thunder, that of tyres over gravel. He was in the car, and he was driving. Of course he was. Searching for her still. Wasn't he?

Again, she was running, listening only for the car, blocking out sounds from a dim and distant past that were once again returning – focusing only on the present, on the moment, visualising herself already within the confines of the car, safe, completely. Leaving the grounds of Drumlin, the castle and the forest, all the pine trees, far behind.

Trees… A few lined the driveway, as did stone ruins of past buildings. Adam would need to be careful driving in this mist, resist the urge to put his foot down. She'd tell him that when she was in the car with him. "Go carefully," she'd say. "She can't hurt us, not now. But even so, go carefully, Adam. You've got to."

At last, she saw them, twin lights flickering as flames might, as the castle lights sometimes did. Not flames, though, she reminded herself, a light that would save rather than devour her. That was coming closer, her already outstretched hands waving madly so Adam would see her.

"Here! Here!" she called, panting again but with hope, crazy hope.

Still the lights were inching towards her and then, what…? It looked as if they swung away, were disappearing. Was Adam turning the car around? Had he not seen her after all?

The lights did indeed disappear, replaced by red, those at the rear, quickly retreating too. She was right; he *was* driving away. Abandoning her. *Because he hasn't seen me*, she reminded herself. *He doesn't know where I am. He's still looking for me.*

She cursed the mist, the very ground she stood on, for it was exactly that, cursed ground, and something in her had known it all along, felt it, from the minute she'd arrived. The castle, the monolith, it must be to her right. A powerful mist if it could hide even that.

A burst of grizzled laughter shook her. It was so close to her ear. A cry followed, one that could break your heart. More hissing, crackling, *sizzling*. A fate no man should foist upon another, that no woman should ever have to suffer.

The car was getting away. She had to run faster.

On the driveway, certain that she was, Kenna was running and screaming, begging Adam to stop, to give her a chance, not leave her alone again.

The further she ran, the more she could see, the mist finally clearing with each step she put between herself and the castle. By the side of the driveway were the trees that lined it, easily spotted now, evidence of the ruined buildings too, including the one that Sal had thought she'd seen someone by once, a figure of some description, and the car, there it was, crawling along but not stopping. Showing absolutely no sign of stopping.

"Adam!" She continued waving her arms, a frantic thing. "Stop! You have to!"

The car was visible, *perfectly* visible. Which meant she was visible too. All he had to do was glance in the rearview or side mirrors. If he was searching for her, he'd be doing just that. His eyes scouring the grounds. *You fucking bastard! Stop!*

She slowed as the car slowed too, as it came to a halt. He'd seen her at last. He would either wait for her or reverse, lessen the gap between them. Hope flared in her once more, as did guilt for doubting him. Of course he wouldn't abandon her! He loved her, had come back to her, finally, wanting to be with her. And she loved him, she did.

Relief, like adrenalin, fuelled her. She was almost there, almost…a few more metres, that was all. They'd leave and never come back, figure out their future elsewhere.

"Never come back," she muttered. "Never, never, never."

All words stopped. There was something behind her. She couldn't see it – her eyes were trained solely ahead – but she could sense it, stronger than ever. She could *smell* it, the stench of something putrid that had been left to rot, but not before the flesh on it had been torn, carved into and blackened. If Rohaise should reach out again, touch her...

Kenna hurled herself forwards, stumbled, then righted herself. The thing at her back, which love had destroyed, which *truth* had, effortlessly kept pace. The car waited, and Adam could see her, she *knew* he could, his head having turned towards the rearview mirror, his eyes trained on the reflective glass. He would know how desperate she was and in how much danger. But he'd do it; he would save her. This thing behind her, this abomination, it belonged here, not in the world that existed outside. It couldn't follow.

The safety of the car was so close.

A car whose engine fired again, that sped off, Kenna herself practically sprinting now as the gap that had been closing once again became wide – *extraordinarily* wide.

Adam was driving *away* from her. Abandoning her after all. Doing so because if he had seen Kenna in the rearview, he'd also seen Rohaise.

"ADAM!" Outrage powered her voice this time. "You bastard!"

Blinded by tears, fear swallowing any sense of relief, she stumbled a second time and fell to the ground. She was powerless now, completely spent. She'd burn like Rohaise had burnt. The shadow, the ghost of her, would see to that, refusing to burn alone.

Have a taste of my despair, drink deep!

Her hands coming over her head, Kenna cowered, waiting...waiting...only once lifting her eyes to gaze at the car ahead approaching the bend, taking it way too fast. Something else she spied, in front of the car. The same something that had been behind her? She dared to peek over her shoulder, all the while whimpering. There was nothing but darkness, the mist weaving its way through it, encroaching again. No hateful figure widening its arms to cover her, but *that* figure – the one in front of the car – had thrown its arms wide, flesh pale in places but black and crispy in others, a patchwork, red hair fanned all around it. A figure that approached the speeding car so damned leisurely.

Adam continued to gun the engine, turned the steering wheel, spun off the driveway. There was an almighty bang as the car hit something hard, the edge of the stone building, perhaps, followed by a whoosh as flames shot up and engulfed them.

Violent shivers tore through Kenna, but she forced herself to stand, screaming and screaming as the tragedy unfolded.

No way Adam could have survived that crash.

Her voice eventually catching, she stared as the figure stared, horror on one face, triumph on the other.

Oh, Adam!

Was this over? Would one death be the end of the nightmare?

The figure then fixed its eyes on Kenna. No. One death would not be enough, maybe not even a hundred or a thousand. Her grief and anger were infinite.

Rohaise began moving back along the driveway to where Kenna now stood rigid. Her eyes never leaving Kenna's face, Kenna's eyes never leaving Rohaise's.

Doomed. All of them.

More sound, this latest taking time to acknowledge, to register, even.

What was it? A ringtone? Someone was calling her? *Gregor?* Oh, to hear his voice! What comfort there'd be in that. Paralysed by shock, however, she was too late reacting, and the ringtone died, a ping following it. Eyes still on Rohaise, she grabbed the phone from her pocket, then had to drag her eyes from the figure to read the new text. If it was Gregor, perhaps he was on his way. If he was, she had to warn him. *Don't come here! Stay away!*

The call hadn't been from Gregor but Sal, who had also sent the text. Not just words, she'd sent an image through, that of Adam in a restaurant or bar – and a woman with hair as blond as his, their foreheads touching and their hands entwined. She frowned. What was this? Adam was here, not in some bar. Adam was…dead.

She quickly scanned the text.

I've been sitting on this for a while, not knowing whether to send it. I just didn't want to hurt you anymore. This was taken a few weeks after my visit – this girl, she's clearly more than a friend. Adam's a rat, a two-timing bastard, and I hope he never bothers you again. He betrayed you, Kenna, and I'm so sorry because you trusted him.

She glimpsed at the photo again, wondered at it, but only briefly. Adam had come to her. Had he done so because his relationship with the blonde hadn't worked out? Was Kenna some sort of rebound? Better than nothing? Who knew?

But what timing Sal had – *perfect* timing.

Her head coming up, she saw Rohaise was no longer moving slowly but rushing at her. Just as quickly, Kenna held the phone up and showed the picture.

"See, Rohaise?" she said, Rohaise virtually upon her. "See?"

Chapter Thirty-Two

The lights were fierce; they burnt her eyes, causing her to lift an arm to shield them.

"It's okay. You're all right. You're safe now."

Kenna lowered her arm. A man had spoken, a voice that made her almost choke on a sob. "Gregor!" she said. "You're safe!" He reached out and clasped her hands, Kenna opening her eyes wider to look around her. "Where am I?"

"You're in hospital, Aberdeen, but don't worry, only for observation. You were found at Drumlin, collapsed on the ground there."

"Collapsed?"

"That's right." Gregor's grip became a little tighter.

"But I'm okay? I'm not…hurt?"

He chanced a half smile. "You're intact."

A memory returned, a shocking one. "Adam?"

That smile vanished. "I'm so sorry, Kenna. Adam's dead."

Kenna had leant forward, but now she fell back against her pillow. Of course he was dead. She'd seen his car in flames. A car she should have been in, had Adam waited for her. But he hadn't. Consequently, she was alive; she was breathing. Her last memory was of Rohaise, who'd rushed at her, but then what? Left her alone? Spared her. Why?

"There was a photo," she began, trying hard to make

sense of it, "sent through on my phone, by Sal. Of Adam. I held it up, showed it to her."

Gregor frowned. "I didn't even know Adam was with you."

"He showed up the night before. Out of the blue. He said he'd rung to warn me, but I didn't get the call, not then. There was a mist, you see, a wall of it surrounding the castle, that came up from nowhere. I think…it affected the phone signal."

"We had fog too," Gregor told her, "but it cleared. It didn't hang around."

"It did at Drumlin. It was stormy. There was thunder in the air, hanging around for a couple of days," Kenna said, frowning like Gregor, "but no lightning." *She* was the lightning. Rohaise. Her strike deadly. "She spared me, though, didn't kill me."

"Who spared you? Who did you show this picture to?"

"Rohaise."

"Rohaise?" Gregor breathed. "Did you…did you get my message?"

"About Alexander?"

"And about not discussing what I'd found out there, at Drumlin?"

Kenna's head hurt as she nodded. "Yes. But too late. We did discuss it there, in Rohaise's bedroom." Tears burst from her eyes as she reached for Gregor, who duly held her close, his embrace as comforting as it had been twice before. "It was her. She did this. Rohaise killed Adam. He was driving away, and she appeared on the road before him, caused him to panic, to swerve. She did this, Gregor! It was her! It was."

"It's okay," he continued to soothe. "I'm sorry about Adam, truly I am. But thank God you're okay."

"It was the photo that saved me."

His arms still so tight around her, Gregor asked why.

"Because she knew I'd been betrayed too."

* * *

After being released from hospital, Kenna didn't return to Drumlin. She went back to Gregor's to rest there. Gregor didn't go back to Drumlin either, not even to collect Kenna's clothes and toiletries. He simply replaced what she needed with new stuff. *No one* went back, not after Adam's body had been recovered. If Rohaise still wandered there, she wandered alone, a 'Closed' sign erected at the beginning of the driveway.

The cottage Gregor rented, on the edge of the village of Tulce, was small and cosy. He let her have the main bedroom whilst he moved into what was effectively a box room, Kenna protesting but those protests falling on deaf ears. A few days passed, quiet days, days in which he stoked the fire to keep them warm, Kenna watching the flames for hours, mesmerised by them, how they leapt and flickered. On occasion, she held her hands out to better feel the warmth of them, a comfortable warmth, but imagining all too easily how deadly it could become. *Knowing* rather than imagining, remembering.

Her mother rang to check on her, as did her father and Sal, all wanting to rush to her side, to visit. "Not yet," she'd said to each of them. "I need some time, some space, to come to terms with what happened to Adam. Soon, though. It'd be lovely to see you soon."

Quiet days with Gregor by her side, someone who understood her and all that had happened, who hadn't doubted her when she'd spoken of Rohaise, and who'd agreed with her that no way could she go back there, not if Rohaise was fully awake. Like her, he was filled with remorse, wishing he'd never found that buried piece of information.

Kenna slept – a lot – and that sleep was thankfully dreamless, her mind just too exhausted to keep contemplating. She cried over Adam, for what she thought they'd had and his fate, sent her condolences to his parents, whom she'd never met, who lived abroad in southern Spain. There'd be an inquest, of course, in Aberdeen, which she'd have to attend, and then a funeral held in the family's original hometown of Essex. *That* she wouldn't go to, or send flowers, but would donate to a charity instead on his behalf. When she'd tried to explain to the police what had happened, she hadn't mentioned Rohaise, just that he'd been leaving, but the weather had been bad, and he'd misjudged the turn.

"Seems awfully late in the evening for him to want to leave," the police officer said, a notebook in his hand, which he was duly writing in. "Had you had an argument?"

"No," she said. "He just...he didn't like it at the castle. Didn't want to be there."

The police officer eyed her. "Then what happened to you, to cause you to collapse?"

"The weather again," she said, "the mist. When his car veered off, I started running. That's when I must have stumbled and fainted."

"There was definitely no argument?"

"Not between us, no," Kenna replied.

With no suspicion of foul play, there was no more questioning. Kenna felt bad for not telling the truth, but as

Gregor confirmed, they'd never believe her version, and Kenna really didn't know all the facts anyway, as there'd been no fire. Adam's car had come off the road and hit a stone outbuilding at speed, which had killed him outright, but at no point had it burst into flames. That, at least, had been an illusion, Kenna having one foot in another world.

On the fifth day, the storm that had been threatening for so long occurred. As she and Gregor huddled inside the cottage, thunder rolled, not in the distance but overhead, lightning striking, a spiteful thing determined to reach them. It was angry weather that reminded her of Rohaise, Kenna shivering so hard in Gregor's arms because she thought it *was* her, lashing out again. But the storm passed in the early hours of the morning, and the day that followed was clear-skied.

After finishing a mug of tea, Kenna was standing on the doorstep, marvelling at the change in weather, breathing in air that was fresher than ever.

A car approached that she recognised, that she'd ridden in before.

Jean. She was the one person she hadn't heard from in the days that had passed, not that she'd thought to call her either. Watching as Jean parked the car, she then hurried towards her. Kenna thought it strange that she hadn't at least texted the woman to let her know, that even Gregor hadn't suggested it. But then, she supposed, she was keeper of the castle now, in charge, or rather she had been. A job – a life – that was now over.

"Oh, my dear," Jean said, "I'm sorry for what happened to you. So sorry. Oh dear, dear, dear, I've only just found out. I would have come sooner, but… Kenna, I'm so sorry."

Having reached her, Jean enfolded Kenna in her arms, a

fresh set of tears bursting from Kenna, Jean as soothing as Gregor had been, as understanding.

They went inside, where Gregor appeared, nodding at Jean, who nodded back.

"I'll leave you ladies to it," he said, glancing at the door beyond them. "It looks like a fine day for a walk in the forest."

A few minutes later and they were alone, Gregor having made a pot of tea first and leaving it on the table for them. The two were silent as Kenna poured them each a cup, Jean taking it from her before asking the question Kenna knew she would.

"Why didn't you let me know sooner?"

"I'm sorry, I've just…I've been in shock, I suppose. So much has happened. I've been trying to get my head around it, understand it. How's your sister?"

Jean looked both sad and remorseful. "She's been very unwell, but she's on the mend. She'll make it. Oh, Kenna, I'm to blame for all this. I should have known."

Kenna shook her head before taking a sip of tea. "No way you could have."

"Kenna, look at me. I *should* have known."

After placing her mug back down on the table, Kenna did as she asked and looked into the woman's faded blue eyes, saw something there, more than an understanding, a *knowledge*. Inhaling sharply, she replied.

"You know about her, don't you? About Rohaise?"

"That something of her remains at the castle? Yes, yes, I do."

"You've what…felt her? Seen her?"

"I've never seen her, no. But I can sense her sometimes, sense…a torment."

"Torment? Oh, she's in torment all right! A torment that's driven her insane."

Jean reached across, took Kenna's trembling hand in hers. "Tell me what happened."

Kenna hesitated only briefly, and then, just as in the restaurant with Adam, words bled from her. It all came out, not just about the night that had so recently passed but before that, all the times she'd sensed something too.

"It's real," she said, finally. "I haven't made anything up. I'm not exaggerating, not one bit. Rohaise is wide awake now, and she's dangerous. She's a murderer!"

"There now, there now. It sounds terrible. It *is* terrible. I pity Adam and his family."

Kenna wiped at her eyes. "How did you find out something was wrong?"

"I sensed it. But too late. This talent of mine, it's not an exact science."

"What do you mean? I don't understand."

Jean sat back in her chair. "Remember I told you about the monk in the wall? The young girl who insisted the wall be examined? Who wouldn't let up?"

Realisation dawned. "That was you?"

"Aye. Aye, it was. As you know, my mother worked at the castle before me, tending to Captain John and Arabella. She'd clean there, cook, and she'd take me along with her. Oh," she sighed. "I've always held a fascination with Drumlin, and, to be honest, for quite a while Joseph Buchannan, the monk, was all I could sense. Stuff had been happening there, unexplained, but after Captain John took me seriously and Joseph's body was found, all went quiet at Drumlin. I took over the role from my mother, then became the custodian when Captain John and Arabella died. Again, as you know, younger members of the family didn't want to follow in their footsteps, had already moved on. Still, that allowed me to live there, at least, which I was grateful for. I was determined to make the castle a success, a place that would fascinate many." She smiled, but her smile soon faded. "We invent ghost stories to keep the customers satisfied. Custodians the world over do it, but I was always careful when I talked of Rohaise. I knew, you see, that there was more to her. I could feel her, but only occasionally, and when I did, oh my…" Jean drank from her mug, clearly in need of fortification. "It was such sadness I sensed, so much so it would make me weep for her loss, her longing, her utter bewilderment."

Kenna couldn't help but contradict this. "She's mad! Not someone to feel sorry for."

"Ah, but she is!" Jean placed her mug on the table and leant forward, her blue eyes faded, maybe, but still able to penetrate. "If she's mad, it was because she was *driven* mad, because of all that was done to her. The information Gregor found about Alexander Buchannan, a man she endured such pain for, I can see how it was the tipping point. Kenna, if they'd made a pact, as you seem to think and which makes sense, he broke it. Kenna"—there was such a plea in her eyes as she repeated her name—"you're sensitive too. You realise that, don't you? You…*acknowledge* that?"

"Sensitive? You mean psychic?" A burst of laughter escaped her, but it soon died away. "I'm not psychic, no. No way."

"And yet, as you've told me, you sensed her, and you did so right from the beginning, when I showed you around the castle, when we stood in her room."

Still Kenna denied it. "I was intrigued by her, that's all.

Her story."

"You know so much of her story, things that no one else does."

"Conjecture. Dreams. Nothing more."

"It was so much more. And then…you saw her."

Kenna screwed her eyes shut. "Don't remind me. Please. I'm trying to forget."

"Not that way, not by denying it."

"I'm not psychic, Jean! Something happened to me there at the castle, but I'm not like you. I'm…ordinary. I'm just me, Kenna Jackson from London, for God's sake. I've never had a psychic experience in my life before now."

"I knew," Jean continued, "as soon as I set eyes on you – before that, even, when we chatted on Zoom – that there was something about you. Ordinary? Oh no, no, no. You're special, Kenna, very special. Like calls to like, something connects and deeply. You were meant to find your way here. Rohaise wouldn't sleep forever. She would wake one day, one way or the other, and she had to be dealt with."

"Dealt with? By me, you mean?"

"By *us*. I'll help you. We can't leave her there. Don't you think she's suffered enough?"

All that she was hearing, all that Jean was saying, was nonsense, pure nonsense, utterly wrong. And yet…when she'd first heard of Drumlin, when she'd looked at pictures of it, when Adam had encouraged her to apply, it was as if she'd been carried along on a wave of something. Fate, perhaps? Determination? As if something inside her had wakened too, slowly, slowly emerging from the chrysalis. *Why are you* really *here?*

Her breath grew ragged as she recalled not just Jean's words but the dream she'd had, how she'd *experienced* the extent to which Rohaise had been abused. When she spoke again, her voice was small, tremulous, one hand reaching up to smooth her own hair.

"I not only sensed her, sometimes it was like…I *became* her. Do you…could it be…?"

"What, Kenna? Say it."

Kenna swallowed hard. She had averted her gaze but now looked back at Jean. "Do you think…I am her?"

"You're Rohaise, reincarnated? Is that what you mean?"

Kenna nodded. "And why I felt the way I did, why I sensed her straightaway? Because I'd come home, in more ways than one?"

Jean didn't answer immediately. A few moments passed, moments as heavy as the weight of history, in which Kenna bit her lip.

"It's possible," Jean said at last. "Certainly you look like I imagined Rohaise to look. There's a similarity there. But *actually* Rohaise?" She shook her head. "I don't know. I couldn't say. Then again, isn't Rohaise every woman who has ever suffered, who's been betrayed or persecuted? She embodies them all. She's you, she's me, she's so many. There's a link between you and her for certain. She's shown herself to you when she never did to me, even when I begged her to. I'm sorry about Adam, but she spared you, and there's a reason for that. She *identified* with you. She may be an abomination now, but she wasn't always. We hold on to that. If someone's in torment, shouldn't we help to end it? Otherwise…otherwise…"

"We're no better than those who inflicted torment in the first place?"

Jean remained silent, but it was clear what her answer would be.

"What's your plan?" continued Kenna. "What do you want me to do?"

It was Jean who swallowed now. "You know as well as I do, Rohaise's only crime was that she was bewitching."

"Yes, yes, she was."

"We have to go back to Drumlin and reason with her, help her let go of the past, to rest and rest properly this time. Release her, just as Joseph Buchannan was released. It's time."

"I'm scared," Kenna admitted.

Jean nodded. "Do you know what your name means?"

Kenna was startled by the sudden question. "Um…it's Scottish. That's all I know."

"I'll tell you what, and it's the *perfect* name for you. It means 'born of fire'. Historically, red is the colour of wickedness, of the witch, but red also signals courage and passion, and you have plenty of both. *She* did, Rohaise. You're a match for each other, and she knows that. She *respects* that, I think. The real reason you were spared. We need to go back to Drumlin, and we need to promise something, something that I think will indeed offer her true release, especially now without Alexander to tie her down, to keep her there."

"Promise what?"

"That we'll find where the king's men buried her, and we'll take her to the forest instead, her first home, her true home. Kenna, I can help, and Gregor too. I'm sure he'll want to. But you're pivotal here. You're the key. Because with Rohaise, you fight fire with fire."

Chapter Thirty-Three

That night the dreams returned. There was the darkness of before, just as complete, something to lose yourself in. Only she wasn't hiding, she was roaming in it, her hands outstretched just as they'd been in the mist, her mouth wide open in a silent scream.

So lost. A wretched thing, a thing that railed, that knew the truth, that tried to deny it but couldn't.

Kenna was this woman, but she was also an observer looking on.

I'm so sorry.

The observer fired those words, tried not to drink deep of despair but banish it.

Sorry for everything.

No use. Despair, like castle walls, could not be breached.

I'm coming back for you. To Drumlin.

Not just this woman, not just an observer, Kenna was every figure looking on, so many – she saw that now as her eyes adjusted. Figures that vied and jostled, that stood stock-still, opening their mouths and silently screaming too. She remembered Jean's words: *Isn't Rohaise every woman who has ever suffered, been betrayed or persecuted? She embodies them all. She's you, she's me, she's so many.*

And all of them were here, trapped.

Kenna as Rohaise continued to wander, always in the

same direction, her shape ever changing, ever shifting. One minute she was red haired, straight shouldered and proud, the next a shorn and twisted thing whose skin bled from the carvings on it.

Unable to bear it, the observer closed her eyes. Behind her lids was yet more darkness, more figures, some raising their hands as if begging her. No escape, then. They were one and they were many, those that had known loss and then, in turn, become lost.

On and on they paced, surging forwards, but where?

The observer reached out, as did Rohaise, felt walls so close, at both sides and above. Rohaise, as the hag she'd been reduced to, began to claw at the walls, to climb them, her limbs bending in the most bizarre ways, wholly unnatural, blood dripping.

Dark, so dark, and yet the observer could see everything, every way in which the figure contorted, that mouth of hers a gash, still open as if shrieking.

The observer rushed forward. "Don't! Don't do that. Please. We'll find a way out."

Oh, how she wished the beautiful Rohaise would return, but she was gone, it seemed. The figure in front of her continued to crawl like a spider might, her head hanging low as she hung from the ceiling, black orbs for eyes staring back at the observer, daring her to come closer still, not a scream on her lips now but a cackle.

The crowd behind the observer cowered, as did she, the observer. All that was human had been stripped from the figure, leaving a creature far more terrifying than any man had the power to create. A creature that continued to crawl, coming for them.

The observer tried to reason further with her.

"This isn't you, your true self. This is what they made you. Come back, Rohaise, as you were before. If not, they've won, don't you see?"

Insane. Too far gone. Unreachable.

She had to escape, find a way or descend into madness too.

The observer turned, issued an instruction to the others. "Run! Get out of here."

As if they were one, not something separate but melded together, the crowd obeyed, the observer in pursuit, hoping against hope for a glimpse of light to guide them, here in a place where all light, all hope, had long since been extinguished.

A wretched smell assailed her, the only thing to find its way in. So fetid it made her choke, the observer bringing an arm up to cover her mouth and nose. Sanity was indeed slipping away. How long had she been in here? Even a second was too long, but for some there'd been countless seconds, minutes, hours, days, years. *Centuries.*

She opened her mouth to scream too, but like Rohaise, like the others, there was no sound, and for the first time she realised why. Because the scream was just too big, too full with grief. If she gave voice to it, she'd explode. Hands reaching out instead, she used the walls to haul herself along. She had to find a way out! Escape this dream, wake up, leave the tunnel she was in…

The tunnel…

Her foot connected with something, and she fell, the pungent smell of earlier more prevalent than ever. She'd landed on the floor, slippery with grime, the filth of ages entrenched. But she'd also landed amongst something, had *scattered* something…

She looked down, her chest heaving, terrified of where the figure was, whether it had reached her, was hanging above her, its jaw stretching, becoming wider, one hand extending... But also, she was curious; she was...excited.

Bones. She had scattered remnants of bones. *Human* bones.

Kenna's eyes burst open at that very moment, trained on the ceiling as she lay in bed.

"I know where you're buried," she gasped. "I know where they put you!"

Chapter Thirty-Four

There was nothing but belief on Jean's face when Kenna told her about the dream, about her certainty, that somehow the king's men had found the tunnel, and there they had interred Rohaise's body before sealing it up, for good this time. Gregor too was nodding as if it wasn't senseless. On the contrary, it made all the sense in the world.

"All that's known is Alexander likely took flight through the tunnel, and if Rohaise went with him, at some juncture she turned back," Gregor said, "to give him the best chance of escape, to stop the king's men from destroying Drumlin too, burning it down."

"Perhaps they should have," Kenna said softly, "because it's a cursed place now."

Jean shook her head. "It isn't. There is history there *besides* Rohaise. But right now, it is about her and how we can help."

This time, Gregor shook his head. The three of them were sitting round the table in his kitchen, just a small room, the table compact, a beam of light shining through the window, something Kenna kept glancing towards, was grateful for, remembering all too well the atmosphere in the tunnel. "How do we help a ghost?" he said.

Jean sighed but in an agitated rather than resigned manner. "Kenna here has made contact with Rohaise. A bond has been forged between them—"

"A dangerous bond," Gregor insisted. "You know I feel for Rohaise as much as you do, and what she went through, but what remains of her there at Drumlin… She killed a man!"

Kenna reached across to him. "Gregor," she began, but again he interrupted.

"I know what the plan is likely to be, that you go back there, make contact with her, try to reason with her, but what if it's just too late?"

As it had been in the dream, thought Kenna. "But what's the alternative?" she said. "That Drumlin remains shut, falls into ruin? Fine, that is an option, except…"

"Except what? Because that sounds pretty okay to me."

"Kids," said Kenna, causing Gregor to frown.

"What do you mean?" he asked, although Jean was nodding, Jean was *agreeing*.

"You know what kids are like," Kenna elaborated. "We all do, being as we were kids once. Kids are…adventurous, they want thrills, they're…reckless. Do you really think people will stay away from Drumlin, from an old abandoned castle with a dark history? They won't. They'll go there in the dead of night and at various times of the year, Halloween, that kind of thing, and they will hunt for her, for Rohaise. They'll call for her, antagonise her. Adam died there because of Rohaise. I don't want another death on my hands."

"It wasn't your fault—"

"No, but if I stay away, if I…I don't know…leave here and go back to London…" Gregor's face fell when she said that, something in her heart lifting to see it. "If I leave," she continued, "then I am guilty. Jean thinks I'm sensitive, and maybe she's right, maybe I am, but I *know* there'll be other deaths if I don't try to help Rohaise, calm her raging spirit. Deaths that *will* be on my hands because I anticipated them and did nothing."

After a few moments of silence, Gregor shifted in his chair. "So what do we do?"

"We?" she questioned.

"If you two are going back, so am I."

Kenna refused. "It's more dangerous for you, I think."

"Because I'm a man?"

"Well…yeah."

"Not all men are evil."

"No, I know," Kenna appeased. "I don't think that, but Rohaise, her views are warped. Shit, *justifiably* warped, but that's why I think you should stay away."

"No," he said, suddenly determined. "I'm coming. So, come on, what's the plan?"

Jean took over. "We believe her remains are in the tunnel because of Kenna's dream. There are many ways connections are forged, and dreams are certainly one of them. It makes sense that she's there, actually, that the tunnel was found. The king's men would have been hunting for it too. It also makes sense because they would have feared Rohaise, what they'd turned her into, something that was indeed demonic, and so, superstition once again driving them, they'd want to bury her deep, thinking to contain her there, that her wrathful spirit wouldn't pursue them, although I hope the memory of her did, at least. I hope it returned over and over to eat away at them in the dead of night, whenever they closed their eyes. I hope they never knew a peaceful night's sleep again." She shook her head. "Sorry, I digress. Easy to, I suppose." She took a breath.

"The tunnel was the perfect place to inter her. An escape route but also a trap."

"So we liberate what remains of her," Gregor said. "Is that what you're saying?"

Jean nodded. "Aye, and, granted, there may not be much left – fragments, that's all – but whatever there is, we remove it."

"One problem, though," he pointed out. "We've still no idea where the tunnel is."

"No records of the castle, no plans ever revealed that information?" Kenna checked.

"No," Jean replied, "and I've asked the Buchannans before. I remember discussing it with Duncan once over the phone. I was just curious, you know? He didn't have a clue. 'Be cool if you found it, though,' I remember him saying, 'the mythical tunnel.'"

"It's no myth," Kenna murmured, remembering how it felt there, so dark, so deep, so…hopeless.

"It isn't," Jean concurred. "So, you're right, Gregor, we have quite the task ahead of us."

Kenna looked at the beam of sunshine again, saw how it had brightened. "If we're going, we go now. Whilst there's daylight enough. And, Gregor?"

"Yeah?" he said, rising like her.

"That pickaxe you use for clearing rocks?"

"Uh-huh?"

"Bring it with you."

* * *

They'd already established that the tunnel would have emerged into the forest, but, again, as to where, they had no idea. As they drove to Drumlin, all three of them so quiet in Jean's car, busy contemplating what lay ahead, Kenna kept her eyes on the pines that ran alongside the roadside. A vast forest. It stretched on and on. Miles and miles of it. The tunnel entrance and exit could be anywhere. Was this a good plan? Certainly, it was the *only* plan. They needed to find the tunnel and liberate Rohaise, and not just because the king's men had deemed it the perfect burial place. The tunnel was also the last place Rohaise had seen Alexander. Now she knew the truth, she'd never be at peace there.

The sky clouded as they reached the start of the driveway, the 'Closed' sign Gregor had erected still hanging there. Jean stopped the car, and Kenna got out and moved the sign to the side, allowing Jean to pass before replacing it and climbing into the front seat again. She was scared to come back; she'd admitted that. Gregor was too, and Jean, their fear something tangible, firing sparks. Greater than fear, though, was determination. She truly believed what she'd said about there being a danger to others here, Rohaise becoming more and more unstable, less and less discriminate.

As they rounded the corner where Adam had driven off the road, she closed her eyes, Jean reaching across briefly to touch her arm, Gregor also leaning forward, both of them endeavouring to comfort her. And it worked. A heart grown icy cold with fear and grief began to thaw. Could the same ever be done for Rohaise?

She didn't love Adam. Kenna knew that now. Even before the text Sal had sent her, she'd realised, deep down. She'd used him for comfort, but, actually, the comfort he'd afforded had been scant. And he'd used her. Lied to her. *There was never anybody else.* But his lie was a comfort too.

It lessened, even if only slightly, the guilt she felt about him.

She glanced over her shoulder at Gregor, a man accompanying her *towards* danger, determined to stand by her side, not leave her as Adam had left her, trying to escape Rohaise alone. Betrayed over and over, but the pain of betrayal, it could fade.

She smiled at Gregor, remembering his face when she'd mentioned she might return to London. Did she mean it? Would she go back? *Could* she? The smile he gave her in return was as gentle, as all-encompassing as ever.

There it was, coming into view. Drumlin. Standing tall and defiant and so, so alone. She scanned Rohaise's window. No figure – beautiful, shorn or otherwise – watching them.

"Where shall I park?" Jean said, breaking silence that was like a shroud.

"In front of the castle," Kenna replied. "Just here."

After she'd done so, they exited the car to stand on the gravel. The clouds had gathered in earnest now, hiding any blue. They were grey as steel and growing darker.

Gregor was looking up at the clouds and frowning. He didn't say why, but she knew: this was weather peculiar to Drumlin. It was Rohaise and therefore a warning.

"Kenna, we're here, by your side," Jean murmured. "Remember we've come with nothing but love and understanding, wrapped in a light that protects us. It's important to also remember that Rohaise is of the light, and that's where she needs to return."

"The forest," Kenna replied, her voice also low. "That's where she's from."

"She is," Jean said. "You're right. And where her bones should lie at last."

They walked forwards towards the entrance, the pickaxe

and a shovel retrieved from the back of the car and Gregor clutching at them, knowing their purpose – not to harm a ghost but to dig as he had dug before, not through textbooks but the cold, solid earth of Drumlin.

With the key in her hand, Kenna, as she had done so many times before, inserted it into the lock of the old oak door. Not as reluctant as before, it gave easily as if welcoming them, *needing* them. The castle or Rohaise? Which was it?

They stepped inside, and Gregor closed the door behind them, a sense of entombment again, just as Rohaise had been entombed. The castle had stood empty for just a short while, but the abandonment felt ingrained. Hard to believe people had ever set foot here.

"At least it's only the ground floor we need to focus on," said Gregor, clearly relieved.

"The tunnel might be outside the castle, remember?" Kenna replied.

"Yes, but we have to have a starting point," Jean insisted and then to Gregor said, "and we only use the pickaxe if we're sure we've found it."

"How the hell will we?" he breathed, looking at a floor covered in flagstones.

"We connect," Jean said simply, her eyes resting on Kenna, Kenna knowing what she meant: that *she* connect, her, not Jean, that somehow, someway, she tune in again.

"Come on," Kenna said, moving further in, her eyes also on the ground and searching.

What furniture there was, they moved – chairs, desks and tables all pushed aside, the flagstones prodded with the pickaxe for any sound of a hollow, Kenna falling to her knees on several occasions, feeling the ground with her hands, closing her eyes, desperate for a revelation. No answer came, and they'd soon covered every inch.

"When they sealed the tunnel, they did a good job," commented Gregor wryly.

"And yet they couldn't contain her spirit," Kenna said. "She's here, somewhere."

"Can you feel her?" Jean's blue eyes were anxious.

"I can feel something," Kenna confessed. "Another storm brewing."

"Perhaps we ought to leave," suggested Gregor. "We can try again tomorrow, and the next day and the day after that, in short sessions rather than one hit. We'll move into the grounds, and I'll study other castle plans, try to learn from them."

Kenna shook her head. "This castle is like no other. You said that, Jean, when I first came here, that Drumlin's unique."

"Aye," Jean agreed, but her voice was tinged with sadness. "It is at that."

"*She's* what makes it so, her history. Rohaise. I have to go upstairs to her room. That's where I'll connect best."

Immediately Gregor protested. "That's just plain dangerous!"

She turned to him. "Gregor, I have to go there, and I have to go alone."

His dark eyes widened further. "Are you mad?"

Something flared in her. "Don't call me that, okay? Don't you dare!"

"Sorry," he said, contrite. "I just…Kenna, I…I…"

"I know," she said when he faltered. "And I love you too, Gregor Lockart. And I'm not leaving; I'm staying right here at Drumlin. This has been more of a home to me than

London ever was. I've been…happier here. Despite Rohaise. *Because* of her. She's a part of me, and I'm a part of her. Two redheads together. I'm going up there, Gregor, alone. This was her home once, but now it's mine. And I won't be driven from it."

Just as something had flared in Kenna, it flared in Gregor too, burst into flame, full of hope. He grabbed her and kissed her, and the kiss was fierce, and then he released her and stepped back, Jean looking on, not saying a word although her eyes glistened.

"I'll be all right," Kenna promised as she turned from them both and climbed the stairs all the way to the sixth floor, entering the Rohaise Room to lie on the bed there.

Chapter Thirty-Five

An observer. Is that all I am now? Someone who stands in the shadows and watches. Who shakes as they take what remains of the creature at the stake and release her, who wonders why the atmosphere has changed, become more...solemn.

Hatred, anger and fear remain, but something else besides. That I struggle to recognise. Remorse? Is it possible...? Could it be that these men, these vile men who have made me a reflection of themselves, something vile too, regret their actions? They have stripped me of my humanity, but is there still a shred left in them?

NO! I want to curse every one of them for what they've done. Damn them as they have damned me. If I'm a witch, then let me haunt them forevermore, let them see my face, the blackened husk of it, in dreams and on waking. Let them clutch at their beating hearts!

There is another in the crowd who clutches at the cape around her neck. Eilidh. She is solemn too as she backs away from the others, from me, unable to witness anymore, her appetite at least exhausted.

Why did she bring the king's men to our door? There has to be a reason other than jealousy. Or am I naïve to think so? Is jealousy the exact reason? Alexander, a man older than me, an experienced man, his gentle hands would have roved over flesh other than mine. Hers? Before me? Was she his lover, his mistress too? And then what? She was discarded. For me? Ah, there it is! Her rage. Quiet but ever burning, white-hot.

I would fly at her if I could and tear her apart. But grief roots me. Fear does too. Where are they taking the remains that have now been wrapped in rags? Where will I be buried? My eyes travel from the men that carry me, from Eilidh too, who has turned, who is indeed running, who will be pursued but perhaps not by me after all. Will they bury me in the forest? That last vestige of humanity steering them? They do not head there but elsewhere, and if I have a heart still, if I have a soul, it howls with despair. Silent despair.

They have found it, the tunnel through which Alexander fled.

That is where they will bury me, my bones, at least. Down, down in the dark. Alone.

If Alexander made it through, emerged into the forest, did he remember the paths I showed him that would lead into the heart of it? Is that where he lingered, where men feared to tread, in hiding? From there, did he hear my cries, my screams, for they would have rung out, they would have travelled far. Did he know how much I suffered for him?

I have been interred. And he is not there, in the tunnel; he is nowhere to be found. The men have gone too, fled, like Eilidh fled. All have left the castle but me. An observer, a wanderer. Since then, I have slept, not in the tunnel in the darkness, but in the bedroom we shared. And yet the darkness clings, the memories do. I have waited because I promised. As did he.

Waited…and waited…and waited.

And there was once hope in the waiting, there was belief. Now there is none.

Alexander escaped, as I wished, and he is never coming back. As Eilidh was replaced, so was I. Yet he heard my screams. I know he did! He lay on the forest floor and heard.

Agony upon agony!

Without hope, without belief, without love, what am I? A husk indeed, a witch, something depraved. A monster! My rage frightens even me. It burns like fire never could. It bursts from me. I have waited in the castle where lies blossomed, not love. Only that.

You said you'd come back, come what may, and I believed you, come what may.

Damn you, Alexander! Every one of you.

You have all made me what I am. You have brought this on yourselves!

Chapter Thirty-Six

"Kenna, wake up! Wake up! Shit, Kenna, listen to me and wake up!"

The room was hot, searing, her skin feeling as though it was blistering again, flesh parting company from bones.

Despite how the voice begged, she couldn't wake, force consciousness to rise. She was caught somewhere in the in-between, a place that reeked of death, of roasting meat.

More crying out, the mention of a God clearly absent from proceedings. There was no God here, only Rohaise, a woman they had all destroyed, betrayed over and over again.

Sorry, Rohaise, so sorry.

She'd apologised a thousand times, it seemed, but now there was no force behind her words, only a tired resignation. What would be, would be. She'd finally made peace with that. The fire – for there was fire this time, real not imagined – right here, in Rohaise's bedroom, could not be contained any longer. It had to burn. Maybe even burn itself out.

Eventually.

"It's okay," she said as arms closed around her. "It's all right. I understand. I do."

How the voice denied it. "No, Kenna, you don't understand, and it is not okay! You will not burn at Drumlin like she did. Be another victim."

She was being carried now. Gregor, that's whom the voice – the arms – belonged to. He'd come for her, fought flames for her. *You are quite bewitching.* What had caused the fire? The light Jean had insisted shine in the window? A guide for someone who had turned his back, was long gone, vanished. It couldn't be. She'd unplugged the lamp. The bulbs above in the chandelier had also burst, been rendered useless. And yet still fire raged.

"Kenna, wake up! You've got to! I can't… Help me!"

Had he stumbled? Were they falling? For that's what it felt like, not into darkness but into the light. Was that a noise she heard? The clash of thunder, so angry, so mighty.

"We can't fight it. Not anymore."

"Kenna, we can! Help me or we burn."

"We have to burn. If it's what she wants."

"No, we fucking don't! Wake up!"

"Leave me. Go. *I'll* burn."

Was she really saying this or just thinking it?

If she was thinking it, then she was connected to Gregor on as personal a level as Rohaise, because he answered right enough.

"I'm not leaving you."

Dear Gregor, sweet, gentle Gregor. Gregor who had turned his life around, from a criminal to a gardener to a student, who loved history so much. Who loved *her*.

Yes! She recalled something about that. He loved her? Or she loved him? Which was it? Had he actually said those words? Had she?

"Gregor?" she said, her eyes half opening, but all she could see was the vividness of orange and the deepness of black. All she could breathe was smoke.

"I'm here," he said. "It's okay, I'm here. Come back to

me. Before it's too late."

But it was too late. That's why they were burning, *precisely* because it was too late.

"Not for us. It doesn't have to be. Please, Kenna, come back. Rohaise is wrong. We don't all have to burn."

Connected. They were. She and Gregor. Because those last words, she hadn't said them. And yet still he'd heard.

"I love you," she tried to say, her voice, like Rohaise's, a croak. She didn't expect a reply, she truly didn't, but one came, the words he hadn't quite managed downstairs.

"And I love you."

Words that didn't burn her, that revived her.

She opened her eyes fully and saw his face, registered finally the extent of what was happening. The room was burning, full of flames. How could they possibly escape?

"Gregor!" she said and saw not just fear on his face but relief. She was back. She was not Rohaise, just Kenna, a girl who was terrified. "We can't get out!"

"We can. We will. We have to run, fast, through the flames."

"What?" Pass through flames and survive? Was he serious? "Gregor, no!"

"It's our only chance."

Again, she denied it, trying to become smaller still, to disappear.

"Kenna!" He took her face in his hands, forced her to look at him. "Do you trust me?"

"Trust you?" She did, but no one could survive the flames, no one!

"We can do this," he continued, "but we have to act now. We have to be quick. We have to run. Get to your feet, hold my hand…and trust me."

No more time to think. All she could do was put her faith in him, believe that his plan would work, because the alternative…no, she couldn't, *wouldn't*, contemplate it.

His hand engulfed hers, and he pulled her forwards into the flames, Kenna marvelling that she was moving as her limbs, conversely, felt frozen. Around them, flames leapt at the drapes, at the window, licked at the ceiling, began to swallow too the bed in which Rohaise had lain with Alexander, the bed he'd had carved with roses in her honour, but which, like real roses, would soon turn to dust. There was heat like she'd never felt it, unbearable, a furnace, and then she was out the other side onto the stone staircase, and so was Gregor. They were still hand in hand, Jean catching them, pushing Kenna to the floor, batting at her – her hair especially, which she could smell had burnt, the bitter singe of it.

"Gregor," she gasped as the sound of exploding glass reached her ears, the very window Rohaise had stood at in life, gazing at the forest. A roar followed on the tide of it, anger fully released, not trapped anymore, far louder than the explosion had been.

"I'm all right," Gregor said, helping Kenna to her feet. "Come on, down the stairs, quick."

With Jean leading the way, all three hurled themselves downwards, Kenna glancing back only once, certain that Rohaise was following them as when Kenna had been in the castle with Adam, something bent and broken negotiating the stairs in a tortured but determined manner, the monster that she'd become, that she'd been made into. But there was nothing and no one, just the sound of more glass exploding and another roar, not one voice, though; it sounded like a million voices combined, all those that had ever suffered, perhaps, as Rohaise had suffered, had been abused. Reaching the entrance, they passed through it and ran to the door, bursting out of it into yet more chaos. Rain and thunder, the weather in sympathy with Rohaise, conjured by her.

"The car," Gregor said, heading towards it, but Kenna stopped him.

"Not the car, not after Adam. We leave on foot."

"The car's faster!" Gregor protested, but she refused.

"I will not get in that car."

He held her gaze but only for a moment before conceding. "Okay, hurry."

No mist, not this time, but the rain blurred everything, made it look every bit as surreal as before. Even now, part of her denied this was happening, but as she glanced back again, saw plumes of fire bursting from the broken window on the sixth floor, she had to admit – the veil had parted, and it had remained that way, let a demon through.

She faced to go, registering her two companions had slid to a halt. What were they doing? Why were they stopping? As Gregor had said, they had to hurry. And then her eyes lifted, saw what had stopped them on the gravel ahead.

A figure.

Rohaise.

"What the hell?" said Gregor, equal amounts of awe and terror in his voice.

"Oh no." In contrast, Jean's voice was barely a whisper.

It was Rohaise as she was after the king's men, after the burning, a demon indeed, blocking their path, their exit, the fury of the heavens on her side, a *righteous* fury.

"What do we do?" Gregor said. "Turn back?"

Kenna shook her head. "She's not just in front of us, she's

everywhere. This is her land."

"No." Jean's denial was stringent. "This is *not* her land. The forest is, not Drumlin."

"We've failed her," Gregor said, "and she knows it. If we can't find the tunnel, we can't release her."

"The tunnel's here somewhere," insisted Kenna. "It is. I was there!"

The blackened, crippled figure moved towards them, each movement an agony to see. Only her eyes remained untouched, but glowing red nonetheless.

More thunder added to the threat.

"There'll be lightning soon," Kenna whispered, Rohaise directing it. A massive bolt that she would divide into three and so effortlessly. Taking a deep breath, Kenna stepped forward, towards Rohaise, not running from her, not anymore.

"What are you doing?" The shock in Gregor's voice deepened. "Come back!"

Kenna turned only briefly towards him, saw how frightened he was, how brave too. He'd come here knowing what had happened and what *could* happen. He'd come not just for Kenna's sake but for Rohaise's. If she killed him, killed *them*, it'd be a travesty.

She asked of him the same question he'd asked of her. "Do you trust me?"

"Of course, but—"

"Then let me go."

Just as she'd hesitated, he did too, but just as she'd also done, he agreed.

"This has to end," she said. "One way or another."

He remained silent, as did Jean, as Kenna faced Rohaise again, drew closer, the past and the present colliding, each one desperate for some kind of future.

She spoke as she walked, her voice not tremulous but powerful.

"I didn't mean it, Rohaise. You're not a demon, you're a woman, only that. I'm sorry for what happened, you know I am, to you and to countless others. You were wronged, and by Alexander too. He knew how you'd suffered, he'd heard, and all to save him. He should have returned, one way or the other, but he didn't. We can't change that, rewrite history. All we can do is forgive. He heard your cries, your anguish, and, Rohaise, those screams must have been torture for him too. Perhaps…perhaps he *had* to forget or be driven mad by it. He lived, and you died. But you wanted him to live, remember? What if that's how he honoured you? By seizing happiness and *truly* living? That vow surpassing all others.

"You weren't the devil's mistress, and Alexander was neither a god nor the devil, both of which you have believed him to be. What he was, was gentle. He would caress you and call you bewitching. He loved you. It was in his touch, in his eyes. You can't feign love. You loved him too, once, for a moment in time. Sometimes that's all we have, a moment, sometimes not even that. You were destroyed, horribly, horribly destroyed, but don't lash out, and destroy too. Don't be like them. Rise above your anger. Rohaise, you have to *soar*. This is about you now, only you. There's so much more to you than anger."

As Rohaise continued towards Kenna, not once did she falter or the expression on her ruinous face soften. She wasn't listening. All would be in vain unless Kenna could think of something else, unless she could promise as Jean had said. There was no other way.

ROHAISE

"The forest was your first love, your enduring love. I'll find your bones, take them from the darkness and return with you there, and you *will* find peace in amongst the pines and the herbs, the ferns and the wild, wild roses. We'll go to the clearing, deep, deep within the forest, the very heart of it, which is your heart too, Rohaise, your soul."

No change in Rohaise, and the thunder was directly overhead. Any minute now, she would lift her arms and draw down the lightning, a hellish creature that was hell-bent.

"Rohaise, I promise!" Kenna cried just as Gregor and Jean screamed out too, Kenna's name on their lips and the last thing she might ever hear.

As Kenna had feared, lightning struck, and it was ferocious, utterly blinding. In it, though, she could see more clearly than ever. She was looking at Rohaise – *always her* – so close now and staring straight into her eyes, her skin no longer burnt or carved or congealed with blood but smooth like porcelain, her eyes flashing green and her red hair a mane. She was dazzling; neither the sun nor the lightning could compare. Resplendent in a dress that matched her eyes. Rohaise in all her glory and bewitching, entirely.

Kenna stared straight back. "I won't betray you. I'll take you home."

The moment held, beyond time, suspended.

"Trust me or the suffering continues, yours, mine, all of ours."

Rohaise, please.

She hardly dared to breathe.

"One chance, that's all I ask. If anyone deserves freedom, it's you, Rohaise."

The light grew stronger, blinding again, then darkness

bore down, and confusion.

"ROHAISE!"

In the darkness there were flashes, like fireworks exploding, a series of them one after the other. There was crashing and banging, ear-splittingly loud, the product of a war zone. Lifting her hands to her ears, then to claw at her hair, Kenna craned her neck forwards, forcing herself to continue seeing. The ground below her feet was blackened and smouldering, lightning having struck perilously close. Further away, though, by the ruined building, the barn or whatever it had been in another lifetime, the earth had split.

The sound of panting replaced all else – not her own but Gregor and Jean running, their hands grabbing at her, hugging her, Kenna holding on to them every bit as tight.

When finally they parted, she looked at one and then the other.

"We've found it," she said, pointing to the barn. "The tunnel. It's right there, the same place Adam crashed the car. Gregor, Jean, I think she's gone. Finally, she's gone."

Chapter Thirty-Seven

Incredibly, the fire didn't spread beyond the Rohaise Room. Jean put in a call to the fire service, and they arrived soon after, some of them baffled the castle remained so intact.

"Aye, well, what can I say?" Kenna heard Jean tell one of them, the smile on her face as enigmatic as the *Mona Lisa*'s. "They built them well in those days."

The cause for the blaze was found to be a lightning strike to the leaded window. Kenna nodded alongside the other two as the firefighters endeavoured to explain this.

The Rohaise Room was shut until surveys and restorations could be carried out by the insurers, but nobody expected any quibble regarding compensation. The Buchannans in LA were, of course, informed. Duncan Buchannan even returned to Scotland, albeit briefly, to check on damage and also because of the tunnel, the excavation that was taking place. That was where all available funds were going, meanwhile, to find Rohaise's bones. Something – Jean told Kenna – Duncan had been hesitant about.

"That's an awful lot of money to spend on a hunch," he'd told her via Zoom.

She'd reminded him of the hunch she'd had as a child. "In many ways, Joseph Buchannan put this place on the map, drew people here when it became a public concern. If we find Rohaise's bones, liberate her, so to speak, and the story spreads – which it will, Duncan, it's bound to – it'll bring even more. It's money worth investing."

"This will be the last person you dig up, though, won't it?" he'd asked somewhat wearily. "Sometimes it's better to let sleeping dogs lie."

"Aye," Jean agreed, "it is. If you can."

Another matter Duncan wanted to discuss face-to-face was a plan to set up the Drumlin Trust, not his family at the helm, financially or otherwise, but castle management.

Kenna, Gregor and Jean sat with him in the café, with Connor and Laura providing tea and sandwiches, and Duncan explained, a little red-faced, Kenna thought, that as much as he loved his family history, would boast of it to anyone who'd listen, ultimately life had moved on. For them, it was all about LA now.

"I know it's a lot to ask, and the last thing I want is for Drumlin to fall into ruin again, but—"

"We'll do it," Kenna said, not hesitating, not for a second, and knowing Gregor and Jean wouldn't either. "If you hand over the reins to us, believe me, this castle will *not* fall into ruin. It'll go from strength to strength, be cherished, by us and many, many others."

"She's right," Gregor said, "it will. It has everything a visitor could want from a castle." He glanced at both Jean and Kenna when he spoke next. "It has Rohaise."

All paperwork was signed, and Duncan, only in his thirties, as dark haired and dark eyed as his ancestors, funded the excavation as a parting gift.

"To appease his guilt," Jean said, but again with a smile.

It was another rainy day when the archaeological team involved in the dig emerged from the tunnel below, such a pitiful collection in their finds-trays, laid out and numbered over paper sheets, fragments of burnt fabric amongst the bones. Kenna was glad it was raining, as it hid the tears that poured down her face as she stared at them.

Although news of the discovery spread far and wide – and did indeed place Drumlin back in the spotlight, the mistress of Alexander Buchannan who had died defending the castle, defending *him*, no longer myth but reality – Kenna wanted the burial to be without fanfare. Just her, Gregor and Jean in attendance. All three keepers of the castle now.

The day they relayed Rohaise to the forest, wrapped in pale satin, it was a bright morning in mid-December, the air cold but crisp, with a white sheen of frost clinging to leaves and ferns, making them sparkle in the sunshine.

Gregor led the way to the clearing, Kenna knowing every step of it too. He had previously prepared a hole in the ground, which was no mean feat, as the earth was solid, but it hadn't deterred him. Now, as they stood beside the grave, Kenna lowering the bones into the earth, tears appeared again on her cheeks and, this time, no rain to hide them.

"Sleep well, Rohaise," she whispered. "Sleep in peace now."

No need for more words; it had all been said. They felt peace too, that of the forest and the harmony that existed all around.

Before Gregor filled the grave, he retrieved something from his jacket pocket.

"What's that?" Kenna asked, intrigued.

"Something I saved from the rosebush in front of the castle," he answered, "the one you wanted me to plant so it could be seen from her window."

"With the red roses," she said.

"Aye."

He unwrapped the small parcel to reveal a beautiful bud, its colour faded, softer.

"Oh, Gregor," Kenna whispered.

"I saved it for her," he said, his voice somewhat choked too, "back before all this happened. I didn't know why, not at the time, only that I wanted to."

"Because you felt her as much as I did. As Jean did too."

"Felt *for* her," he amended, gently placing the rose on the satin, following it with earth.

Rohaise was home, where she belonged, buried deep still but free.

As they walked home, a bird sang.

"That's the—" Gregor began, but Kenna interrupted him as Jean smiled.

"Scottish crossbill. You told me once, remember? A bird unique to these parts."

"That's right," he said, also smiling. "That belongs."

* * *

Kenna's idea for Christmas was to host festive lunches in the café and also to display more local arts and crafts, not just in reception but utilising the main hall too. Aiming to get the Rohaise Room reopened as soon as possible, she threw herself into these plans and more, presenting ideas to Gregor and Jean for Valentine's Day, Easter, summer and beyond. First, though, there was Christmas, the blue skies that had been present the day they'd buried Rohaise turning gunmetal grey and snow falling. Despite this, visitors still came, food was eaten, gifts were bought, and questions were

ROHAISE

always asked about Rohaise.

"Miss, Miss," said one little girl, "tell me about Rohaise! About the witch!"

Kenna had bent slightly and looked into the girl's brown eyes. "Now why d'you think she was a witch?"

"Because…because…she was, though, wasn't she? That's the rumour."

The extent to which Rohaise had suffered would go to the grave with them; neither Kenna nor Gregor or Jean had told anyone else about the torture she'd endured or that she'd been burnt at the stake on the grounds of Drumlin, and neither would they. If Kenna got around to writing a novel one day, if it was indeed about Rohaise, she'd focus more on the woman she'd been, a brave and noble figure, a child of the forest. But, as the girl had said, rumours had sprung up. A fierce woman buried in a tunnel, *sealed* in it, tended to fire the imagination. No harm in enlightening her, though.

"Sweetheart," she said, "what's your name?"

"Lily."

"Lily? That's such a lovely name. You have something in common with Rohaise. She was named after a flower too, a rose. A beautiful wild rose."

Lily scrunched up her nose. "Rose isn't a witch's name!"

"That's because," replied Kenna, "she wasn't."

"Oh." How crestfallen Lily looked, how disappointed.

"What she was, was bewitching."

Still the girl frowned. "What does that even mean?"

"It means…it means…" Kenna paused before continuing. "It means she was beautiful, certainly. But more than that, she was kind. She was trusting. Like you, she was full of life, full of dreams. She was brave, really, really brave!

And she was selfless. It's because of her that Drumlin still stands. It's here for us all to enjoy centuries later. She was a hero."

Lily also paused. "So, she wasn't a witch but…a bewitching hero, is that right?"

"Absolutely right," declared Kenna. "And there's no crime in that, is there?"

Resolutely, the girl shook her head. "No! No, of course not." Abruptly, she turned from Kenna and ran back to her mother, who was busy reading an information sheet.

"Mummy, Mummy," she yelled. "Rohaise wasn't a witch, she was a bewitching hero!"

Kenna grinned widely to hear it, caught Gregor's eye as he came into the room, his amusement at hearing the girl too.

At her side, he gently squeezed her. "You're good at this job, you know that?"

"You think?" she teased back.

"Uh-huh. Born to it, I'd say."

"An extraordinary life after all," she said, a lump in her throat as she turned to gaze out the window at icy grounds and a rising mist that clung to the surrounding trees.

"Kenna, are you all—"

She peered harder, frowned. "Gregor, is that someone down there, just on the edge of the lawns, in the trees? Look."

Gregor duly moved closer to the window.

"Can't see anyone," he said after a few moments.

"Yes, in the trees," Kenna insisted. "It's hard to see because they're also dressed in white, but it looks like a woman, a…distressed woman. She's wringing her hands."

Still Gregor denied it. "There's nothing but mist."

ROHAISE

About to protest again, Kenna quietened. There *was* someone there, becoming more and more defined. But who? Joseph had woken, Rohaise had, and perhaps others that slumbered, a thought she'd had when fleeing from Rohaise. Did no one sleep forever?

With Kenna still staring, the figure turned, inclined its head and locked eyes with her.

"Eilidh," she whispered.

"What?" Gregor said, clearly confused.

Something stirred within Kenna, a surprising anger.

"It's just come to me. Her name. It's this. It's Eilidh."

A note from the author

As much as I love writing, building a relationship with readers is even more exciting! I occasionally send newsletters with details on new releases, special offers and other bits of news relating to the Psychic Surveys series as well as all my other books. If you'd like to subscribe, sign up here!

www.shanistruthers.com